Magic at Work

Fated Lovers – Book 1

SOTIA LAZU

This book is a work of fiction.

While reference might be made to actual historical events or existing locations, the names, characters, places and incidents are either the product of the author's imagination or are used fictitiously, and any resemblance to actual persons, living or dead, business establishments, events, or locales is entirely coincidental.

...Does true love exist?

Table of Contents

Chapter One

God, his eyes were blue.

Lexi had never seen him before. He certainly wasn't there on Monday or Tuesday. She'd remember a pair of eyes blue so startling even from a distance and behind a pair of wire-rimmed glasses.

He was talking to Edmond but studied her as he passed by her desk. And his eyes were mesmerizing.

Maybe he was a client?

But no. Her stepdad patted him on the shoulder and continued to his office, while the guy turned left and parked his butt behind a desk that had been empty on Lexi's first two days at work.

She should stop staring now. He'd notice.

Oops. Too late. Their gazes met, and he arched an eyebrow in challenge. She blinked and looked away. Her gaze fell on the clock mounted on the wall across from her.

Eleven forty-three.

Only five hours and seventeen minutes to go.

Only.

Lexi crossed her arms and turned her yawn into a fake cough. She had color-coded the department folders, sharpened all her pencils, and reorganized the files on her

PC for the tenth time that day and was ready to go home now, please.

She propped her elbows on the desk and rested her face in her palms. No. That looked less than professional. She squared her back and sighed. She was supposed to be working hard on the latest instructions-for-use translation, which she'd already finished even though it wasn't due until Friday. It was her single work assignment this week.

And it was still Wednesday.

Proofreading and translating marketing materials for the Sales department wasn't what she'd signed up for. She told Edmund—owner and general manager of Pedelty Electronics—she felt underutilized, and asked for more to do, but he wanted to ease his little girl into things. His words, not hers. Lexi tried to get him to see people wouldn't appreciate the preferential treatment, but he would have none of that.

"They all know you're here because you deserve it, honey, not because you're my stepdaughter. You just have to become a part of the team first."

She didn't tell him *honey* felt like a blow at her Business Economics degree from UCLA.

Lexi glanced at the paperwork supposed to help her grasp the nature of the products the company designed and sold. The formatting wasn't what she'd choose, and she didn't love the phrasing in some instances. And the charts could be clearer. She had access to the electronic files. She'd play with a couple of things and show her suggestions to Pedelty. She pulled up a folder marked INSTRUCTIONS FOR USE and opened the top file. A message window appeared in the center of the screen. *Insert Password*. She tried the access code she used

2

for her PC, but the window buzzed. Angry red letters read, *Wrong Password. Access Denied.*

Great. So much for her having a say on things. Edmund didn't trust her not to mess things up on her first week.

She was grumbling to herself about parents who never realized their kids grew up, when she sensed someone watching her. It could be anyone. The first floor of the company offices housed the Sales and IT departments in an open L-shaped space, and the lack of cubicles — while great for enhancing teamwork — offered no privacy. In Sales, desks were placed in two parallel rows of five, one along the windowed outer wall, the other facing it. Lexi sat with her back to the foggy San Francisco sky.

She raised her gaze, but John, the guy opposite her, wasn't looking her way.

While she hated sales with a fiery passion, he was a born salesman. Just yesterday, Lexi saw him go from disinterested to mellow, to cheerful, to a customer's best buddy within a few seconds. Chilling to watch.

He wasn't on the phone now, so he was in off-mode, his face bland.

Next to John, Matt munched on chips, typing something with his free hand. He caught Lexi's gaze and flashed her a goofy grin. She returned the smile and kept scanning the room.

The rest of her department were out, pitching sales, but the glass pane that separated Sales from IT offered her an unobstructed view of most of the floor.

Everyone seemed fixated on their computer screens.

3

The IT Crowd.

Boredom made her easily amused. She almost chuckled, before she zoomed in on Mr. Blue-Eyes staring at her. She chanced a smile, but the guy's face seemed set in stone. He didn't even blink.

With a shrug, Lexi returned to her reading.

She smiled again when she passed by his desk on her way to the restroom. This time he acknowledged her with a nod that was nowhere near friendly. *Ouch.* Every workplace had to have at least one weirdo. Pity this one was so cute.

A couple hours later, she decided a coffee refill was necessary. Mug in hand, she walked the short distance to the fully stocked kitchenette, only to find the weirdo there, washing his own mug and humming some tune Lexi didn't recognize. He didn't seem to notice her, which allowed her to notice him. A few shoulder-length honey-blond curls had escaped his ponytail and hid part of his face, but not enough for her to miss those razor-sharp cheekbones. The company policy didn't insist on formal wear except for the salespeople who met clients, so his shaggy T-shirt wasn't against regulation. His faded blue jeans held a few rips and tears, and although baggy, gave a good hint of his toned butt as he leaned forward to scrub the cup with fervor.

And *that* brought her gaze to his muscled arms and long fingers. Lexi sucked in her lower lip. She knew better than to allow herself to be attracted to a coworker, but she couldn't help thinking how nice he'd clean up.

*

4

Ric wasn't having a good day.

He should have taken Edmund's offer to take a day off, after flying back from Germany. And coming to work jetlagged wasn't the worst part of his Wednesday. That spot went to his morning meeting with Edmund, who more or less told him he'd hired the stepdaughter he'd been raving about for years, to do a job irrelevant to her studies and experience.

During the past two years, Ric listened to Edmund talk non-stop about the brilliant young woman he'd help bring up. Edmund couldn't have loved her more if she were his biological daughter, and was extremely proud of her, but instead of having her involved with the company's operations, he stuck her with paperwork.

When Ric argued she'd be buried in that position, Edmund insisted she needed the experience. *Plus she seemed content.*

How could she feel content with something she could do with her eyes closed?

Pedelty Electronics started off as a single store. When Edmund decided to have a line of hair trimmers contracted under his brand, he didn't expect to one day be the owner of a company that designed anything from flash drives to toasters. Additions to workforce came as they were needed, and the result was a patchwork of people and skills. Edmund was an excellent leader, visionary and inspiring, but he led by trial and error. It worked at first, but at its current size, Pedelty Electronics needed a manager with solid operational skills.

It pissed Ric off that Lexi didn't step up to the plate.

She seemed more interested in him when he walked in than on what was on her screen. Part of him was flattered, but that was the part that didn't realize Edmund's daughter was so far off limits, she wasn't even a blip on his radar. She might be beautiful, but she was Edmund's family, and Ric didn't mess with that after all Edmund had done for him.

She kept glancing his way, and it amped up his irritation. Was she flirting with him? He huffed.

His body begged for caffeine. He didn't enjoy drinking coffee when he couldn't have a smoke, but concessions had to be made. His I-heart-London mug wasn't in the drawer he usually kept it. He went looking for it in the kitchen, and found it in the sink. *Dirty*. Pissed him off when people used his stuff without asking.

He was furiously washing the otherness off it, when Lexi walked in. He didn't have to look, to know it was her. She'd been clacking those heels all morning, making him glance at her long legs despite himself.

Ric was torn between being the polite man his mother raised, and showing Lexi what he thought of brats who let down people Ric cared about.

And that was harsh, coming from someone with his past. Edmund had given him a chance. Ric would show Lexi the same courtesy. He'd play it by ear. Wait to see how she'd introduce herself.

But she didn't.

Ric waited, but she stood there. When he turned to face her, he saw she was studying him. And not his face. Her gaze was trained to his arms. She licked her lips, and Ric arched an eyebrow.

"Do I get the seal of approval?" he asked.

6

She gave a tiny shake of her head, but it wasn't a no, judging from the brilliant smile that curved her plumb lips and made her green eyes sparkle.

"You're British." She sounded pleasantly surprised.

"You're perceptive." And her voice was as sexy as the rest of her. Shit.

She held out her hand. "Hi, I'm—"

"The boss's daughter, who just moved back from New York. Yeah, I know." He left his mug on the drying block and grabbed a paper towel. Anything to keep from touching her. Her gaze felt like an electric jolt, and he was afraid if he took her hand he'd forget he was pissed, and fall under her spell.

"Yeah, that too, but I have a name. It's Lexi." Unfazed, she opened her palm wider.

He reached for it with a smirk, the shields he'd crafted for years coming up. It was about time his self-preservation instincts kicked in. "From Alexandra. Your mother calls you Xandra, and you're brilliant and not just another Californian bird."

Lexi stared at him, wide-eyed.

"I told you, I know," Ric said. "Ed's been talking about you like you're the second coming or something. Make sure you don't disappoint him."

Her smile cracked. "Well, I'm not about to. Not that it's any of your business, Mr...."

"Richard Ackart. Ric for short. Head of the IT department, and not about to make your life easy just because of your relationship to the big man. Got it?" So he went a little overboard. Blame it on the jetlag.

Lexi nodded.

7

"Good." He brushed past her, and was at the door when he remembered he needed coffee.

"Got it, jerk," Lexi muttered behind him.

He kept walking. Time he weaned himself off caffeine, anyway.

****

The clock showed nine minutes past one.

Lexi'd been with the company for two working days, four hours, and nine minutes, and she was bored to death. Doing translations and typing other people's business trip reports weren't what she'd signed up for. She wanted more.

She wanted something that would require her to think and put her business degree to use. Sadly, Edmund had made it clear she wasn't getting that anytime soon, which meant she was looking at more than two days of doing nothing and feeling uncomfortable about it.

Everyone else seemed pretty busy. She needed to find something to do.

Right on cue, her phone rang. Caller ID came up as Richard Ackart.

"Hello?"

"Come here for a sec, will you?"

"Huh? Here, where?" She'd know it was him even if it didn't say so on the phone display. His voice and accent stood out… and made her skin flush with desire. Still, it was rude of him not to identify himself, and so she played dumb.

"To the desk of the Brit who *isn't* your dad," he said and hung up.

Great. Now she felt dumb. She took her time standing, smoothing her skirt in back, and walking to his desk in small steps. By the time she reached him, she'd managed to plaster a disinterested look on her face. "Want something, Richie?"

He clenched his jaw, which she considered a personal victory until he turned the tables on her. "It's Richard or Ric. If that is too much for your pretty little head, you can call me *hey, you*. Are we clear, Xandra?"

She nodded and tried not to stare when he folded his arms behind his head, stretching the white T against his muscled chest.

"Wanted to pick your brain about something," he said.

"You mean my pretty, little, blonde brain?"

"That one. Good ideas sometimes hide in the most improbable places." He seemed pleased with himself. "Ed wants me to upgrade the operating system of the PCs to the latest version that came out just three months ago. What do you think?"

She was astonished he'd ask her that. He was the head of the frigging IT department. It was his job to know these things. Still, it wasn't like she didn't have an opinion. "I think it'll be a waste of money. We could change to an open-source system. It's free and compatible with all other programs." She shrugged. "It may take a while for everyone to get used to it, but I don't see why we'd pay so much money for something I hear is harder to operate than the one we have now, without offering enough perks to make up for it."

9

"That's what I thought."

The way he looked at her didn't indicate whether he agreed with her or he meant her opinion proved as useless as he'd thought it would be. When he turned back to his twenty-three-inch monitor, she saw it as her cue to leave.

"You're welcome," she said in as sarcastic a tone as she could muster, and went back to her own desk.

Her short exchange with Richard brought her spirits even lower. So much for Edmund's reassurances that everyone knew she deserved to be there. Did she even want to be there? Once upon a time, she had plans about a career, but now she'd settle for doing a job she didn't hate and being recognized for it.

The computer screen tempted her. If people thought she was a slacker anyway—and right now, she was just that—maybe she could surf the web for a few minutes. Take her mind off how her life passed her by while she sat at her desk, doing things that didn't challenge her.

Yeah, that might help.

But what to surf for?

She'd always been into sultry romances. When she was younger, she read them and hoped the perfect guy would swoop into her life and open her eyes to the magical world of love. He would prove not all men were like her dad, who—true to the middle-age crisis stereotype—left her mom for his secretary when Lexi was four.

Lexi met her Prince Charming right after college and followed him across the country. He promised they'd build a life together.

He lied.

Sickeningly sweet love stories were now Lexi's secret little indulgence. They helped her escape the cynical outlook she'd forced on herself, and kept her company on long, lonely nights. Reading those improbable happily-ever-after stories was the only time she permitted herself to hope there was someone out there who could be her other half. Her soul mate.

Not that she'd ever admit it to anyone. As far as she was concerned, true love didn't exist in the real world. The rare exceptions were for the extremely fortunate, like her mom and stepdad, who still swooned at each other.

Lexi took a deep breath, placed the cursor in the browser's search bar, and typed, *Does true love exist?*

She gasped at the hundreds of thousands of pages reported as results, but it was the first entry that made her do a double take.

Exotic Beast: the Saga of Xandra and Rex – a FREE Erotic Romance novel by Xopi Chilli
Will Xandra allow herself to fall for Rex, despite the generations of hatred between them? Is she even capable of true love, and will she fight for it if she finds it?

Maybe it was that her secret nickname was there, or perhaps the second question struck a chord, but Lexi clicked on the link and was directed to a page showing a man and woman in the shadows. A cornflower-blue mist lit up the darkness surrounding them and enhanced their features. The man was the hottest specimen of the male species she'd ever laid eyes on.

Of course it was true love. Everything about him looked loveable.

The jet-black hair and leather outfit made him look dangerous, and his blue eyes were familiar, as he stared at the woman in his arms with breathtaking intensity and adoration.

A bad boy with a soft side. "Yum," Lexi muttered under her breath.

From what she could see of the woman's face, Xandra looked a little like her. More than a little. The woman in the picture was her spitting image, except for the hair. Lexi's was a darker shade of blond.

Her name *and* her face on the page were too much of a coincidence. Her best friend, Angie—computer-wiz and self-proclaimed witch—had to be playing a practical joke at her expense. How did Angie know what Lexi would be browsing for, though? Lexi clicked on the *Next Chapter* button, and sure enough she was led to a new chapter. She did it again and again, until she was satisfied that what was on her screen was a real paranormal-romance novel. Angie couldn't have had the time to write one, just to mess with her.

The summary of the story read,

Xandra Eves has been taught to look down at everyone but other shifters. She has no reason to doubt vampires are her natural enemies, until she meets Rex and is forced to work with him, to uncover a conspiracy that threatens to destroy both their species, as well as creation as she knows it.

It didn't seem all that tempting, but a romance novel featuring her doppelganger was too hard to resist. Plus, *Xandra Eves* had a weird connection to *Alexandra Adams*.

She could see what other people thought of the book. Everything was searchable online. She entered the names *Xandra* and *Rex* into the search bar but came up with nothing. Odd. The novel's read count was in the thousands, according to the webpage's meter.

It was free, it was there, and it intrigued her. She would read a couple of pages, and then get back to… something work-related.

With a shrug, she clicked on the first chapter.

The two pages became several, and soon Lexi was entranced by the characters. Xandra was every bit as messed up as Lexi, and Rex oscillated between adorable and smoking hot—a perfect mixture of shy and cocky, sure to make any woman drool.

And he was British.

Lexi flickered her gaze to Richard, who was busy typing. He was hot and British too, but far from adorable.

She pretended to type and click for a couple of minutes, and then returned to reading.

Rex tied Xandra to a tree, to keep her from alerting her pack to his presence. He was washing himself in a lake, while she pretended to keep her eyes closed.

He had to know she watched. Why else would he push out his chest, stretching his pectorals, just to wash his dark hair? Water gleamed on the well-defined abs that rippled under his skin. But what made Xandra's breath hitch in her throat

13

were the twin arrows of corded muscle that ran at the lower sides of his abdomen, over his hipbones, pointing at his cock...

He could have been carved in marble.

Lexi didn't know about that Xandra chick, but she craved the guy. And she had to get back to work. She could print the read-only versions of the manuals and jot her notes on them.

She would just read to the end of the chapter. No more than that. She glanced around, afraid someone might notice what she was reading. Just to be safe, she opened a couple more windows on her desktop and arranged them so the tab with *Exotic Beast* took up a small part of the screen.

Sparks flew, but it took a couple of chapters for Xandra to give into the vampire's charm. The sex was hot and tender at the same time — hotter and more tender than anything Lexi had ever done — and there would be more, because Rex wanted to know as much about Xandra's body as possible.

Lexi gulped.

"…now."

She snapped up her head so hard, something clicked in her neck. Richard stood in front of her desk, looking at her expectantly.

"Huh? I mean, I didn't catch what you said." Did he know what she'd been doing?

"I said I think you should get off now." He intoned each word separately, as if speaking to a child.

"Excuse me?" Her eyes felt wide as saucers.

14

"It's five thirty. Shouldn't you be going home?" he asked in a bored tone. "Or is that big, bad translation giving you trouble?"

"Ah." He meant get off *work*. She was so flustered, she didn't even return the sarcasm. "Um, no. No biggie. Yeah, I'll go now. Thanks."

He frowned, shrugged, and swaggered to the stairs, his laptop hanging from one shoulder and bouncing against his ass with every step.

Lexi packed up and left, but not before jotting down the web address of the site, as well as that of the particular page she'd been on before the interruption.

Chapter Two

"I'm home." Not waiting for an answer from her mom, Lexi rushed past the kitchen and up the stairs to her room. Her *old* room. She let go of her old apartment when she followed the jackass to New York, and was staying here temporarily, while she looked for a new place. The lack of personal space was already grating on her nerves, but at least her folks tried to be as discreet as possible and gave her the privacy she needed.

She locked the door behind her and hurried to change into a T-shirt and a pair of shorts, before switching on her PC.

"Come on, come on, come *on*." The darned thing took ages to connect to the wireless network, but she was finally online. She felt like a hormonal teenager for wanting to read more Rex goodness in the privacy of her own room, but it wasn't like she could be doing something else instead. She lost touch with most of her friends when she moved away, and hadn't been back long enough to make new ones. The guys at work were friendly and talked about going out as a group, but they hadn't arranged anything yet.

She typed in the address of the page she'd been on, but got an error message for her trouble. She tried the site homepage again but to no avail. She typed, *does true love exist?* in the search machine, like she had earlier. Instead of getting the direct link as she expected, she was directed to a blues band's Myspace page—that thing still existed? Searching for the e-Book by name also came up with nothing useful.

She repeated all steps on her smartphone, with the same result. Nothing.

To say she was annoyed would be an understatement, but what she'd read at work earlier was more than enough to call for a hot shower session.

Now where was Lexi's little purple helper?

She stuck her hand in the back of her bottom drawer and pulled out her small vibrator. Not the most satisfactory of her toys, size-wise, but the most discreet. It was barely visible when she stuck it inside her waistband and pulled her T-shirt over it. She left her room and entered the bathroom, making sure to lock the door before taking off her clothes.

The shower was refreshing but offered too tame a release. Neither the showerhead nor her vibrator managed to send Lexi hurtling into ecstasy, like Rex sent Xandra in the novel. Not that it surprised Lexi. She knew earth-shattering, mind-blowing orgasms were just a legend. After all, she'd been around the block, and no man could provide that. It was just fiction.

The niggling thought that maybe she hadn't met Mr. Right yet knocked on the door of her mind, but she refused to let it in. To do so would mean believing in the existence of a Mr. Right, and therefore hoping to one day meet him. Lexi knew, sooner or later, hope led to heartache.

"Dinner's served." Her mom's voice drifted upstairs and brought Lexi out of her reverie. There was the one perk of living at home. Her mother's cooking was out of this world.

She brushed her wet hair quickly, changed out of her fluffy bathrobe and into a different pair of shorts and a tank top, and bounced down the stairs to the kitchen. She'd have to remember to ask Angie how that thing with the book was possible. Maybe see if her friend could access it from her PC.

She'd reached the kitchen door, when she heard Edmund say, "...insists she doesn't fit there."

That didn't sound good.

"Who doesn't fit where?" She could tell she had that bubblegum-blonde smile on her face—the one her friends knew to steer clear from.

"You, according to Richard in IT. He says I've made a mistake with you." Edmund obviously didn't think his words would affect her temper. His attention was on his plate, but he wasn't avoiding her gaze; he was taking in the meal in front of him. His manners didn't allow him to just dig in before the ladies got seated.

Lexi was bristling. She didn't get how her stepdad could be so calm about it. She widened her fake grin, hoping to mask her anger. "Well, good thing it's not his decision to make, huh?" Oh, Mr. High-and-Cocky was in for a world of pain tomorrow.

"No, it's not, but I do wonder if maybe he was right. He made a valid point."

What was Edmund talking about? Firing her? And why was her mom so cool? Lexi kept looking from Edmund to her mom. "What point could he have made?

18

He's seen me all of four hours. He doesn't know me *or* what I do. He's not even in my department." She didn't care she hadn't wanted the job to begin with or that she didn't find it even half interesting. She was just pissed off at the thought of that jackass trying to interfere with her work and her family.

"So you're saying you're happy where you are?" Her mom looked at Lexi with the eagerness of any mother who wanted her child to be happy.

Lexi couldn't find it in her heart to mention how she felt under-utilized. "Of course I am. Why wouldn't I be?"

Edmund smiled and bobbed his head. "I thought so but wanted to make sure." Lexi's world was safe as long as she got that smile. That was the way things had been since she was six, and Edmund had promised to be the best husband her mom could ever want and the best father Lexi could ever need.

Someone still had to pay, of course, and now that her footing at the company was secure again, Lexi could start by collecting info about Richard the Meddling.

"So, who is that IT guy, and how come he has opinions about me?" She frowned and pouted. That always got her way with Edmund.

"According to Edmund, he's a very nice, clever, and hard-working young man."

Lexi didn't like the dreamy look in her mother's eyes. If she asked why Lexi never got involved with guys like that, Lexi would bolt.

"Edmund?" Her mother looked at her husband, who removed his glasses, vigorously wiped them with a corner of the table cloth, then placed them back on the bridge of his nose and took a deep breath.

"Richard is the son of a very good friend of mine, from the old days. His father, Anthony, and I grew up together. We moved here together after college, and I was his best man when he got married, but hadn't seen him since the family went back to England. He called me a couple of years ago, to say Richard was in San Francisco, looking for a job. The boy's credentials were excellent, and I thought he'd be an asset to the company. I can safely say I was right. He's brilliant."

Pride shone in the man's eyes, and for the first time since Edmund became a part of her family, Lexi felt a real pang of jealousy. He talked about Richard as if he were his own son. Her pouting lip jutted out a bit more at the thought. "Well how come I never heard of him before today? And why doesn't he want me working with you?"

"I saw no need to mention him while you were away, Lexi. You never showed any interest in the company until you joined us. And dear, you've misunderstood. What Richard said — "

"No. Forget it." She shook her head. "I'm sorry. I'm being childish. I'm sure Richard had his reasons for saying what he did." Nasty, mean reasons, for which she'd somehow get him back. "Mom, dinner looks great." That signaled an end to the conversation, and they all dug into their plates.

After dinner, Lexi once more tried to access the site and failed. She thought about calling Angie and asking her to give it a go too, but that would lead to a series of questions Lexi had no answers to.

20

Sleep was elusive that night. Her mind raced between flashes of a hot Brit worshiping her body and thoughts of how she could make a certain other Brit's life hell.

****

During the drive to the office the next morning, Lexi kept repeating in her head, *'I'm not going to log into that site till I'm off work.'* She felt bad indulging herself by reading erotic scenes while on the clock. There wasn't much to do during those long eight hours, but maybe she needed to pressure Edmund more about that.

In the end, she decided she'd log into the site before she left work, and copy the next few chapters of *Exotic Beast* to a document she could take home on a flash drive.

The first thing she did once her PC connected to the network was type in the site address, to check that she hadn't just dreamed of it. Sure enough, the book showed up. Lexi went to the last page she'd read, in order to make sure she had the right URL.

It all went downhill from there.

She had nothing urgent to do at the moment, so she could dedicate fifteen minutes to read the next chapter. Right? Only, then she really, really, had to know what came next, so she kept reading, throwing an occasional glance around to make sure no one was watching. She promised herself she'd make up for the lost time the next day. Or she could print those manuals and take them home with her.

She made sure to keep a constant frown of concentration on her face, so nobody would figure out she was reading steamy sex scenes instead of doing her job.

All thought abandoned Xandra the moment Rex began trailing his wandering fingers up her legs. He pushed his hands under the hem of her dress and lifted it to her waist, so he could nuzzle her inner thigh.

All thought abandoned Lexi, too. Her heart pounded hard inside her chest. She felt the moisture between her thighs seep through her panties, until she had to rub her legs together, to alleviate the throbbing in her pussy — if only a little.

She was snapped out of her lusty thoughts by a deep, rumbling voice that sounded way too close.

"Bloody Californian legislation. What is so wrong with smoking, I can't even do it out on the balcony anymore?" Richard wasn't yelling, but his tone was far from conversational.

"I know for a fact that smoking isn't allowed in workplaces in most of Europe, either," Lexi said.

He turned his bored gaze to her. "You know European law, then?" The sarcasm in his voice was more than evident, and she just wanted to punch the smirk right off his face.

"It's a filthy habit." Her voice was shaky. "Even if it isn't banned everywhere now, it should be." She was far from satisfied with her reply and felt a blush creeping up her cheeks. Why did she open her mouth to begin with?

Then she remembered she was pissed off at him. Like *really* pissed off. "And you're not in Europe now

22

anyway, Richie, so I guess you'll have to deal." She immediately knew she'd made a mistake, calling him by the nickname he disliked.

His eyes darkened, and the muscle in his jaw ticked. The room cleared around them. Even thickheaded John must have felt the storm brewing, because he left his desk, mumbling something about checking on a shipment with the logistics department.

Richard approached Lexi's desk, leaned over it, and slammed both his palms on it. "Not Richie, Xandra. Are you too dense to remember, or do you just want to be an annoying little chit?"

"I'm not annoying or a—a chit. You, on the other hand, are a jerk *and* an idiot. Which of us do you think is better off?" She leaned forward too, the distance between their faces mere inches, as they stared each other down over the narrow desk. Lexi was proud she didn't flinch or back off when he lowered his voice to a near-growl.

"What are you on about? Just because I'm not going to roll over for Pedelty's little girl, I'm a jerk and an idiot? Hate to break it to you, but I'm not rolling over for anyone. You want me to be nice to you? Earn it."

His accent sounded rougher, less refined than usual, but she was too chagrined, to care much about the change. He thought her problem with him was so shallow? "Be nice? I don't give a fuck about you being nice. Nobody expects you to roll over. I don't want you to. But you're a jerk for going behind my back and telling Edmund to fire me, and an idiot for not expecting him to tell me about it." She leaped to her feet, pushing her chair back with such force it would have toppled if it didn't have wheels, and mirrored his posture.

Richard just looked at her. And then the bastard chuckled.

Shocked at his reaction, she recoiled, straightened up, and planted her hands on her hips. "God, you're damaged."

"So I tried to get you fired, huh? Guess that would at least make me an idiot." His expression grew serious, as his accent reverted to the more cultured one she always heard him use. "Is that what old Ed told you?"

"He said you thought I didn't fit in here. Are you going to deny that?"

"No. No, I'm not. Though next time you might want to get your facts straight before blowing a fuse." With that, he turned and went to his desk.

"And what's that supposed to mean?"

No answer.

The subject was apparently closed.

Lexi was fuming, to say the least. How could he disregard her like that? He didn't even try to defend himself or give her an explanation. He wanted her to get her facts straight? Well, he should get his head straight, the arrogant ass.

She sat back down with a huff. God, she needed a good yelling match with him. One which would end with him groveling for forgiveness and her with a smug smile on her face. That wasn't in the cards, so she went back to *Exotic Beast* and hoped for some fun sexy times.

"*Look at you, all flushed for me. Bet you're still wet.*" *Rex's hands were on her thighs, thumbs tantalizingly close to her pussy, but not touching. "You've been wet for me all night.*"

24

It wasn't a question — and even if it were, he already knew the answer.

"Yes," Xandra whispered, trying hard to keep her hips from bucking against his hand.

"Do you want to do something about it?"

Lexi caught herself nodding. Arguing with Richard didn't seem to have gotten her any less hot and bothered, after all. She squirmed in her seat and felt her cheeks burn when John returned and sat opposite her with a wink. The guy did nothing for Lexi, but her hormones seemed to be wonky. Heck, she even found Richie-boy attractive, in an angry, wanna-bust-his-head-in-for-being-a-jackass way. Yup, definitely wonky hormones to blame. Richard was *not* hot. He was scruffy and infuriating and… looking at her.

Fuck.

He smirked like he knew she was appraising him, and found it amusing. She glared and turned back to her monitor. Rex was waiting, after all.

Also, she should be working. What was wrong with her?

"You're mine Xandra," he leaned to whisper in her ear. He tugged at her nipple through her bra. The lace rubbed against her sensitive flesh, enhancing the sensation and making her body tingle with anticipation. He sneaked his free hand under her skirt, twisted his fingers around her panties, and ripped them off in one violent yank. He pushed a finger inside her pussy. "Say you're mine."

When Xandra let out a moan, he caught her lips in a rough kiss and slid another finger inside her. "Say it."

25

The man was sex on legs. Lexi couldn't stay still. She needed to touch herself. Close her eyes and imagine Rex sliding his fingers in an out of her. She needed some privacy, and she needed it now. She made sure to minimize the browser window, restore the Word document with the finished translation, and lock her computer, before heading to the ladies room.

She noticed Richard looking at her. His gaze was soft for the first time—an expression so unlike him, she had a hard time recognizing it. Was it concern? Nah. He opened his mouth to say something, but she held out a hand. "Not a word." With a shrug and a shake of his head, he turned back to his PC. As she passed by, he made a show of putting on his headphones.

In the ladies room, Lexi was torn between splashing some cold water on her face and locking herself in a stall, to take the edge off. Her brain took over the decision-making process, and she went with the first option. Whether she liked it or not, this was her place of work. She drizzled some water on the nape of her neck, trying to shock her body out of its excited state. It might have worked, but the moment she was back at her desk, she went right back to reading and didn't stop until it was time to go home.

Despite loving the way she'd passed the day, she felt horrible for not working. She'd ask for something more to do tomorrow. She got ready to leave, but not before copying the next three chapters of *Exotic Beast* into a Word file and saving it on a USB drive to take with her.

She was surprised and a whole lot more than a little pissed off when she opened the file at home and found it blank.

"What the fuck is up with this thing?"

Her empty bedroom offered no reply. She had to stop visiting the site. It was spooky how it only appeared on her work computer, and Lexi always made a point of staying away from spooky stuff—hormonally-induced attraction to assholes included.

She had no idea where that last thought came from.

Chapter Three

When Lexi all but ran to the ladies room, looking flushed and upset, Ric couldn't help thinking it was his fault. He saw her look at him with those big green eyes, and he made out the accusation in them.

He hadn't expected her to take it that hard. She shouldn't care what he thought—and he hadn't said what she thought he did, anyway. He wanted to ask if she was all right, and even considered apologizing, but the way she cut him off made him want to hide under his desk. Instead, he put on his headphones and pumped up the volume to "I Wanna Be Sedated," while returning his focus to his latest project.

He didn't spare her a glance the rest of the day, and was sure she equally ignored him.

When he passed by her desk at five and wished her a good afternoon, she was too entranced by her translation to reply. Or she liked pretending he didn't even exist. He didn't care either way. He didn't care if she hated his guts.

He wasn't there for her to like, after all.

The thought seemed too sulky for his liking, but he brushed it off and tried to occupy his mind with work thoughts on the way to his apartment. It was a short drive, and thinking about computer systems and the glitch he found in their newest software purchase should have kept his mind busy, but worry over whether he'd overdone it with Lexi kept sneaking in.

He tried to convince himself that wasn't what drove him straight to the bottle of scotch in his kitchen.

He sank into his favorite armchair — worn out to fit the lines of his body — and downed a hefty gulp of the amber liquid, relishing the burn down his throat. He hadn't craved a drink first thing after coming home in a long time. He hadn't needed one since that day almost two years ago, when Pedelty rang his doorbell and saved him from his miserable excuse for a life.

Back then, Ric called himself Rex, and was a borderline alcoholic who made a living selling his services to people and companies looking for information they couldn't obtain through legal means. His broken heart led him from one bad decision to the next, and he wasn't seeking a way out because he didn't feel he deserved one.

Until Edmund straightened him up.

There was nothing worse than waking up with a hangover because some sick bastard decided nine o'clock on a Sunday morning was a good time to be ringing your doorbell with vehemence.

Rex dragged his feet to the front door and threw it open. Without looking at his visitor, he walked to the kitchen and grabbed a beer — the best medicine for hangover. He popped the bottle open on the countertop and drank a couple of sips, before turning around.

An older man stood on his doorway, wiping his glasses. His cardigan and corduroys screamed wrong part of town.

Rex scratched at his crotch. Sleeping in his jeans wasn't the best idea. He should remember that next time he passed out.

He chuckled at his inner joke and approached the man, who made no move to come inside. "You sure you got the right apartment, mate?" Rex asked.

"Are you Richard Ackart?" the man asked in a cultured British voice.

Rex had heard that voice before, although he couldn't place it. "What if I am? Do I owe you money? If I do, good luck getting it." He shielded the entrance to his apartment with his body.

"So, are you Richard or not?" The man sounded impatient.

"Was. A long time ago. Now I'm Rex." He ran the fingers of one hand through his gelled hair, tussling the curls loose. Trying to look cool and menacing, despite the Heavy Metal concert in his head, he hooked the thumb of his other hand through one of his belt loops and squared his shoulders.

The man shoved the door in, hitting Rex's ribs and nose at once. A cracking sound let Rex know his nose was busted, seconds before the pain kicked in. Hell, it wasn't the first time that happened. He tasted his own blood before he saw it drip to the floor. He cupped his nose, pressed, and pulled to set it straight. He gave no thought to protecting his body from another assault – his mind was too fuzzy for that – so he did nothing when the man grabbed a fistful of his T-shirt and shoved him backward, following him inside.

"I'm a friend from the past" – the man kicked the door shut – "and I'm here to make sure you're Richard again long enough to go visit your mother in the hospital."

Rex didn't realize he'd passed out again until he woke in his bathtub. He was fully clothed, and the man splashed cold water on his face.

30

"Mum... What happened to her? Who are you?" Rex tried to get out of the two inches of water pooling in the tub, lost his footing, and slipped back inside.

The man held him in place with a hand on his shoulder. "I told you, I'm a friend. I used to know you when you were a boy." He shook his head when Rex made to rush out of the tub again. "Sit back down. We have to stop the bleeding. Pinch your nose and tilt your head back." He narrowed his eyes. "Whatever made you want to pierce an eyebrow, for heaven's sake? No matter. Our flight isn't until tomorrow morning. Enough time for you to clean up, and for the both us to have a nice, long chat."

It was the glint in his eye and the tone of his voice, not the cold water, that made Rex shiver. He'd done something the man didn't appreciate, and Rex was sure he didn't want to remain on his bad side. "Just tell me if she's all right." He sighed with relief when the man said she would be.

An hour later, Rex was too sober. A pair of sweats and a clean T-shirt had replaced the skin-tight black jeans he favored these days. Nose no longer bleeding and eyebrow stud removed, he sat and watched the man who'd screwed up his morning, as well as his nose, make tea.

"You'd think a fellow Brit would have better taste in tea," the man said.

Rex — no, he was Ric again now, properly scolded and worried about his mother — was hit by a sense of the surreal, when he found himself answering in the same conversational tone. "I wasn't able to find anything better in the local supermarket. I should have kept looking."

Tea served, Ric looked into the man's grey-blue eyes and asked, "Now will you please tell me what's wrong with my mother?"

31

"*After you tell me what happened to change* Richard of the Brush *to* Rex the Alcoholic Punk.*"

His tone wasn't mocking. It was concerned. The phrase triggered an old memory, and the pieces clicked in place. The man's hair was grey now, he wore glasses, and his attire was different. Still, Richard wanted to smack his forehead. He should have recognized him. "Edmund?" he asked in a whisper. His face felt hot with embarrassment. Edmund shouldn't see him like this.

Edmund Pedelty bought Ric his first crayon set. He was the one person who'd never treated him as a child, always as an equal. Ric remembered how hard he cried when he and his family left for England, and Edmund stayed behind. He felt alone in the world in his new home.

It wasn't that Ric's parents weren't understanding or supportive, but he never felt he could talk to them about his hopes and dreams, about science and the stars and the girl who sat in front of him in class, whose pigtails he wanted to pull, because she wouldn't give him the time of day.

He was eight the last time he saw Edmund, though they kept in touch a few times a year until Ric went to college. Now he wanted to hug the man and tell him how much he'd missed him, but held back. He'd let everyone down.

He let out a sigh of relief when Edmund stood and grabbed him in a bear hug. "Son, what happened to you? What is this?"

How do you tell someone dear to you how you royally fucked up your life, and then ran away from those who loved you, to avoid facing the aftereffects of your fuck-up?

Easy. You start at the beginning.

"I was weak." Ric pulled back from the hug.

Edmund retook his seat with a frown on his face. "You were never weak. You were a sensitive, good *lad."*

32

"Yeah, well, good lads don't get to have a lot of fun, now. Do they?" Ric used the rough brogue he'd adopted during his third year in college as part of his effort to be a badass for Bridget.

To become Rex for her.

Edmund's frown turned into a scowl, but Ric didn't revert to his real, upper-class accent. "I fell in love. Had to make her interested in me. She was a punk chick, and I went punk for her." He kept his tone even, as if he weren't describing the love that shattered his heart into a million pieces and screwed up his future. "I became a bad boy, though I still went to my classes. I hoped to make a good life for the two of us after I finished my studies. Was going to ask her to marry me." He let out a pained chuckle. "Didn't know she had a badder boy on the side. Didn't find out until graduation. She showed up with him at the party afterward, the both of them stoned. Never touched the stuff myself. Alcohol is my poison."

He took a sip of his tea, and felt ridiculous after his last sentence. "Got home late that night. Three sheets to the wind. Dad started shouting at me for waking them and for being in that state. He said one word too many, and I punched him." He hid his face in his palms. "I punched my dad, Edmund. Couldn't face him after that. Took the first plane here. Been doing odd jobs since."

"Odd jobs?"

Ric forced himself to meet Edmund's gaze. "Yeah. Kept up the bad-boy routine. Did some bouncing at night clubs. Then met a guy looking for a hacker. I was always good with computers, so that was it."

Edmund tapped his chin. "I may have a plan to make right of this mess of a life you have here."

33

"I don't care about that. I told you what you wanted to know. Now, how's my mother? What's wrong?"

"She and your father have been looking for you since you disappeared." His voice held no accusation, and Ric was grateful for that. "They only thought to contact me a few months ago. I called in some favors to locate you, but you're a hard man to get a hold of."

"She's been in a hospital for months?" Ric jumped out of his seat.

"No, boy. Sit down." Pedelty waited for him to do as he was told. "It's been six years since they last heard from you. Her health had been... deteriorating. You know she never had a strong constitution. She suffered a heart attack five days ago. The doctors said it was a close call, but she will be fine as long as she has the will to get better. I called today to say I found you, and she's expecting you tomorrow. You are what she wants to live for."

Ric nodded, but his panic was rising. "But I'm a mess. Can't let her down again. I can't!"

"You won't."

At the certainty in Edmund's voice, something fluttered in Ric's chest. Hope. "I have to get a clean change of clothes," he mumbled.

"Better throw away your entire wardrobe. I can lend you a suit for tomorrow, but you'll need more than that if you're going to work for me." Edmund grinned when Ric gave him a startled look. "We have no dress code, but your current stylistic choices are a tad over the line. With your... experience, you'll fit right in the IT department. Of course you'll have to cut down on the slang."

"Mate?" Ric didn't know if he should thank the man or grab his shoulders and shake some sense into him. He'd done nothing to deserve such an opportunity.

34

"You can't call me that at the office; I'll be your boss. But you can call me Edmund."

Edmund did more than straighten him up — he offered him a way out, a job, and the chance to reconcile with his parents. A chance to become a new man.

Ric swirled what was left in the bottle. He'd had... what? About half a bottle? He'd better stop. Edmund went above and beyond to help him out with his life, and Ric wouldn't screw it up. He wasn't going to disappoint the man now, after being an exceptional employee for this long, by showing up at work with a hangover because some silly bint thought he didn't like her.

He realized he still had his shoes on, and kicked them off. One tackled the loaded ashtray to the floor. Ric groaned and picked it up. He should vacuum. God, he hated the idea. Sometimes he missed being a bad boy. Missed talking like Rex. Not giving a damn about consequences. Doing what he wanted.

Funny thing was Rex gave a damn about consequences after all, or he wouldn't have rushed to England, to see his sick mother. He wouldn't have cleaned up his act. Wouldn't have disappeared in the shadows and let nerdy Richard resurface.

He got up and fetched the vacuum. After cleaning, he'd make dinner. He always cooked for himself these days. It was normal and nice, and he needed some normal and nice in his life, to remind him he had a life now — even if it consisted of little more than work, the gym, and the occasional outing with Pedelty for a couple of beers at the sole place nearby that vaguely resembled a pub.

Part of him knew he kept his life empty on purpose. He still didn't forgive himself for how he acted when Bridget left him, even though his father had.

Thinking of Bridget somehow led to thoughts of a perky and pesky blonde. She was everything he wasn't — bubbly, with no baggage, and unburdened by a sense of responsibility. He shook his head and started preparing his dinner. Lexi was free to do as she pleased, as long as she didn't let Ed down. This was the only reason Ric ever spared her a thought. The only reason she was on his mind, with those annoying smiles she gave to everyone but him, and her infuriating temper even when she was wrong.

He didn't care that she didn't know she was wrong. She bloody well *should* know. She should have cared to ask. He took out his frustration on his meal, wolfing it down without registering its flavor.

That night, lying in a bed that was too big for just him and wishing for some company, he pushed all thoughts of Lexi out of his mind and had a wank with his eyes closed.

He didn't realize the exact moment her face crept into his fantasy, blond tresses whipping his chest, green eyes blazing with passion. He came thinking of how she'd look riding him. His eyes flew open as strings of his cum landed on his stomach and fingers. He'd never come that hard before. Not by himself. Knowing her face had caused it shocked him.

He grabbed a fistful of tissues from his nightstand and wiped himself clean. *That* would never happen again. He just didn't see her that way. Sure, he found her pretty,

36

when he first saw her picture on Pedelty's desk—and she was stunning in person—but that was all.

He told himself the same thing over and over the following morning... after he jerked off in the shower, thinking of her.

He was screwed.

He got dressed, grabbed his laptop, and stormed out. Sliding inside his car, he took a deep breath. It would be okay. His thoughts were private. Nobody had to know.

Besides, Lexi already thought he was a jerk, and that was when he wasn't trying to be one. There was nothing there on her side, which would make it easier for him to forget his fantasies.

Right.

****

It was finally Friday, hours away from the weekend, and Lexi wanted to join her co-workers' happy buzz but couldn't. *Exotic Beast* kept her occupied. She wanted to stay late and read more. If she went home, she'd have to study the paperwork she kept putting off. She couldn't think about that when Xandra was getting what seemed to be the oral of the century in the novel.

Lexi didn't notice Richard was talking to her, until he stepped next to her and cupped her shoulder harshly.

She could have jumped right out of her skin, but had the presence of mind to press the Windows key and *D* and minimize everything on her desktop before turning to him. "What?" What did he want now? He had no business in her department, and he definitely had no right to sneak up on her. Hadn't the man heard of personal space?

And was she upset at him, or at almost being caught reading smut at work?

She was going to hell.

As if he read her thoughts, he took a step back and sat on the corner of her desk, still at an angle that would allow him to see her screen. She wanted to close the site's window, but that might seem conspicuous, and she'd rather die than have him of all people find out what she did in her spare time at work. Or that she had spare time.

"Are you all right?" His question seemed to startle him as much as it did her, because he hastened to elaborate. "I mean, is that translation too hard for you, maybe?"

Ah, now this was the Richard she knew and disliked. His mocking tone made her want to put her finger on that raised eyebrow and lower it to its normal height. "Nothing is too hard for me. I can take it all."

Incredibly, Richard blushed. Then he scowled. "I doubt the *all* you're getting here is much of a challenge, little girl."

Lexi felt her own skin flush. Not only did his words reflect her thoughts about her position, but also his *little girl* remark made her feel like she was twelve. She couldn't let that slide. She scowled back. "So what? You think I'm doing nothing difficult? You'd be surprised. This translation isn't easy. It has all these technical terms. I'd like to see *you* tackle it."

She didn't have time to feel bad about the lie, because Richard's eyes grew darker. If she knew what pissed him off now… she could do it again. Unfortunately for her, she couldn't help but notice how good *pissed off* looked on him. The muscle ticking in his jaw made his

38

cheekbones and hard-set angles of his face more prominent.

"I was thinking you should start coming to meetings. You know Edmund's planning to reorganize some interdepartmental processes, and there's no time like the present for you to get more involved."

Edmund wanted her more involved? That was great. Although attending meetings meant she wouldn't be at her desk as much as usual. "But—but my work. I'll fall behind."

"I'm sure you'll more than manage both paperwork and doing something useful."

His tone implied she wasn't doing something useful at present, and maybe she wasn't, but only because she'd finished sooner than expected. Her ire rose, but she managed to once again wear her custom-made grin for dealing with assholes. "I'd love to be useful. It'd be such a change from being the waste of space I am now. Oh, wait. That's not for you to decide. You're not the manager of this department, are you?"

Richard narrowed his eyes.

She bit on the inside of her cheek. Should she attack or be ready to defend herself? And why was he silent? The man was never silent when she was snarky.

And then he was right in her face. Close enough for her to... smell the smoke in his breath. Filthy habit. And that was most definitely all that came to mind about him.

"I don't need to be your manager, to see you're too fucking good for this." He spat the words out and left, while Lexi opened and closed her mouth like a fish, trying to grasp what just happened.

Did he just pay her a compliment?

If he did, if he thought of her as better than an airhead, thrown his way by nepotism, he didn't show it again. If anything, he looked at her with even greater disdain every time she flicked her gaze his way between chapters.

She didn't care. She was feeling hot. As in, extremely-horny hot. She'd just finished a deliciously wicked chapter and was tempted to go to the ladies room, to seek a little release of her own. No. Bad Lexi. There would be no taking the edge off during work hours. It was wrong enough that she got horny while at the office.

Should she even still be there? A quick glance at the clock showed her it was half past six.

It was official—she had no life. If she were still in New York, she'd be getting ready for happy hour with her friends, and here she stayed late at work on a Friday afternoon just to read smut. Her stomach chose that moment to protest. She should go home. *Nah.* Even though she had plans for Saturday, the prospect of spending a weekend without feeding her addiction to hot, passionate make-believe sex was the opposite of alluring.

There was a way she'd yet to try, to take her new favorite reading with her. She opened her personal e-mail account and copied one of the chapters she'd already read into a new message which she sent to herself. Aware she was bordering on paranoid, she checked the room yet again, and when she was sure nobody else was there, went to John's desk and switched on his PC. Username and password. What could they be?

She slid open his top drawer, and on a small piece of paper read *John_Rocks* and *God_s_Gift.*

40

He needed a cheat-sheet for that? Lexi typed the words with a snort.

She wanted to kick John's PC to smithereens when she saw her inbox did in fact have a message from her, but the message was empty. Had she really expected it to work?

And what was it with that website?

She sighed. She'd just stay at work longer. If anyone showed up, she'd say she wanted to get a better grasp of operations. Actually, she'd do that anyway. Starting on Monday, she'd start getting more involved with things. If she wanted to spend time reading *Exotic Beast*, she'd either come in early or stay afterhours and find a way to explain her long hours to Edmund without appearing to work overtime.

Yeah, that sounded easy. Not.

Eh, she'd figure it out after a couple more chapters. She returned to her novel and kept reading.

"I hate that he's touched you first." Rex withdrew his fingers and took in the sight of her, splayed and ready for his pleasure. She whimpered a pitiful plea in response, but he continued down the possessive road he'd chosen. "Have you ever begged him, like you do me?" His need became more heated, more urgent as he unbuttoned his jeans and freed his already rock-hard cock. Without further preamble, he plunged inside her to the hilt.

Lexi gasped, feathering her fingertips over her neck and collarbone, through the opening in her shirt.

The next few paragraphs broke her resolve to not be too naughty at work.

41

"Did he make you scream, Xandra?"

"No. Only you." She opened her eyes, caught his gaze, and said it again. "Only you."

Pleased with her answer, he pushed back inside her and used one of the fingers he'd soaked in her wetness, to stroke her ass. "Did you let him in here?" He slowly pushed the slicked finger inside the tight hole.

Lexi scrolled down. She inched her free hand under the hem of her skirt and caressed her thigh in ever widening circles, inching the fabric upward until her thumb brushed her soaked thong. She closed her eyes, took a deep breath, and brushed the thin fabric aside, to run a finger along her slit.

Chapter Four

Ric felt shaky since Lexi said she could take *anything*. His mind turned her words into a sexual innuendo, and he barely refrained from indulging in yet another fantasy of her taking all of something hard he had to give.

He was planning a peace offering when he went to her desk, but she was so defensive, he had to clench his teeth to bite back the same words he'd been telling Edmund since she set foot in the company.

Her being in that position was a mistake.

It didn't take a profiler to recognize the bored sighs and dazed looks. One translation a week wasn't letting her live up to her potential. He'd bet his ass it wasn't her task giving her a hard time. No. She excelled in what smart people did when they found no interest in their work—slacking off.

And she did a right good job of it too, the way she made sure to always look preoccupied and stay late. His inner Rex was almost proud of her, although he wouldn't let that show.

She was frightened at the prospect of more responsibility, but he couldn't guess why that was. Perhaps she doubted she was capable of more. Or maybe she wasn't just pretending to be busy. If it was the latter, what was she busy doing?

He wanted to grab her shoulders and shake her. Yell at her that she was being wasted. Tell her to ask Pedelty — hell, demand of him — to be given more responsibility. Maybe become her stepdad's assistant. Couldn't she see Ric was hard on her because he expected more? He could just…

Kiss her.

He shook off the thought. He wouldn't go there. Pedelty had treated him better than anyone he'd ever known. Ric shouldn't fuck with the man's stepdaughter. Unless she —

No.

He gave up trying to get through to her and returned to his desk, but couldn't stop wondering what she was doing. For some reason, he doubted it was the translation. Seriously doubted it. She looked too flushed and half-hid silly grins. Maybe she was just reading her email. He'd ogled her enough, so he turned back to catching up with his own work.

When she showed no sign of leaving at five, he didn't even try to convince himself he had a valid reason for deciding to also stay late. It was because of her, and he didn't give a fuck. He'd finally see what her extracurricular activities were.

Someone had turned off the overhead lights except for the one right above Lexi's desk. That was no surprise; everyone at the office knew Ric disliked fluorescent light. Taking advantage of the shadows, he sat back, made himself comfortable, and waited.

And waited.

44

And waited.

Lexi just looked at her screen, on occasion pressing a few keys.

He ducked under his desk to tie his shoelaces, and heard the clackety-clack of her high heels. He never understood how women could walk around in those torture devices. Still, they made Lexi's shapely legs look miles long. He had to lean down a little lower, to look at those legs through the opening at the front of his desk.

But what was she doing with the asshole's computer?

A couple of scenarios ran through Ric's head. Lexi could be making a practical joke on John, screwing up his settings, or she could be leaving him a message. Ric snorted. She was too good for the likes of John. If she were anyone else, Ric might suspect she was logging into files she had no access to on her own PC, but he doubted she'd be selling out company secrets.

The thing was, she didn't seem like the kind of girl who'd make practical jokes, either.

Wanking off to thoughts of her a couple of times was no reason for him to feel the rage he did at the thought of something going on between her and John, but he felt it anyway—and then some. He tried to be a good man. Tried hard not to give in to his urge to just walk up to her and bend her over the nearest horizontal surface. At the same time, he was the only one seeking a way for her abilities to be put to the best possible use at work. All because he owed it to Pedelty to look out for the man's and the company's best interest.

But he wasn't about to sit back and watch *John* swipe Lexi away.

John was a prick, and even if he treated Lexi right, they wouldn't know whether he cared for her or was making his best sales pitch ever by selling himself to the boss's daughter. And that would be bad for the company.

Yeah, that was all.

Ric didn't convince himself, but he didn't need to. He didn't care.

Even if she was so bloody beautiful and flirted with him when they first spoke. She shouldn't be flirting with him. She was off limits, and he had to respect that. Was trying too buggering hard to respect it…

And he had to stop looking at her legs.

He carefully sat up, slid forward so he his screen hid him, and tucked his legs underneath his chair. Peeking around the side, he saw Lexi smack her hand on John's desk before marching back to her seat to once again lose herself in whatever spell the screen held over her.

When she caressed the creamy column of her neck, her eyes hooded, Ric thought she knew he was there. He grinned. She was putting on a seductive show for his benefit. Disappointment replaced glee, once he noticed how riveted she was by what she was watching.

He had half a mind to stand, to see what Lexi was doing. Whatever it was, she enjoyed it. It was evident in the way she threw back her head, her chest heaving, her breath coming out in short pants of pleasure. Her upper arm moved faster and faster, and — oh, yeah — he got a very good idea of what she was doing. He inwardly cursed at her desk, for preventing him from zeroing in on her activities.

His cock stirred, but he ignored it in order to satisfy his curiosity. She was touching herself, but what had prompted it? Was the golden girl watching online porn? He could use the company's tracking system to check her activity. Nah. He didn't want her internet history recorded on the log, plus the company monitoring system didn't work around the clock on all computers.

With barely a second thought, he fell back on the skills he'd accumulated during his brief tenure as a hacker.

It took a few minutes, before he could see on his screen what she saw on hers. It would have taken less if Lexi didn't let out those sexy little mewls every once in a while, forcing him to readjust his jeans and want to crawl to the restroom for a quick hand-job.

She let out a moan and shuddered with release, and Ric looked away. It was weird to draw the line here, when he hadn't minded watching her get to that point, but this wasn't for him. *He hadn't earned it.*

His gaze landed on a random line in the text filling her screen. His jaw dropped, his straining cock forgotten, as he took in what was before his eyes.

"Did he fuck you like I do, Xandra?"
She was incapable of answering him, only managing to *exhale his name in pleasure. "Rex..."*

What the hell was that?

Deep breaths. He took slow, deep breaths and tried to remain calm. She was reading about sex between her and him... or another Rex.

He read back, trying to find a description of that other Rex, but none was available in the part of the page visible on Lexi's screen, and therefore on his. Then his screen showed her desktop. She was shutting down her PC. He considered making his presence known to her — ask her what it was he'd seen — but he somehow doubted that conversation would be in any way favorable to him. He remained quiet while she packed her bag and left, and then he waited another ten minutes or so.

When he was sure she wasn't coming back, he got up and walked to her desk with a plan in mind.

He planted his ass in her chair, hoping she hadn't bothered to change the username and password set up for her PC by the IT department. Namely, him. Only a few employees changed the codes they received, but even that wouldn't be a problem to crack. It would stall him, however, and Ric was in no mood to be stalled.

He needn't have worried. Her codes were the standard ones assigned to the position of her PC — $23\$\$68b$ and *sal!!un9*. No challenge there. When he opened the browser, it loaded the last page visited. The one that had shocked him. He pressed *Home*, and was directed to a page showing the front cover of an e-Book.

What the actual fuck?

He was seeing what had to be a Photoshop manipulation of him in the good old days. He sported the spiked hair and full-black outfit — the whole façade he put on when he was going around calling himself Rex, for Bridget's sake. But it wasn't his ex in his arms. The one he held was a slightly blonder Lexi. They both had such passionate looks on their faces, Ric couldn't tear his gaze from the picture.

He shook his head. He had to focus. He entered the book and skimmed through bits and pieces, suppressing his arousal in favor of figuring things out. He tried to

48

make sense of it all. The picture. The story. His old name in it. Not possible. He clicked on the author's name, Xopi Chilli, and was directed to a page that listed her as the author of several online novels, all about Xandra and Rex. He could get none of the links to the novels to work, and the search engine he used came up with no results.

Having seen his picture with Lexi, he no longer doubted the story was about him. He didn't know whether to be ecstatic or horrified. He had to trace the poster's IP to be sure, but the whole thing screamed *stalker*. For fuck's sake, the woman was making manips of the two of them and writing about a version of him fucking her. He ran his fingers through his hair and squeezed his eyes shut. A smoke would clear his mind. He fumbled in his back pocket for the crushed packet of Marlboros.

Did Lexi have the hots for the punk version of him? Pedelty shouldn't have fucking told her about his past.

She shouldn't fucking want him as Rex, when she disliked the real Ric.

Sucking on his unlit cigarette, he tried to calm down.

There was no Rex. Ric invented that persona to convince the girl he loved he was enough of a bad boy for her to give him a chance. Months had passed before he realized Bridget didn't do exclusivity. He'd reacted badly, hurt people he loved. He'd tried to become Rex after that. Be bad. Stop caring.

Until Pedelty had smacked some sense into him.

The cigarette's filter turned soggy. He swiveled around in the chair and pulled the window open far enough to throw the useless cancer stick outside. Then he turned back to the screen and clicked on *History*.

There were several pages with the words *Xandra* and *Rex* in the last couple days. Ric took a deep breath and let it out slowly. Why would Lexi do that here, especially if she didn't know he was watching? What was more, why would she write a whole book, just so *she* could read it? It made no sense. He read the rest of the author's bio and realized she bore no resemblance to Lexi. That didn't say much; the bio could be bogus. Still, something didn't fit.

This was going to be a long night.

It was three in the morning by the time he reached the page Lexi stopped at. He didn't have time to read it all, just skim it, but he knew one thing—she hadn't written it. According to the word count on the first page, the novel was about eighty-six thousand words long, and that was a bit much for her to have written in the three days she'd known him. He barely ever saw her type anything.

Lexi probably had no idea he was Rex, and something fishy was going on.

That an author happened to write about a couple so similar to him and Lexi, names included, wasn't probable, but weirder things had happened. He tried to think of one, failed, and finally admitted it was the oddest thing ever. Nevertheless, he'd always been a practical man. He wouldn't focus on how the book had come to be, but on what it meant that Lexi was so hooked on it.

On Rex.

Having jotted down the website address, he made sure to return to the page she'd last visited, then shut down her computer and went back to his desk to pack his laptop. He didn't care what Lexi had been doing with

50

John's computer, after all. She couldn't be interested in John, since she wanted Ric. Well, Rex, but still…

The grin that blossomed on his lips stayed there until long after he left work. He ignored the night security guard wishing him a nice weekend, though he heard the guy mumble *asshole* under his breath.

Ric no longer cared who wrote the book. He had a plan.

****

He didn't feel like going online or sleeping when he got home. What he wanted to do was take care of his throbbing cock, which had been rubbing against the inside of his baggy jeans for what seemed like an eternity. He left his laptop on the armchair and walked toward the bathroom. Without breaking his stride, he kicked off his sneakers, peeled off his T-shirt and jeans, and sent them to land on the floor in careless heaps.

He adjusted the temperature of the shower with one hand, the other caressing his cock slowly, almost absentmindedly. His mind couldn't have been more present or more focused on his erection, but he loved the anticipation and wanted to enjoy getting off with thoughts of Lexi free of guilt, for a change. Now he knew she wanted him on a carnal level—that she was more than just flirting with him—all thoughts about staying away from her for Pedelty's sake vanished. He'd go after her, and he'd make sure to treat her right, whatever that meant. He wouldn't fuck with her.

He stepped under the water spray. What did he want from Lexi? He didn't know. He just knew he wanted her and wanted to keep her best interest in the forefront. That would have to suffice. For him, for her, and for Pedelty.

It felt so good being able to admit he wanted her. So good to want someone again. And he wanted her right now, kneeling in front of him, looking up at him with those huge green eyes, the water soaking her hair and running down her naked breasts. She'd shiver and run her tongue over her lips.

He wrapped his hand around his thick, long shaft and dropped his head back against the tiled wall. Out of the water's way. He drew his fist from the tip of his cock to the base and back again, swirling his thumb over the head and grazing the slit on the upstroke. He could almost see Lexi taking him in her mouth. Feel her licking the underside. Tracing the vein there. In his mind's eye, she gave him that cheeky, infuriating look she'd given him earlier, when she was all snark and fire.

The look that said she knew she had him…

She had him by the short hairs, and he didn't care. He trailed his fingers along the sensitive underside, before tightening his grip on his dick. His movements became faster, as he envisioned Lexi's rosy lips stretching to encircle his width. Her tongue caressing him, as she sucked him as far as he'd go into her mouth. Her heat engulfing him, while she caressed up his inner thigh, finding her way to his balls.

He used his free hand to play out her part in his fantasy, cupping and tugging at his scrotum and putting pressure on the place underneath that always drove him wild, while he pumped his length furiously. His release approached, throbbed inside him, and he wished Lexi

52

were there with him, so he could tangle his fingers in her golden locks and let go with her gaze locked to his.

He came harder than ever before. Harder than when the woman he'd deemed to be the love of his life used to ride him to oblivion. All because he was thinking of those green pools of fire staring up at him. He didn't come with a yell or a roar, but with a chuckle that reverberated off the walls of the small bathroom. If it was this good when Lexi's memory was with him, he couldn't begin to imagine how the real thing would be. Then again, he didn't have to imagine. He'd make sure to have the real thing soon enough.

He showered quickly, steering clear of thoughts of Lexi, lest he go another round, and went to bed not bothering to pick up his clothes or shoes from the hallway. The cool sheets felt tantalizing against his naked skin, his senses awakened from a deep, long slumber. He hadn't paid attention to sensation since he came to the States. He'd only cared for the touch of anonymous strangers, before he'd given up on it all together two years ago. The single pleasure he allowed himself was smoking, and that was permitted almost nowhere.

"Sod it." He shook a cigarette out of the soft pack he always had on his bedside table, and lit it. He folded one arm under his head and blew rings of smoke while he went over the finer details of his plan.

Lexi had given him something more than a way to get through the next day. She'd stirred things in him he'd thought long dead. It was time he started stirring things in her.

He left the cigarette in the ashtray and reached for his cock. With his other hand, he grabbed one of the bars of the headboard.

He didn't think it weird that he called out *Xandra* when he let go. She was Xandra, and he was Rex, and there was nothing wrong about that.

Chapter Five

Lexi hit her alarm clock with the flat of her palm, but the stupid thing wouldn't stop ringing. She tried again, with no success. What…?

Not the alarm clock. Her phone, and the sound came from under her bed. She must have thrown it to the floor sometime during the night. She half-mumbled, half-sang her ring-tone, while reaching for it. When she closed her fingers around the phone, she blinked the sleep from her eyelids and looked at the screen. She'd accidentally already accepted the call. "*Shit.* Hello?"

"Hello? Lexi? Good afternoon. Or is it still morning to you?"

"Huh?" Lexi didn't know who it was, but she didn't mind him repeating himself. His deep voice and British accent sent tingles from the back of her neck all the way down her spine.

"Is that little brain still sleeping? Want me to call later?"

She was all but swooning at a man she didn't recognize. "Who is this?" she asked rather abruptly.

"Don't tell me you don't know." The voice sounded familiar, but the accent sure didn't.

"Well, I don't." She took the phone away from her ear and checked the Caller ID. Withheld. "Tell me who

55

you are, or I'm hanging up." She really, *really* didn't want to hang up, because his gruff voice made her feel warm all over, but she would. Even crazy, loony stalker guys could have sexy voices.

"It's Ric, from IT."

"Ric?" She hoped she didn't sound as astonished as she felt. She probably did.

"Yeah, it's me. Sorry to wake you —"

"You're not Ric," she said. "You said *sorry*."

He chuckled. "Miracles do happen, you know."

"I guess they do. So, to what do I owe the displeasure?"

This time he didn't laugh. His tone was all business, but his voice was still sexy. Why didn't he talk like this at the office? "Wanted to ask if you've been having any trouble with your computer this week."

She wouldn't call it *trouble*. It had been providing her with delicious smut. "What kind of trouble?"

"Browser crashing or redirecting you to random pages? I know it's weird, calling you about it on a Saturday, but I stopped by the office earlier, and my PC seemed to be acting up. My internet connection was especially slow."

She frowned. "So you're calling all employees, to ask how their computers are faring?"

"The system showed you left last yesterday, and since no issues were reported while I was there, I thought whatever happened must've been after I left." He paused. "While you were the only one there."

Lexi's pulse thumped faster. If there was a virus, they might search everyone's browsing history. She'd be found out. "Nope. Didn't notice anything out of the

56

ordinary. Not that I was online for longer than it took to check my e-mail." She prayed to every deity she could think of that he didn't check the internet log. "So, whatcha gonna do about it? About fixing it?"

"Don't know for sure there's something in need of fixing. I'll let you know once I find out. Keeping all PCs tamper-free is the best way to ensure we have a smooth business operation, but some people consider internet safety to be some exotic beast."

She sucked in a breath. It was a turn of phrase. Nothing more than that.

"You still there?"

"Yup. Thought—thought I saw a cockroach." It was a stupid response, and she knew it, but couldn't do much better for the moment.

His voice turned huskier. "And you went silent? I'd expect that to make you scream."

The line went dead, and Lexi was left staring at her silent cell. Richard's—Ric's—words slammed into her conscious mind with force. *Exotic beast? Make her scream?* It had to be a coincidence. No way he'd know about her new... hobby and not rub her face in it openly. He didn't know. Couldn't.

Going back to sleep proved a lost cause, so she took her purple helper and went for a long bubble bath. The voice she imagined guiding her hand as she pleasured herself was Rex's, not Ric's. She repeated that to herself until she almost believed it.

Clean, relaxed, and a bit more satisfied than after her last session with the toy, she called Angie and arranged to meet her for coffee.

****

Angie was already at their favorite table. She fidgeted with an imaginary piece of string on her sleeve, straightened her neckline, sleeked chestnut hair down both sides of her face, and made sure the cornflower-blue stone of her ring was centered.

Lexi smiled. She knew and loved all of her friend's quirks. The two had been friends since Angie straightened Lexi's scrunchie in second grade.

Lexi snapped around and met two big blue eyes.

"I'm sorry. Your scrunchie — it wasn't…" The girl took a deep breath and closed her eyes briefly. "It was wonky," she finally said, as if that summed up all that was wrong in the world.

Lexi couldn't help but giggle. "I'm Lexi, and you can save my ponytail from wonkiness any day."

And Angie didn't stop at saving her ponytail. As the years went by, they grew closer instead of apart, despite the differences in their interests and the distance during and after college. Angie flew to New York when Andrew proved to be a two-timing bastard, and again to help Lexi pack for her return to San Francisco.

A couple days ago, overwhelmed by loneliness and lack of prospects, Lexi broke down in this café, and Angie once more helped her collect the pieces.

Lexi was glad to have something other than personal woes to share this time. She took a seat, and Angie beamed that brilliant smile of hers that still held traces of the shy kid she'd been. "Spill," she said.

"Huh?"

Angie crossed her arms over her breasts. Her ring caught the light and cast a filigree of brilliant dots over her face. For a moment, she looked ethereal. "Don't play coy with me, or I'll turn you into a frog, and good luck finding a prince to save you in this century."

Lexi giggled and held up both hands in mock surrender. "Oh, please don't. I'll talk." Angie claimed she had magic powers, and Lexi always pretended to believe her. No harm done by letting Angie do her thing, even if Lexi thought mid-twenties was way too late for such fantasies. "Just lemme get my caffeine fix." She asked the waitress for a latte and turned back to her friend. "Don't you want to go first? My news could take a while."

"Sure. Why not?" Angie shrugged. "The living together thing is working out perfectly, Sarah is as much of a keeper as they come, and I couldn't be happier or more in love. Your turn."

"I'm so happy for you two." Lexi'd seen the sparks fly between them when Angie introduced her to Sarah at Lexi's Welcome-Home party. "She's wonderful, honey, and you seem to be made for each other."

"Yes, yes. She and I are soul-mates. Now *tell me*."

"Tell you what?"

Angie twirled her right index finger in the air and squinted at Lexi. "Frog."

Lexi widened her eyes in mock-fright, before she leaned in closer. "Can you keep a secret?" At Angie's raised eyebrow, she scrunched her nose. "You're so gonna think I'm crazy, once I'm done telling you."

"Lexi. Seriously. Have I ever judged you?"

59

She never had. Hoping she wouldn't now, either, Lexi told her all about the book.

"I have no idea what's up with it," she said finally. "I'm so hooked, and I'm afraid someone at work may find out."

"Then just stop visiting it when you're in the office." Angie bit on her lower lip. "Oh, but you can't access it anywhere else. It can't be a coincidence that your nickname is there, and I don't know why anyone would go through so much trouble... We'll get to the bottom of this. I'll have to do some research. Find the IP address, the site administrator—*something*. Everything leaves traces on the internet. I'll just follow the trail." And there was that class-nerd-slash-whiz-kid sparkle in her eye.

"I love it when you go into research mode." Lexi grinned. "We have to figure it out soon, 'cause I'm getting paranoid. Just this morning, I freaked out when Ric called because something he said was too close for comf—"

"Wait. Ric? Who's Ric?"

"You know. Richard. From IT? Annoying Brit? I told you about him over the phone."

"Yes, you did. But on Wednesday he was IT-Richie. Now he's just Ric?" The arching of both eyebrows was meant to show incredulity, but Angie's eyebrows were so round, the expression gave her face a cartoonish quality.

"Yes, well, he's still IT-Richie. Still a jerk. But maybe we can coexist." He said she was too good for her current job, so at least he was perceptive. "He may not be as determined to get me out of there as I thought. It doesn't mean I like him, of course." Though he was easy on the eyes, and his accent during that call made her want to—

60

"Ah, I get it," Angie said.

"What?"

Angie gave a lopsided grin. "What *what*?"

"Why do you have that look? You know I don't like the guy."

"Did I say you did?"

"No, but you said, 'I get it,' when I said I didn't."

"And how did agreeing with you mean I didn't agree with you?"

"Oh, I know all your acting-like-you-believe-me-till-I-snap-and-tell-you-the-truth techniques."

"What truth? I thought you *were* telling the truth."

"Well, I was. I don't like IT-Richie."

"Good for you, sweetie. Now about the site..."

Angie obviously itched to solve the Internet mystery. She hated anything being beyond her understanding.

"All I need is time with your PC," she said.

"I'm just as eager to find out what's going on, if not more. I want to make sense of it. To see if this is the mother of all coincidences" —

"Yeah, right."

—"or if someone's messing with me. But we need a cover story. Not like I'm so swamped, I need to be there. And I can't just bring my BFF with."

"But I need *that* computer, to look into this thing. Weekends are the only time I can come by without people asking questions."

Lexi's resolve crumbled. Angie's persistence and stern voice were her most trusted weapons, once she made her mind up about something.

"We'll still have to explain it to security. There's always someone there, even during the off hours. And I'd like us to get it over with as soon as possible. I have plans tonight."

"Interesting plans?"

Lexi shook her head. "A couple friends from college are in town. Said I'd meet them for drinks."

"Alexandra Adams" — there was the stern voice — "drinks can wait. Now finish your coffee, and let's go."

"Okay, okay. But if we're caught looking at that stuff, you'll be the one coming up with an excuse to give Edmund." Lexi paid for both of them, and then spent most of the ten-minute cable-car ride to Pedelty Electronics grumbling about what they were about to do.

She ran her key-card through the slot at the right of the door, and they went inside, both squinting to adjust their eyes to the sudden change in lighting. Lexi couldn't hold back a groan when she saw the security guard standing behind the front desk.

"What?"

"You and your brilliant ideas. This guy's been hitting on me from day one. The big lump's too stupid to understand *no*, and now we show up on his shift? God."

"Then it's a good thing it's his shift. Go and charm our way upstairs."

"But—" She didn't get to say more, because Angie elbowed her forward. With a huff, Lexi dragged her feet in his direction, with Angie hot on her heels.

"Hi Lexi," the ogre said, while she was still several feet away. "Come to keep me company on a long, lonely shift?"

62

His grin was so goofy she felt the urge to smack it off his face but for the thousandth time this week, she restrained herself. It would be inappropriate. Plus, if she were to smack anyone in there, it should be IT-Richie. "Um... No, actually. Just wanted to copy some files from my PC." She held up her keychain for him to see her flash drive. "Do you mind if my friend comes with me?"

"I don't know. You two ladies may be planning a heist." Ugh. He was irritating as hell.

Lexi batted her eyelashes and forced a giggle, like she thought he was the funniest thing since the Three Stooges. "Oh, come on, Chad. Like I would do that to my own company?" She sounded like a brat, but the end had to justify the means.

"Can't say no to the boss's daughter, can you?" Angie tilted her head.

All mirth left Chad's face. "I suppose I can't. You may go upstairs, Miss Pedelty."

Lexi ignored the formality, except to make a correction. "It's Ms. Adams, but thank you." She graced him with a beaming smile, took Angie's hand, and all but dragged her toward the stairs.

An hour later, when Lexi's office phone rang, Angie had come up with zilch. Lexi frowned. Nobody knew she was there. "Hello?"

"Are you two okay up there, all by your lonesome?" The guy had an extremely short memory span. His voice held what he must have considered a teasing quality.

"We're fine. We'll be right down and out of your way."

They left, still no closer to solving the mystery of *Exotic Beast*.

Angie muttered something, once they'd exited the building. Lexi caught the word *option*, but she was used to her friend mumbling when she was deep in thought, so she made nothing of it. Angie typed furiously on her phone while they waited at the bus stop and for most of the ride to their neighborhood.

She gave Lexi a tight hug when they got off the bus. "We'll figure it all out."

Lexi promised to keep her updated on any news. She didn't miss the deep vertical line between Angie's eyebrows before they went their separate ways. Could Angie know more about the site than she let on? *Nah.* Lexi felt bad for even entertaining the thought. Angie wouldn't keep something like that from her. She texted her college friends, to find out where they'd meet up, and went home to get ready.

Chapter Six

Ric hummed to himself while taking another shower. A cold one this time. He kept humming while making an onion-and-peppers omelet, as well as while eating it. On more than one occasion, he considered calling Lexi again, to let her know he'd solved the imaginary computer problem. In the end, he preferred to let her stew and worry she'd get caught.

What was more, calling her again was what a lovesick puppy would do, and while he was certain he wasn't lovesick, he was a hundred percent positive he wasn't a puppy.

The big bad wolf, maybe.

He howled — a fairly impressive imitation of a big dog, if he said so himself. He chuckled, shook his head at his own silliness, and then howled once more for good measure. If he didn't have to clean up his place, he'd say this was a good day.

When he was done, he went for the wireless phone. A number was written on a post-it stuck to his refrigerator door. He knew it by heart, but double checked while dialing it. He punched the numbers in his phone and brought the receiver to his ear. If he couldn't call Lexi again, he'd settle for the next best thing.

The phone was answered on the second ring. "Hello?"

"Hey, Ed. It's me. Want to go for a drink?"

Pedelty always talked about Lexi's achievements, but Ric didn't need anyone to tell him how brilliant she was. He knew that. There were other things he wanted to find out about her. He could do some in-depth research — he had the means to — but he didn't want to invade her privacy, just to find a way to approach her.

****

Ric was two bottles of beer behind Pedelty, and a galaxy away from learning anything useful about Lexi. All he'd found out was that she loved monkeys and her favorite color was pink. His best fishing tactics had been in vain. Edmund seemed to work around his questions, almost as if on purpose.

Ric had to be more direct. He bought Edmund his fourth beer for the evening, and tried once more. "Must have been hard being a stepdad to a teenager, yeah?" He leaned forward conspiratorially. "Having to fend off the boys with a broomstick? I bet Lexi wasn't an easy one to handle during the rebellious years."

Outside the workplace, he always reverted to his less polished self. It made him feel he had some control over his life. That he hadn't gone completely soft yet.

Pedelty shrugged. "No. Not really. She was a hit with the blokes but never made any trouble for me or her mother. We trusted her to make the right choices, and she made a point to keep her dating away from home. Joy insisted on meeting her" — he arched both eyebrows

66

briefly—"dates on several occasions, but Lexi said only Mr. Right would have to undergo the Spanish Inquisition. She did introduce us to her prom date. Nice young fellow, but his handshake left something to be desired. Like shaking a cold fish, it was. I believe she stopped seeing him after that night. And then there was her fiancé. Right pillock, that one. Wish I'd told her I expected it to end badly."

"Fiancé? Lexi was engaged?" And Pedelty had never mentioned it before?

"Yes. Sore spot with her. The bastard moved her to the other side of the country, before he made a right mess of things."

Ric was surprised by his instinctive need to find the guy and teach him it wasn't polite to mess with beautiful, funny, and smart young women. "Was that why she came home?" If the breakup was so fresh, he wouldn't make a move yet. Lexi'd need some time to herself.

"Partly. It's been over for a year now, but—" Edmund waved his hand in a dismissive gesture. "I shouldn't have said anything. Lexi had me promise nobody in the office would know her personal business. Forget we had this chat."

"Forgotten already." Ric was such a liar. He wanted to find out exactly what happened. Pedelty seemed a bottle away from answering more direct questions, but Ric thought he'd better not push him to drink more. He didn't want to have to explain it to the man's wife. He'd met Joy a handful of times, during her brief visits to the company, but he didn't need to ask who Lexi inherited her fierce glare from.

67

Edmund downed the bottle in a couple of gulps, mumbled something about it *not even remotely resembling British ale*, and ordered another.

Ric waved for the check. "I'm good, thanks. I'm driving you home after this one. All right?"

"What's the rush? The night's still young, and you've yet to tell me why you wanted to see me—let alone get me drunk." Yup, someone's words were slurred.

"I didn't..." Ric felt all of five years old under Edmund's scrutiny.

"Save it. You did. Now, what's the problem?" Pedelty's accent had slid closer to the one Ric adopted as Rex. He hadn't always been the respected family man and business owner he was now. Ric's dad had often mentioned Edmund's promiscuous and alcohol-soaked *dark years*, but never got into further detail about that era.

"There's a girl," Ric said.

"When isn't there one? Come on, mate. Tell me about her."

"Not much to tell, really. She's nothing like anyone I've met before. And she hates my guts."

"There's passion, then." Ed leaned back and crossed his arms. "What are you going to do about it?" He squeezed his eyes to slits, and Ric hoped it was because of the poor lighting in the establishment, and not a warning. It couldn't be a warning. Edmund didn't know who the talk was about.

Did he?

"I want her." Ric too crossed his arms, feeling nowhere near as nonchalant as his boss appeared. He turned his gaze to the ceiling, afraid Edmund's would read the truth in his eyes. "So, I guess I should go after

68

her. Yeah. I *will* go after her, Edmund." He chanced a glance the man's way.

Pedelty nodded. "You do that." He raised his beer upside down and caught the last drops with his tongue, before setting the bottle on the table with a thud. The talk was apparently over. "Glad to have helped, boy. Now let's get out of here before Joy makes me sleep on the sofa, shall we?"

The grace with which he unfolded himself from the chair and draped his jacket over one shoulder was at odds with the slurred speech from moments ago. So was his swagger, as he led the way out the door.

Ric followed after him, dumbfounded. He had no idea whether the man believed him about the random girl that tickled his fancy, or whether he understood and gave Ric the green light to go after his stepdaughter.

****

Joy threw the door open, just as Pedelty pushed his key into the lock. Her scowl put her daughter's to shame. "Edmund Pedelty. Coming home later than Lexi, reeking of alcohol and unable to find the keyhole? Honestly."

She ignored Edmund's protests that he was perfectly able of letting himself in his own bloody house, and turned to Ric, her gaze softening. "Thank you, Richard, for making sure he got home safely."

Pedelty leaned sideways on the doorframe and graced his wife with a naughty smirk, as she stood there full of passion and fire.

Ric smiled. "He isn't drunk, Mrs. Pedelty. Just a bit tipsy."

69

"Call me Joy, honey. He could have been mugged if he'd walked home. Or worse. You must let me make it up to you." She paused and did that thing with her nose that Lexi did when she was deep in thought. "You should come to lunch tomorrow."

Edmund chuckled. "Good luck with that one. I've asked him over time and again, but he keeps saying he doesn't want to impose."

"This time it's the lady of the house asking." As if Ric would miss this opportunity. "I'd love to, Joy. Can I bring something?" He hoped his smile wasn't frightening. It had been a while since he had reason to smile this widely, and it felt foreign on his lips.

Edmund gave him a surprised look for a split second, before his face settled on his previous smirk.

"Just bring yourself, dear," Joy said. "We'll be expecting you around one. Good night, and drive safely."

"Thank you. I'll see you tomorrow." He nodded to Edmund, who was pulled inside by the lapels and definitely in for a tongue lashing.

Ric bounced down the porch steps and opened his car door with a chuckle. Lexi would *freak out*, as America's youth put it.

Chapter Seven

Lexi had to remember to switch off her phone before going to bed. She'd drunk a little too much last night, and couldn't endure the noise pounding inside her head.

She accepted the call. She'd chomp Ric's head off, if it was him again. "What?"

"Um… I woke you, didn't I? I'm sorry. I'll call —"

"Hi, Sarah. No, it's okay. I'm up."

"You sure? 'Cause I can —"

"It's fine. Really. What's up?"

"We wanted to see if you'd come over for lunch at our place. Angie's cooking."

"And you don't want to risk food poisoning all by yourself?"

"Never said that." Sarah's smile carried in her voice. "Her cooking has come a long way."

Eh, that was true. Angie tended to — in time — excel in everything she busied herself with. "Let me pour some coffee into my body, and I'll call you back. Okay?"

"Sure."

"Talk later." Lexi hung up and rolled onto her stomach. The idea of going to Angie and Sarah's for lunch wasn't unappealing, except for the fact that she didn't feel like getting up and getting dressed.

There was a knock on her door, followed by her mom's voice. "Xandra? Honey? Are you awake?"

Uh-oh. Use of *Xandra* was never good. There had to be chores in the immediate future.

Lexi pulled the covers over her head, praying her mom would give up. In her twenty five years, she should have learned there wasn't much chance of that. She snorted when her mother knocked harder. "Xandra? It's almost eleven o'clock. Rise and shine."

No way she'd go back to sleep now. With a groan, she kicked the covers off. "I'm up," she mumbled.

"What was that, honey?"

"I'm up, Mom." She had to step up the search for an apartment, or she might have to kill her mom to keep her sanity.

Her mother's footsteps echoed down the hall, and Lexi forced herself out of bed. She looked through her drawers for a set of underwear, a pair of jeans, and her favorite sleeveless top. "Of course I'm up," she said aloud. "Why would I want to stay in bed on a Sunday? The only day this week I had no reason to wake up?" As she pulled out a pair of lace panties, her vibrator rolled forward. There might be hope for her morning yet.

She didn't feel like a bath, and from the way her mom tried to get her up, it was obvious she had an itinerary Lexi wanted no part of. Her best bet was a quick shower and a quicker getaway.

Well, the shower didn't have to be that quick.

She stepped under the spray, Mr. Purple already buzzing at the lowest setting.

She ducked, for the hot water to fall on her head and back, her mind rehashing scenes of Rex and Xandra

72

making love. She imagined fingers running down her spine and caressing her hips along the path the water made, while she traced her slit with the toy, letting it linger on her clit. She slid the vibrator inside her pussy a fraction of an inch at a time and clamped her thighs shut to hold it in place. Letting the low hum build up her arousal, she poured some of her jasmine-scented shower gel in her palms, and massaged her body from the neck downward. She cupped her breasts, grazing her sensitive nipples with her thumbs, and couldn't stifle a moan.

By the time she feathered the fingers of one hand over her mound, the accumulated sensations made her lightheaded. She had to find purchase on the wall. A quick twist of the vibrator's base between index and middle finger, while she pressed on her clit, and her release hit her with a force that buckled her knees. She leaned her forehead against the cool tile and bucked her hips into her hand, riding out her pleasure.

When she caught her breath, she extracted the plastic phallus, washed it clean with jerky movements, and set it aside. She felt grumpier than before, while lathering her hair and rinsing, but couldn't find a reason for the deterioration of her mood.

No reason other than the fact that what sent her over the edge was the memory of Ric—IT nerd and asshole extraordinaire—saying, "I'd expect that to make you scream."

She wrapped a towel around her head, pulled on her clothes, and left the bathroom. Back in her room, she applied some light makeup and her favorite strawberry-flavored lip-gloss. She pushed all annoying thoughts from her mind, slipped on a pair of loafers, and stormed downstairs. If she was lucky, she'd make a clean exit.

She threw open the front door and turned to yell that she'd be at Angie's, when she bumped into a hard body.

A strong hand coiled around her right upper arm and kept her from toppling over. "Steady there, love. Were you in such a hurry to greet me?"

Lexi's breath hitched in her throat. The endearment was one Rex had used in the book, and she knew the voice, even though the accent wasn't his usual one. She looked up, and found Ric's bluer-than-blue eyes.

Shit.

Lexi took the opportunity to study him as much as their respective positions allowed. He stood on her porch in a charcoal button-down shirt and slim-fit light-blue jeans. She almost swooned at his closeness, his strength, and the firm muscles bulging in his arms. The boy sure cleaned up *nice*. She shook her head, to snap out of it. Hot or not, he was a jerk, and she was leaving

"What — what are you doing here?" And why had he called her *love*? It had to be a British thing… though Edmund never used it.

She scowled, channeling her surprise and grudging attraction into anger. It was either that or acknowledge the heat inside and try to make sense of it.

Whatever showed on her face was enough to make him let go. She took a step back and poked his sternum with her finger. "Don't tell me you're making surprise house calls to check on Internet Explorer."

"Actually, I was invited."

"Oh? Edmund asked you to come over on a Sunday, to talk shop?" She gave him her best and-I'm-the-Queen-of-England look, but her mother's voice made her spin on her heel.

"I asked him, Lexi. For lunch. And where are you going? Last night you said you'd be eating with us."

Lexi had been tipsy enough to agree to anything last night, but she knew better than to say so. She took in the box Ric held. *Cupcakes?* "I forgot I'd already made plans with Angie and Sarah, Mom. Didn't know we'd have guests."

"It's perfectly all right, Joy. I'm sure we'll have fun without Lexi. There's no reason for her to reschedule on my account."

Lexi turned back to him with frown. Had he just been *nice*? For the second time in two days? Oh, he was up to something. Maybe he wanted to convince her mom Lexi didn't belong with Pedelty Electronics, since he couldn't get Edmund to fire her. "I guess I could stay," she said.

"No, Richard is right. Hold on. I have some cake you can take with you to the girls."

"Mom, I'm riding my bike there. I need the exercise."

"I'll put it in a bag for you. Come in, Richard." Before Lexi could protest, her mom left for the kitchen.

Ric winked and walked past Lexi, but she caught his sleeve. "Not so fast. I don't know what you're doing here, but you better not..." Better not what? Not *be in her home*, unsupervised—by her. "Just don't, okay?"

"I wouldn't."

His simple reply left Lexi speechless. She wanted the last word, but her mom brought out a platter with half

75

a round cake covered in tin-foil, told Lexi to give Angie and Sarah her best, and all but shooed her away.

****

Angie opened the door, and Sarah rushed to gather Lexi into a tight hug. Even visually, they completed each other. Where Angie was petite and lean, Sarah was plump, taller, with an ample bosom and round rosy cheeks. Sarah's soulful brown eyes and the air of calmness she exuded added to a wholesome, nurturing image that came at odds with Angie's wiry, nervous energy.

They were both smiling, and Lexi once more wondered at how perfect they were for each other.

Lexi muttered a subdued greeting and dragged her feet to the couch. She planted her ass on it, clutching the cake which had miraculously survived the hugging. "IT-Richie is at my house," she said. "He's probably charming my mom and planting alien spawn in her and Edmund's bodies, to use them as mindless soldiers in his battle against me."

Sarah elbowed Angie, who patted Lexi's shoulder but didn't speak.

"Would you like me to go?" Sarah asked. "Maybe you want to talk to Angie alone?"

Lexi shook her head. "It's not a secret. This guy from work seemed to dislike me till—like—five seconds ago but is now all nice and alone with my parents. He has to have an evil plan."

"Hon, maybe you're overreacting?" Despite her sweet tone with Lexi, Sarah gave Angie a stern look. She mouthed something Lexi didn't even try to catch, and Angie shrugged, a smile tugging at the corners of her eyes.

Whatever.

Any secret communication between the two lovebirds wasn't her concern. Ric was at her house, planning her fall.

"Can't let him do that." Lexi stood again, thrust the cake toward Sarah, who barely had enough time to close her arms around it, and rushed out the door.

As she pulled it closed behind her, she heard Sarah say, "Tell me again what you did."

They had to be arguing before she walked in. Her leaving was for the best.

Chapter Eight

Lexi was happy to discover she wasn't totally out of practice from her cycling days in school—she rode at full speed for the entire seven blocks, and was only *nearly* out of breath when she burst through the front door.

She checked her appearance in the foyer mirror and waited a couple of minutes for her heart rate to return to normal. When the twin red blotches on her cheeks faded, she entered the dining room with a slow, confident stride.

Her mother was loading Edmund's plate with vegetables, while Ric helped himself to the baked potatoes.

"I'm back."

They all looked up, but showed no surprise. Ric must have already inserted the alien spawn in their brains and killed the human ability to display emotions in the both of them. Lexi stifled a giggle.

Edmund ruined her theory when he winced and massaged his temple. "Could you be a tad less cheerful? I have a blasted headache."

"It's called a hangover, darling."

"So you said. Repeatedly."

"Not my fault you're developing a drinking problem." Her mother kept piling greens on her husband's plate.

"I don't have a sodding drinking problem. I had a few beers with a friend."

"Really, Joy" — Ric seemed uncomfortable — "he didn't have that much to drink. He just had an empty stomach."

"He still should know better at his age." Her mother patted Edmund's shoulder.

"You know, I don't believe my headache has anything to do with last night," Edmund said. "I believe it was caused by your fussing about, clanging pots, and yelling this morning. You'd think we were having royalty over."

Lexi had the distinct feeling Edmund was about to bang his head on the table. Before he could do so, her mother turned to her. "Join us, honey."

Ric stood and pulled out the chair next to his, and Lexi noticed an extra set of cutlery and a plate. Weird. Her mom expected her to come back for lunch?

She took her seat and graced Ric with a smile. "Thank you." She tried to suppress a shiver of pleasure when his hand grazed her naked shoulder as he pushed the chair in place.

She noticed her mother nudging Edmund, who looked at her and nodded. What was that about?

Ric wore a rather self-satisfied smirk. Without much thought, Lexi swung her leg so the heel of her foot connected with his shin under the table. Her behavior was about two decades off, but he brought out the worst in her.

He kicked her back in the same manner... and just as hard.

The bastard *kicked* her.

79

Pretending to bring her chair closer to the table, she stretched out her leg, stepped on the toes of his trainer, and pushed down as hard as possible. *Ha.*

Her victory was short-lived. Quick as lightning, Ric snaked his hand under the table and clamped his fingers just above her knee like a vice.

With his other hand, he raised his glass. "Thank you, Joy." He squeezed Lexi harder, digging his fingers into her flesh when she tried to move her leg. "I'm honored to be part of your family's Sunday meal. It's nice to feel included, and it means more than you can imagine. Here's to you." He loosened his grip on Lexi's knee long enough for her to pull free.

"No need to thank me, sweetie. We're happy to have you. If anything, I'm sure you had better things to do with your Sunday." Lexi's mom beamed at him.

"All I had planned was to sleep in until about now." He looked a little sheepish at the confession.

Lexi's anger boiled inside. The man was a natural actor. Well, she wasn't going to fall for it. She made a show of ignoring the conversation around her, and shoveled mouthful after mouthful of meat, veggies, and mashed potatoes in her mouth. No one had questioned her return, and she prayed things would stay that way.

"Lexi, I forgot to ask. Was everything all right with the girls? I thought you wouldn't be back till after lunch." Her mother smiled, and Ric turned toward Lexi with a triumphant look in his eyes. Edmund glanced at her from over his glass as he downed some water.

That made for one hundred percent of Lexi's prayers going unanswered today. And they said Sunday was the Lord's day. "The girls are fine, Mom. I just

80

thought I should be here, since Richie was invited. I mean, 'cause we work together and stuff." Ric's jaw didn't give the tell-tale sign of irritation when she uttered the name he hated, so she braced herself for payback.

When it came, it was so subtle, she didn't recognize it for what it was at first.

Ric smiled and thanked her for her consideration, before he began raving about Joy's cooking. "I'm amazed you managed to prepare this elaborate meal on such short notice. Unless you eat like this every Sunday." He spread his arms wide enough to indicate the two kinds of salads, steamed vegetables, baked and mashed potatoes, pasta al' forno, and veal casserole strewn on the table.

Lexi couldn't help but snort at his wide eyed *gosh, ma'am* look.

"Joy is an excellent cook," Edmund's said.

"I can see that." Ric toyed with a pea, chasing it around his plate with his fork until he finally snagged it. "You're mine, pea," he whispered. "Say you're mine." His tone was light, and Edmund and Lexi's mom cracked up.

Lexi, on the other hand, was shocked. He'd used a line from the e-Book almost verbatim. Did he know?

He couldn't.

She sat there, watching as Ric brought the pea to his mouth, rolled out his tongue, wrapped it around the green morsel, and pried it from the fork. It was the most obscene thing ever—and would have been erotic, if she weren't so taken aback by his words.

Ric tilted his head back a fraction and drew the pea in his mouth with a wink. "I mean, such a feast is an exotic beast to me..."

81

The rest of what he said was lost to her. Her mind was stuck on a loop. He'd now used that phrase twice. Coincidence? She doubted it, after his lusty words to the pea. "Exotic beast?" she asked.

"Of course. I'm used to preparing meals for one." He reached for the platter of greens.

Her mom rushed to push the platter closer to him and jumped into the conversation.

Lexi was lost in her own thoughts. It was him. Ric was doing this. She narrowed her eyes at him. She'd kill him. *Correction* – she'd go all *Xandra* on his ass and rip his stupid head off, come next full moon. Her mind was going a mile a minute, trying to figure out the *hows* and *whys*.

How could he know she'd find the book? Read it? How did he manage to write the entire thing? Did he get someone else to? But why? He hadn't even met her before the day she discovered the story. Was he planning on getting her hooked and then telling everyone about her work faux pas? Did he hate her enough to go through all that trouble?

Too far-fetched, even for him.

She took a deep breath and pushed her chair back from the table. "I need a diet soda. I think we all do, after all this food. Ric, help me get clean glasses?" Stupid excuse to get him alone, and she felt like a hypocrite, batting her eyelashes, but the end justified the means.

"Glad to." He was up and following her to the kitchen without hesitation.

She could kill him, there and then, but she had to be as sneaky as he was, to win this game. Stalling for time, she opened the refrigerator's door, stuck her head in, and grabbed a large bottle of pop.

82

"Where are the glasses, pet?"

She turned to him so fast she felt light-headed. "I don't know why you're doing this, or even how" — she shook the arm holding the bottle at him, to emphasize her words, since she couldn't yell with her mother and Edmund in the next room — "but you better stop it, or else." The threat was left hanging in the air.

He frowned. "Doing *what*? What are you talking about? I'm just making small talk. It's only polite."

"Yeah, well, you can't fool me." Lexi took a step toward him and closed the refrigerator door behind her. She leaned against it and squinted at him. "You know I'm not talking about the small talk. I mean *you* are the one who's doing *it*." The dick was trying to make her spell it out.

"*It*? What *it*?"

"Oh, don't act so clueless. You know what I mean." She whispered the words. "*Exotic Beast? Tell me you're mine?* Come on. You're the one behind the site."

*

Ric had followed her to the kitchen, curious to hear what she'd say. Not for a moment did he believe she'd asked for his assistance without good reason.

He tried to sound casual when she swayed her luscious ass in front of him, the denim stretching over curves so perfect he longed to trace them with his hands. He forgot all about her ass, though, when she faced him and threw her accusations at him.

She looked furious — a magnificent look she wore well. He was tempted to touch her cheek. Slide his finger

83

along it to her jaw line. He wanted to know if her face was hot with anger or chilled from the fridge.

Then her words sank in.

She believed he was the one behind the website? That he'd written the story? "Whatever you think I did, I swear I didn't." He wasn't lying.

"Oh, God. You really don't know." Her hand flew to her mouth, and in that second, he found his way out of this whole mess.

"You're into exotic beasts? Sexually?" He widened his eyes. "I—I'm sorry, I didn't know." This was counterproductive, let alone childish, but he couldn't resist goading her.

She turned an even darker shade of crimson and fisted her free hand at her side. She opened and closed her mouth, but no sound came out.

She raised the bottle and swatted at his head. 'I'm *not* into bestiality, you... you idiot. You moron. You—"

He chuckled and managed to still her hand before the bottle hit him. He wrapped his palm around her wrist, lowered her arm, and moved closer in the same motion. "Then what is it you're accusing me of, pet?" Her breath hitched when he called her *pet*, and he smirked. "What's this site you're on about?"

He had her trapped between his body and the fridge, and those damned gorgeous eyes of hers were burning him.

"So? Care to fill a bloke in?" He cocked his head to side and licked his lips.

Her gaze zeroed in on his tongue, and her body tensed. If he had her figured out, which he thought he did, she'd be shoving him away and bolting any minute now.

84

Instead of pulling free, though, Lexi grabbed his neck and pressed her body to his. Before he knew what was happening, she pulled him down and crashed her lips to his.

He couldn't process what was happening, so he didn't even try. Instead, he lost himself in the wonderful sensations her unexpected kiss evoked. Her lips were soft, still carrying a fruity flavor although nothing but a few traces of her lip-gloss remained. He craved to devour her. She moaned against his mouth, but he resisted the urge to slip his tongue past her lips—drink her in, get drunk on her. His resolve wavered the second her tongue traced his lower lip. He couldn't hold back. No longer had the will to. He deepened the kiss, inhaling her breath and savoring her taste.

Her whimpers made him more desperate to consume her. He cupped her cheek and ground his hips against her. He needed more of this connection. More of her.

She rested her hand on his chest, giving him pause. She didn't push him away, though. Just held on to his shirt.

She didn't feel close enough, though her body was flush against his. He wanted her inside his skin. Letting go of her wrist, he moved to wrap his arm around her waist.

He was a heartbeat too slow.

The moment her arm was free, Lexi brought the plastic bottle down on his head and shoved hard against his chest. His stunned step backward was all she needed, to hightail it out of the room without a backward glance.

Ric wanted to run after her, grab her, drag her back to the kitchen, and finish what she'd started. He wanted to

85

be pissed off she seemed to regret kissing him, or that the most likely reason she did it was to shut him up.

But he wasn't pissed off. He was ecstatic. Because in the middle of an argument against the fridge, in her family's kitchen, for whatever reason, Lexi kissed him, and he sensed her hunger.

A hunger strong enough to rival his.

He took a moment to adjust his crotch, and then located the glass cupboard and placed four glasses on a tray he found by the sink.

Maybe he needed to stay there just a second more, to catch his breath and lose the bulge in his jeans.

Chapter Nine

Silence met Lexi when she re-entered the dining room. Not the normal, don't-talk-while-you-eat silence, but a suspicious one. Like people being quiet after trying to listen in on what was happening in the next room.

She sat and placed the bottle-slash-assault-weapon as far toward the middle of the table as she could reach.

Her head spun. Ric had smelled so fucking good, and his voice had been deliciously gruff, like on the phone yesterday morning. She'd needed to get out of their talk. Had to get away from him and his stupid cheekbones, the heat of his body, that plump bottom lip taunting her…

Kissing him had been her only viable option, really.

Oh, God. She'd kissed him.

She wanted to disappear.

Wait. This was her house. She wanted him out of there. Out of her house, out of her life, and in her —

Whoa, hold up.

She just kissed him to distract him, and it worked — *boy*, did it ever — but she never expected it to feel so good. It shouldn't have felt good, because it was wrong. So totally wrong. Made of pure wrongness. And it would never happen again.

Ever.

"What is keeping Richard?" Edmund asked. "Maybe you should go back in. See if he needs anything." The smirk on his face was new to Lexi. Her mom giggled and made a jerky move that gave Lexi the impression Edmund's hand wasn't in his own lap.

Lexi rolled her eyes. Lunchtime kept getting better. She didn't feel like witnessing her mom and stepdad's saccharine sweet, adolescent-like displays of affection, but she couldn't return to the kitchen either. Not after Ric made her heart race and her body tingle.

Which, by the way, were not normal reactions to IT-Richie. Loathing and disgust? Yes. Tingles? No way.

Still, her gaze was riveted to his fluid motions as he rounded the table to place glasses to the right of Edmund and her mom. When he got closer, she stopped watching, afraid to see the look in his eyes. Afraid she'd get lost in them.

He wasn't afraid to lean into her and press the hard evidence of his arousal against her as he placed her glass beside her. "Here you go."

She managed not to flinch, and most importantly, not to mold her body to his.

He smiled, left the last glass by his plate and the tray at the end of the table, and reclaimed his place by her side.

This lunch was endless.

Ric asked her to pass the soda. She turned her body halfway in his direction and hoped the whirlwind of emotions warring inside didn't show in her gaze. Watching him from the corner of her eye, she steadied the bottom of the bottle between her knees and unscrewed the cap.

88

Ric squeezed his eyes shut a split second before the cap was off, and foamy spray bathed his entire upper body, including his hair and wire-rimmed spectacles.

She'd forgotten she shook the bottle in the kitchen. Now she tried to juggle apologizing profusely, which she meant, and laughing hysterically, which she felt like.

Ric laughed. Uproariously. His chest shook with it, and a warmth spread inside Lexi's belly. It was a good laugh. Happy. He took his glasses off with one hand and smoothed his hair back with the other.

Lexi gasped.

His bright blue eyes, with those sinfully long, dark lashes were even clearer without the glasses covering them. Way more intense. And with his hair pushed back from his face for a change, his cheekbones were more prominent. Sharper. His face reminded her of…

Rex.

She felt the blood drain from her face. The bane of her existence was identical to the man of her dreams — and daydreams — were as alike as two drops of water.

He narrowed his eyes, his gaze darkening for a split second before he grinned and shook his head the way a wet dog would. Driblets of pop flew her way, and she let out a surprised squeal which made her mom and Edmund laugh, too.

With Ric's locks in disarray again and his glasses back in place, it was hard to spot the previously glaring similarities. A weight lifted from Lexi's chest as she resorted to her favorite way of dealing with things. Denial. The resemblance had never been there. Her over-Rexed mind was just messing with her after that brief kiss in the kitchen. Yup, that was it… even if the memory of the kiss sent liquid fire through her veins.

Her mom, who wasn't gawking at Ric, had the presence of mind to deal with the situation. "Richard, you should take a shower. Edmund can lend you a change of clothes."

"No, need, Joy. I'll just go home now."

"Nonsense. We can't let you go like this."

Ric refused several times, but the woman was unrelenting. "You're not leaving yet, anyway. Lunch isn't over, and I've made apple-pie. And you brought cupcakes. If you don't want Edmund's clothes, I'm sure Lexi can spare a pair of sweats and one of those oversized T-shirts she wears to bed. Lexi, will you show him to your bathroom?"

Ric gave in, and Lexi led him upstairs and then ran to her room to look for clothes. She was already over feeling guilty for getting him wet, and wanted to find something silly to give him, but her mom wouldn't appreciate that.

She decided on a pair of pale pink pants and the largest white T-shirt she owned. Not like she could be blamed for owning only girly clothes, and she didn't want to see more of the well-defined muscles she'd spied under Ric's shirt when the liquid made it cling to his torso.

This wasn't the day Lexi got what she wanted.

She held the clothes against her chest and knocked on the bathroom door. "Ric? Are you decent?"

"Not when I can avoid it, love."

Did he have to make even the dumbest remark sound so hot? "Well, I'm coming in, whether you are or not." She opened the door and froze at the sight before her.

He didn't have his glasses on, and his hair was wild around his face. His shoulders and biceps were sculpted, and the effect they had on her didn't fade when she glided her gaze downward, over his toned pecs and ripped abs. His upper body was that of a Greek God, forming a wide *V* from his broad shoulders to his slim waist. A towel barely clung to his narrow hips, and all that dreamy maleness was wet, as if he wasn't sinful enough without her wishing she were a droplet of water gliding down his smooth skin, into the downy line that began right under his navel, and inside that towel.

Never before had a towel been so hated... or so appreciated.

Her gaze bounced off the fluffy white barrier and back to his face, where she expected to see a leer. That would shake her out of her lusty haze much faster than the serious look he appraised her with.

"You call that decent?" was all she could come up with.

"That word's never described me, kitten." He remained solemn, not teasing or provoking her, but his words sent a bolt of desire through her entire being, raising her heartbeat and body temperature, and making her breath labored.

"My bad," she whispered and held out the clothes.

He took them and thanked her in the same hushed tone.

As she exited the bathroom and closed the door behind her, Lexi didn't know why she felt like something big and not altogether good had just happened.

When Ric showed up back in the dining room, her mother and Edmund made valiant efforts not to giggle. Her pink pants ended well above his ankles, and the T-shirt—although long on her—stopped right at his midriff, letting a sliver of skin show with every step he took.

He had his hands in his pockets, so nothing was outlined in the front of the pants, but Lexi had to try not to stare at how the thin material stretched over his ass when he sat down. Or at how there was no underwear line in sight.

The rest of the meal and afternoon went by on a much lighter note. Lexi's mom asked questions carefully constructed to seem like she wasn't prying. Ric indulged, and Edmund jumped in from time to time, with anecdotes from Ric's childhood.

Lexi couldn't believe she enjoyed IT-Richie's company. She reminded herself tomorrow was another day. One during which all balance would be restored in the universe. The kiss they shared would be deleted from their memory, and they'd revert to their mutual disdain.

She didn't realize how fast the day went by, but it was a little after seven when Ric said he didn't want to overstay his welcome.

"Too late for that," Lexi muttered, not to lose her edge. It came out half-hearted.

Ric thanked her mom repeatedly for the meal and Edmund for the company, before turning to Lexi. "See you tomorrow."

"See ya." She pretended not to look at his ass while Edmund walked him to the door.

****

Lexi didn't want to help her mother clean up. She hoped to avoid listening to her rave about what a nice boy Richard was, as Lexi knew she would.

They hadn't even picked up one plate, when she was proven correct.

"Richard seems nice."

Lexi said nothing.

"He minds his manners. He didn't even yell when you almost ruined his clothes."

"Didn't do it on purpose," Lexi mumbled under her breath.

"And he was helpful, too. He didn't let me wash his clothes for him, and he went to the kitchen with you. To help you…" Her mom emptied leftovers from the plates into the empty salad bowl and stacked them on each other, all the time not even glancing at her.

Lexi braced herself for a more direct line of questioning as soon as her mother realized fishing around wouldn't bring results.

She sighed with relief when Edmund called from the upper floor, "Joy? Can you please come here for a minute?"

"In a minute, sweetie."

"Now, Joy. Please."

Both women looked toward the stairs. Lexi heard the urgency in the man's voice, and apparently so did her mother, who stopped what she was doing, to rush upstairs.

Lexi went back to cleaning up, bringing dishes to the kitchen and trying to keep her mind free of naughty fantasies that included the towel falling from around the hips of a certain half-naked, wet Brit.

Great. Now she couldn't stop thinking about the jerk. Could the day get any worse?

She knew that was one of the things she should never wonder. Thinking such thoughts meant jinxing herself, challenging her luck, drawing in negative energy… Asking for something worse to happen.

That *worse* now headed her way in the shape of her mother, who held in a firm, full-palmed grasp something Lexi had left in the shower and forgotten all about.

Oh, God.

"Lexi" — her mother held up Mr. Purple, two feet away from Lexi and too damn close to her own face — "is this a vibrator?"

Fuck.

"Um, yeah…" Lexi worried her lower lip with her teeth for a split second, before saying what belonged up there with the ten worst lines to say when your folks find your sex toys. "It was a gift, and I thought I'd try it."

It wasn't a lie, but she wanted to hit her head against the closest surface. Couldn't she have come up with something better?

Her mom handed her the still-buzzing thing. Something must have jarred it and switched it on. "Edmund was passing by your bathroom. The door was open, and when he heard the vibration, he thought it was your cell phone. Told him it's one of those battery-operated razors, for deep shave. I doubt he believed it, but I'm sure he appreciated the lie."

Lexi clasped the vibrator and turned it off. Without another word, she ran upstairs and shoved Mr. Purple all

94

the way in the back of her underwear drawer. Though mortified, she couldn't help but also be grateful Pedelty's discovery stopped the Ric-centric talk with her mom.

And hey, at least it wasn't on while Ric was in the bathroom. She recognized a silver lining when she saw one.

Chapter Ten

No person in their right mind likes going to work on a Monday morning, and no one is ever in a hurry to get there unless work entails palm trees and exotic fruit.

Or maybe hot guys with washboard abs.

There was such a guy at Lexi's workplace, but he was far from the reason she busted her ass out of bed and managed to shower and get ready in record time. She just wanted to make sure she'd be gone before either her mother or Edmund woke up. She still couldn't face them.

She started her car and put both hands on the steering wheel, barely refraining from banging her head on it. How did she always get herself into such messes? This time she didn't hold back, and let her forehead meet the wheel full force. The blare of the horn snapped her out of her thoughts long enough to set the car in reverse and maneuver out of the garage.

She got to the office at twenty to nine. That was a first, but she needed to have a cup of coffee on her own and clear her thoughts before everyone else got there. And she could think of no better way to clear her thoughts than by reading a bit more of *Exotic Beast*. She felt like she'd missed a fix—or several—during the weekend.

Coffee was forgotten the moment she reached the next chapter. By the time she was done with it, she was attacked by images of IT-Richie in the shower, naked and dripping…

She should be thinking of Rex, damn it.

"Had a good night?"

Lexi snapped up her head to see brilliant blue eyes looking at her behind glasses that should be taking something away from their startling beauty, but weren't.

Startling beauty?

IT-Richie?

Shit. She needed to be medicated.

She readjusted her posture, so she no longer slumped, and looked him straight in the eye. "Huh?" That was as witty as his accent let her be. What was up with that? He sounded different. Or maybe she was more susceptive to him.

"I asked if you had a good night." He spoke slowly, as if to a child.

"I did. As a matter of fact, my night improved vastly once you left."

"I just bet it did. Didn't have to see my hot body wrapped up in those tight pants anymore—"

Lexi gulped audibly at the memory of how tight those pants had been. Her temperature rose.

"Besides, pink's my color." He winked.

He was being ridiculous on purpose. Ridiculous was good. Much better than sexy.

He leered and bent forward, to plant his palms on either side of her PC monitor. "Never thanked you for the kiss, by the way."

"Kiss?" Couldn't he have stayed on the ridiculous track? "What kiss?"

"Ouch. I didn't know I was so forgettable. Maybe I should remind you?"

He licked his lips, and Lexi could swear she felt it at the apex of her thighs. Just like that, she was wet.

She had to do something about it, so she got mad. "I don't know what you're talking about, and there will be no reminding—thank you very much. Now if you don't mind, I've got work to do."

He straightened and took a step to the side. The way he hooked his thumbs in his belt loops had his fingers framing his groin. "I hope your work changes your mind, kitten." He waggled his eyebrows and bounced on the balls of his feet, the movement tilting his hips forward. When he smirked and turned to go, he left behind a very distraught Lexi.

Kitten did it. She knew why his accent was different. Whom it reminded her of. She couldn't believe she hadn't figured it out the first time he'd used the nickname. Maybe she'd never heard the other's voice in reality, but it was there, in her head twenty-four-seven since the first time she read of him.

Rex.

Glad nobody else was at the office yet, she pushed back her chair and hurried after him. She reached him after a few steps, grabbed his arm, and made him spin toward her.

"What?" He seemed pissed off, but she'd done nothing. Mere seconds ago he'd been annoying her, and now he was upset she'd rather forget the kiss? He didn't even like her.

She didn't care. He had no reason to be upset. She was the wronged party.

98

"What?" he asked again. Now she noticed his eyes were darker. She could swear it wasn't anger, but something else.

"Why did you call me kitten?" Lexi glared.

"'Cause I bloody well felt like it. Is that all?"

"No. Why *kitten*?"

"You remind me of one. With those green eyes and claws…"

Lexi nodded and let go without moving from where she stood. She was far from convinced of his innocence, but she couldn't accuse him of having anything to do with the book just because he sounded like she thought Rex did.

Well, if he was behind it all, that kiss had been a complete waste of time. Or it would have been, if its purpose was to silence him. In all honesty though, it was one hell of a kiss, and she wouldn't mind a repeat performance if Ric wasn't such a grade-A idiot. But he was, and so she did. She minded so much, she had to get away from him that very instant.

****

He wished she hadn't touched him. When he approached her, he meant to… Well, hell if he knew what he meant to do. He wanted to be a five-year old and pull her hair. Make her acknowledge the kiss they'd shared, or just make her uncomfortable. What he didn't expect was to be more uncomfortable than her. Including inside his pants. Going commando in tight jeans could be unpleasant when he got hard, but at least his cock was held in place. Not wearing underwear under the loose-fitting pair he had on today was torture; his cock that was previously hanging comfortably was now painfully pressed downward by the crotch seam. Her touching him only made things worse.

And the way she looked at him, all fire…

Ric rushed to the men's room to fix his not-so-little situation.

He knew trying to get rid of his hard-on would be useless. It would take no more than approaching Lexi, to reestablish it. With a deep breath, he readjusted himself so the seam cradled his length, instead of suppressing it. He threw some water on his face and smoothed back his hair. In the mirror, he saw what he believed Lexi had when he was doused in Coke. Rex — or as close to Rex as he could be these days.

He chuckled at what an idiot he was, thinking of himself as two separate entities. He was both Ric and Rex. There was no need to try and get the girl as one, when the other was better equipped for the task. Once he had her, he'd grow on her. Yes, his old badass self would be his key to the kingdom. He messed up his hair with his fingers, allowing damp strands to frame his face.

He snorted. Like bloody Superman. Stick a pair of glasses on him and let a curl hang down his forehead, and his secret identity was safe. He flexed his biceps one at a time and took the trademarked Superman-pose — fists resting on hips, legs spread at shoulder width, chest pushed outward.

"Faster than a speeding bullet."

Superman himself couldn't have spun around his axis as fast as Ric did when he heard the chuckle.

"Ric, my boy, are you finally coming out?"

100

John, of all people, had to be the one to see him preen like a peacock. The way the dark-haired hulk sneered made Ric pray for super-strength, to kick him all the way back to Chicago and make sure he never laid eyes on him again.

He settled for a glare as he brushed by him on his way out.

****

Lexi heard Edmund's voice before she saw him coming up the stairs. She sank lower in her chair, praying her monitor would hide her.

She hated having to minimize the browser window when spanking was on. She felt like a very dirty girl for how wet she got at the thought of a big, calloused hand smacking her ass. Even dirtier for how that made her almost giddy.

"Good morning." Edmund passed by her desk, and she mumbled the words back, itching to return to her reading.

She waited to see the doors of his office close behind him before restoring her browser. She'd finish the chapter, and then go tell him she needed more out of her job.

By the time she reached the point where Rex was all growly, she'd almost forgotten where she was as well as any reason why she should be feeling bad.

"I'm not your toy, Shifter." Another slap added to the fire already burning her skin. *"You cannot discard me when you're done playing with me."*

"I'm sorry." Xandra could see his insecurity under his dominant façade. "I'm sorry," she said again, hoping he saw the truth in her words.

"I don't believe you."

She was about to apologize again — keep apologizing until he believed her — when he twisted his fingers in her hair and pulled her head back. "You're going to have to convince me," he said with a smirk.

Lexi chanced a glance around. Matt and John clicked on their keyboards like crazy. She felt bad that all she could think of was getting off, while the two men were hard at work. She had to find something to do.

Something to focus on, other than the throbbing need between her legs.

She rubbed her thighs together. She had to stop reading, before someone noticed her panted breaths or the flush she felt spreading from her cheeks down the front of her blouse.

She didn't care.

****

Ric was just back at his desk, when he noticed Lexi exhibiting the same signs she had on Friday, right before she'd driven him wild by masturbating while he watched. He hacked into her system again and started skimming over the page she was reading.

Spanking? She'd be the death of him.

He didn't dare touch himself, even though he was dying to. The on-screen Rex was having a much, *much*, better time.

102

"Do you still think you're better than me? Still think you're doing me a favor?"

Xandra mewled. She wanted to scream at him to move faster, drive harder inside her, but this was his game. He made the rules, and his rules said she had to go crazy with anticipation before he let her climax.

His hand landed hard on her ass.

Ric wanted to cup that magnificent ass. Have the taut flesh against his palm. Feel it heat under his touch.

He needed release, and he needed it now.

He couldn't get it.

Instead, he spent the day reading what she read, thanking God and cursing his luck at the same time that there was no pressing matter to be handled at work. He didn't dare move from his desk, because he'd be unable to hide the erection stretching his jeans.

Time went by excruciatingly slow. He watched Lexi stifle gasps and squirm on her seat, while he got a good idea of everything that made her hot and bothered. It seemed his girl wasn't all vanilla, and he didn't mind that one bit.

****

Lexi crammed in as much naughtiness as she could until half past one. When she was about to talk to Edmund, she saw him leaving. He was meeting a client, and she cursed herself for spending so much time with *Exotic Beast.* Upset and more than a little guilty, she started preemptively translating the manual for a product

103

supposed to launch in the local market next month. They'd need it in German at some point, anyway. Who'd have thought studying foreign languages for the fun of it would pay off more than her Master's?

When she looked up again, it was half past five. The office was almost empty, though Ric was still there. She wished he weren't. She wanted to read some more and didn't appreciate the company.

She returned to her book anyway, and soon wished she hadn't. She needed to come, or she'd explode. She'd have to go home and have a one-on-one with one of her toys. Not Mr. Purple; the thought of it in her mom's hand killed the allure.

She switched off her PC and shouldered her bag before turning to Ric. Saying *goodnight* was only good manners.

Ric looked up before she could speak. "Leaving already?"

"My work here is done. Good night." She didn't want chit-chat. She just wanted to go. Reach home with delicious Rex-thoughts intact, while the Rex in her head still had a voice that wasn't Ric's.

"Is it?" He cocked his eyebrow in that infuriating way that heightened her arousal.

No, no, no, no. There would be no naughty thoughts about him. No IT-Richie-lust. "Yes, it is."

"Well, if you're sure you've done all you could... You wouldn't want to leave things unfinished, would you? Not finishing my work always makes me feel like someone's doing me a favor, keeping me here. Like I need a smack on my arse, to get back on top of things."

104

The eyebrow almost reached his hairline, but Lexi couldn't even bother with an internal jest about it. He knew. *He knew.* She felt like a deer caught in headlights—wanting to run but unable to move.

Ric seemed oblivious to her panic. "Well, hope you get off all right. 'Night, kitten."

"I'm sorry?"

"Get off *work*. Unless you were thinking of something else…" He ran that sinful tongue of his over his front teeth. "Be glad to help, you know."

Lexi bit back a venomous response about how he could never do it for her, and not only because it would be a lie. She spun on her heel and fled, his low rumbling chuckle following her down the stairs.

So Ric was behind it all. Until she found out how he managed it and what he was trying to accomplish, all she could do was become a model employee.

That meant no more *Exotic Beast.*

Shit.

Chapter Eleven

Even as Ric laughed at Lexi's indignant retreat on Monday, he had the distinct feeling he'd messed up. He considered running after her but dismissed the thought at once. It'd be better to let her cool off and see how she played it the next day. She'd confront him. They'd fight. They'd make up.

He knew she wanted him. He'd tasted it on his lips. If all went well, he'd soon be tasting more of her.

He should have remembered his plans never panned out, and done something, instead of shrugging off her fury and concentrating on his erection.

By Wednesday afternoon, he had to admit he'd fucked things up. Royally.

Instead of gathering her courage and confronting him, making him confess, and saving him the trouble of telling her how much he wanted her, Lexi had ignored him for the past two days. What was more, she'd constantly been on Pedelty's case for more workload, which she'd handled strictly within work hours, leaving the office at exactly five in the afternoon.

She didn't visit the site anymore.

Ric was getting worried by Thursday at noon. Well, that was a lie. He'd been worried on Tuesday morning. By Thursday, he was flat out agitated he'd scared her out of

106

visiting the site. That made him even more reluctant to approach her the way he wanted to.

When he first formed the plan of getting to Lexi, he meant to keep letting traces of Rex seep into his demeanor. At some point, she'd realize the similarities were overwhelming, find him irresistible, and throw herself at him. Messing with her and irritating her in the process would just be an added bonus.

In retrospect, his plan wasn't what one would call brilliant.

Sure, he had no doubt she wanted him, but only in the strict sense of *want*. She wanted his body, was turned on by him, but that was all. His behavior had put more distance between them, and now she wouldn't even go near the site. Ric hated to admit he was hooked on the book, as well as on how she looked when she read it — pupils dilated, breath shallow and fast, cheeks reddened, nipples visibly peaking.

He pictured her reacting like that beneath him.

He remembered jotting down the address of the site and decided to check it out himself. Maybe reading more about Xandra and Rex fucking could do it for him, if he imagined Lexi and himself in the leading roles.

Ignoring the little voice that insisted doing so would be tantamount to torture, he typed in the address and hit *Go*.

All he got was an error page.

No matter how many times he reloaded the page or typed in the address from scratch, he got the same result. He must have copied the address wrong, to begin with. A tension headache blossomed behind his eyes. He had to do *something*.

Then she was in front of him, and he knew exactly what he wanted that to be, only there were people at the office, and he'd earn himself a slap or worse if he tried to bend her over his desk and fuck her.

"I'm done with my work for the day, and Matt suggested I ask if you need anything." The disdain in her voice reached her eyes, and Ric masked his discomfort behind a smirk he didn't feel.

"Anything, *translation-wise*." She rolled her eyes and sent an arrow through his heart at the same time he felt a stirring in his groin.

It was official. He needed to be institutionalized. The woman of his dreams hated his guts, and all he could think of was how much he wanted to make her his.

Wanker.

He couldn't bite back the juvenile response that jumped to his lips. "How much work do you want, kitten? Enough to make you stay late and enjoy a bit of after-work fun?"

Her eyes threw daggers at him as she rounded his desk. "I knew it was you."

"Knew it was me doing what?" He kept his voice low, aware people around glanced at them.

"The whole e-Book thing, you asshole. What I can't figure out is how you knew I'd be searching for anything related to it. Or was it supposed to pop up, no matter what I searched for?"

He was scared by the intensity of her gaze, yet more turned on by her anger and her proximity than ever before. "I didn't—"

"Yes, you did. I may not know how, but I know why. You were hoping for proof I was slacking off, so

108

you'd get Edmund to fire me. And what proof could shame him into throwing me out, if not my reading porn at work? Right?" She was whispering, but her tone was full of emotion.

"Lexi, love—"

"Do *not* call me love, kitten, or anything of the sort, ever again. I'm on to you, *Richie*, and you don't scare me."

He should be more worried about what she thought of him, but that last part was his chance to make things right. "If you're not scared, how come you gave up what you were doing?" She recoiled as if slapped, and he rushed to explain. "Why did you stop reading? Staying late?" He did his best to return her fierce glare.

"I just felt like it."

"I say you chickened out. I do scare you."

"You so do not."

"Prove it." There. He had her. She wouldn't back away from a challenge.

"Why? Don't you have enough incriminating evidence against me?"

"Wasn't looking for any."

"Right." She sucked in her cheeks.

It made him want to crush his lips against hers. "Kitten—" He cleared his throat when she flared her nostrils at the endearment. "Lexi. I'm not the one doing this. I know what you've been reading, but I didn't—"

"Take your glasses off."

"You going to punch me?" He tried to look more nervous than he felt, to gain some time to figure out what she wanted to do. And then he knew. He remembered the look on her face when he took off his glasses and slicked back his hair the other day. He didn't want her to know, though. Not when it would reaffirm her belief he was behind it all.

"Take them off. Now."

He shook his head but did as she asked anyway, making sure to squint more than necessary.

"Now look at me."

He did, and his gaze wandered to her rising chest as she gasped.

She tangled her hand in his hair and held the unruly curls back from his face. "Oh, my God."

Ric pulled away and hurried to put his glasses back on. "What's wrong?"

"You don't know?"

"No, I don't. Care to share?" He hoped his snideness would mask his fear that she'd never again give him the time of day if she believed he not only wrote the e-Book but also cast himself as the leading man.

"You're Rex." She sounded resigned, instead of livid.

"Yes, I am. But it's not what you think."

"What is it, then?"

He opened his mouth to say something. Anything. Whatever it took, to keep her from hating him.

"Never mind." She straightened up, turned on her heel, and hightailed it to the ladies room.

Ric was left watching her back and wishing no one else was there, so he could run after her and tell her the truth. Hold her to him — chain her up if he had to — until she believed him.

*

110

Lexi leaned against the closed door, unsure why she was crying. Not like she didn't already suspect the man whose goal in life was to torment her and make her lose her job was the same as the fictional character she pined over. No. Not *suspected*. She'd been *convinced* it was him. He said he wasn't behind the site, but there was no other reasonable explanation, and it stung that he wanted to hurt her like this. What had she ever done to him? Not like she even asked to be there.

And did he have to make her lust after him? Was that another thing to rub her nose in?

By the time she returned to her desk, her eyes were dry and her mind made up. She'd do whatever she felt like, and if Ric wanted to tell Edmund about it even after she'd confronted him, she'd deal with the consequences.

She signed onto her instant messenger account, glad the company proxy didn't block it, and clicked on Angie's avatar.

Blondes_Rule: Guess what I found out.

Angie didn't reply immediately, but a new window popped up.

Rex_is_sorry: I swear I'm not behind the bloody thing. You have to believe me.

She closed the popup and pinged Angie.

MagicA: I'm here, I'm here. What happened?

Blondes_Rule: Richie-boy was behind the site with the book

MagicA: How do you know? Did he fess up?

111

Lexi started typing her response, but Ric's window reappeared.

Rex_is_sorry: right. Ignore me. I'll just say what I have to say. I didn't do it, but I've known about it for a while.

Blondes_Rule: never talk to me again

Rex_is_sorry: HOW could I have done it, you crazy woman? The thing is hundreds of pages long. How could I have written it? Even if I wanted to do what you said, I'd have to be writing non-stop for more than a year.

Lexi scrunched her nose and chewed on the back of a pencil while she pasted that last bit to the window she chatted in with Angie.

MagicA: He's right, you know. Maybe it wasn't him.

Whether he was telling the truth or not, Ric was persistent.

Rex_is_sorry: didn't say I'm not wrong for knowing about it and not telling you, but I swear I'm just as shocked as you. Someone's been writing fiction about *me* and *you*, for fuck's sake

Blondes_Rule: 'someone' *snorts*

Rex_is_sorry: I'm telling you: *Wasn't me!*

Blondes_Rule: whatEVER. Blocking you now. Buh bye.

112

She waited until he looked up, and waggled her fingers at him.

*

Ric wasn't fazed by her dismissal. He didn't expect her to believe him. He'd tuned in on her screen to see if she'd taken him up on his challenge and gone back to reading. When he saw her on her messenger, he gave it a try. Nothing ventured, nothing gained, and all that.

Now he sat back and waited, while Lexi said goodbye to that MagicA bird, signed out of messenger, and returned to *Exotic Beast*.

Ha. He knew she wouldn't be able to resist, and maybe getting back into the story would make her forget for a few minutes that she hated his guts.

It did. For the rest of the day, Lexi went through page after page, only occasionally glancing up from her screen.

When she did so a little after five, Ric expected her to log out and go. She didn't. Instead she blew him a kiss, flipped him the bird, and resumed her reading.

Ric was twisted for finding that so erotic, but he decided not to focus on it. What mattered was that Lexi had been playful with him, even for a split second.

Maybe he could work with that.

Chapter Twelve

Lexi saw Ric gather some documents and shut down his laptop. She'd won. She'd shown him she wasn't afraid, even if she was still worried about what he'd do with the information he had on her.

She didn't look up when he switched off all overhead lights except for hers on his way out. Good riddance. Now she could read her book undisturbed and be as naughty as she damn well pleased. And she'd be extremely naughty. It was her reward for being so good for so long.

Still, her release was the furthest thing from her mind once he'd left. Her gaze was locked to the screen, but all she could think of was his face when he swore he didn't do what she accused him of. He looked innocent. And writing an entire book in mere days, to get her out of his hair, was a Herculean task. Let alone a stupid one, since she wasn't even *in* his hair.

"Nobody said Richie was clever," she mumbled, folding her arms over her chest.

She wished Angie could meet him. She'd always been a better judge of character than Lexi was.

But she'd spent enough time on that menace of a man. Especially when Rex was once more about to have his wicked way with a very willing Xandra. She clicked on the next page and shifted to raise her skirt a little, in anticipation of what was to come.

She wasn't disappointed.

Rex let his canines elongate, and Xandra's skin prickled, as it always did when her lover reminded her of his real nature. "Do you need to do this?" she asked.

"I do, because you love it. You love being reminded of how different we are, of how bad *everyone thinks we are together. You love being bad, Xandra." He dragged a fang along one side of her neck, and a growl rose in her chest. She loved being bad with* him.

"Feel free to tell me I'm wrong." He kissed her behind the ear, and she shivered.

"You know you're not." She clasped his wrist and led his hand up her inner thigh. "Now shut up and help me be bad."

Lexi stopped her hand halfway up her own inner thigh when she heard heavy footsteps approaching. She hurried to smooth down her skirt, and looked toward the entrance, praying it wasn't that brain-dead Chad.

It wasn't Chad.

It was worse than Chad, even if she'd never thought that possible.

It was Rex.

Rex.

In the flesh, complete with the short black hair, tight black jeans and shirt, leather bomber jacket, and steel-toed boots.

"Hello, Xandra." He smirked, approaching her with panther-like grace. "Miss me?"

115

Her head felt light, her brain short-circuiting in an effort to reconcile the truth she knew with the sight facing her. This was Ric — *IT-Richie* — and he looked like sex personified. She was aroused because of the book, and not the way his muscles rippled beneath his tight outfit.

Luckily, when her brain short-circuited, her snarky mode kicked in.

"I did miss you, *Rex*" — Lexi spat the name out with enough contempt to mask the tremor in her voice — "but give me a stake, and I will try again. Promise my aim will be better this time."

"I love it when you talk dirty, love."

Ric — Rex — rounded her desk till he was right beside her, but she refused to turn toward him. She gripped the armrests of her chair. If she let go, she might melt into a puddle. "Do you have a point there, *Richie*, or has Halloween come early this year, and no one informed me?"

He grabbed her arm and tugged, spinning her chair so she faced him. "You look at me when I talk to you, *Shifter*. And the name is Rex. Better remember it, 'cause you'll be screaming it soon enough."

Lexi lifted her chin defiantly, suppressing the wave of lust that rose inside. The man tempting her was her enemy. "Oh, cut the crap." The knuckles of her hands hurt with tension. His proximity heightened her desire, despite the anger his behavior sparked in her. "You're not Rex, and I'm not Xandra. You're nothing but an IT nerd, and I'm the boss's daughter, whom you dislike. Snap out of it and leave me alone."

"Oh, but you *are* Xandra, kitten, much as I'm Rex. At least for tonight." He touched a finger to her lips when

116

she parted them to voice her thoughts. "Don't fight this. I know how your body reacted to me in your kitchen." He waved a hand toward her monitor. "I know how hot and bothered you get every time you read that. You want to hate me? Do. But don't deny your body what it wants. I can give it to you, Xandra."

"I don't want you. I could never —" That was as far as she got, before he leaned down and closed his lips over hers. He cupped the back of her head with one hand, the other still holding on to her arm, not allowing her to break free.

Not that she tried. Or even considered it.

She clutched his shoulder. He wasn't wrong. She needed this. And if it wasn't about her and him, if it was about Xandra and Rex, maybe she could have it.

*

The way she clung to him, the way she devoured his lips as though he tasted of nectar and ambrosia, made him dizzy with a euphoria he'd never known before.

She pulled away, and he groaned. "Bloody hell, not again."

He let go, straightened his body, and turned to go. He didn't want to push her too much, and he knew if he opened his mouth that moment, he'd forget his bravado and beg her to pick up where they'd left off.

Lexi stood up so abruptly, she sent the chair rolling backward. The noise made him shoot a questioning look her way.

"Well, I was craning my neck for so long, I could have sprained it," she said.

117

With a growl, he wrapped his arms around her and pulled her against him.

She surprised him further by linking her arms around his neck and rising on her toes, to kiss him once more. When she moaned into his mouth, he couldn't resist grabbing her ass to press her against his erection, aware he risked a slap or a knee to the groin. The expected blow never came. Instead, she swiveled her hips from side to side, rubbing against him.

He pulled back from the kiss and made the biggest boo-boo he could have, while trying to convince her he was a bad boy.

He spoke.

It wasn't dirty talk, but stupid, sentimental Richard, who surfaced in the most passionate moment of his entire life. "You're so beautiful... Your eyes—I've dreamt of your—"

"No." She dropped her arms to her sides, trapping his where they still encaged her body.

"No?"

"No, you haven't. You hate me. You're a vampire, and I'm a shifter, and we don't do sweet talk."

So that was how she wanted to play.

He fisted his hand in her hair and pulled, baring her neck to him. He licked a trail up the side of her neck and grazed her earlobe with the tip of his nose, inhaling her scent before giving her hair a second, harsher tug.

"You want rough? I'll give you rough. Think you can handle it?"

"Told you before, nothing is too hard for me. I can take it all."

118

Yes, she'd told him, and it turned him on now just as much as it had then.

She didn't shy away when he slid his free hand under her skirt, to knead her flesh where her thighs met the curve of her ass. He brushed his fingertips over her soaked thong, and then let go of her completely, pulling his arms free and taking a step back.

*

Lexi whimpered at the loss of his touch.

He smirked, and this time she didn't want to slap the expression away. She wanted to taste it. Pull his lower lip between her teeth and nibble on it.

When she stepped closer, he held up his palm, fingers splayed. "Turn around."

"Ric—" She wasn't prepared for the coarseness in his voice when he cut her off.

"It's Rex. You said so yourself. Now turn around and bend over." He indicated her desk with a tilt of his head. "Don't make me say it again."

She wanted to yell. She wanted to smack him upside his stupid head and make it clear that he had no business ordering her around, and she would by no means do what he said. At least she wanted to want that. Truth was, all she cared for at that moment was finding out exactly what he had in mind for her.

There was only one way to go about that.

She turned and bent over the flat surface. Unsure of where to put her hands, she ended up placing them on either side of her hips, holding on to the edge of the desk.

She shivered with anticipation, praying the build-up wouldn't lead to an anticlimactic — pun intended — end.

It took a couple of heartbeats, and then Ric or Rex — or whoever the fuck he pretended to be — pressed against her backside. He draped his body over hers and ran his fingers up her sides to her shoulders.

His breath was warm against her skin, his touch soft when he caressed her cheek, his cock rock-solid against her ass.

She needed to feel him naked on top of her. Inside her. *Now.* The book had taken care of foreplay, and she was ready for him. She writhed under him, but he only feathered touches along her arms. He was so gentle, she didn't resist when he locked his fingers around her wrists, pulled them both above her head, and closed her fingers over the farthest edge of the desk.

"I know you want me, Xandra" — his words sent a tingle down her spine — "but this isn't happening unless *you* know it too. Tell me you want me, or be a liar and deny it."

She bucked, enraged by his gall, but she couldn't throw him off. She was pinned underneath his body because she wanted to be. Once more, she went for the snarky option. "You want to get a confession on film too, or are you just recording sound?"

She didn't expect the hard slap on her ass.

"Ri — *Rex!* What the — "

"Either tell me you want me or that you don't." He straightened, no longer restricting her with his weight, though he knotted her hair in one hand. "Which is it?"

"Yes."

120

"Yes, what?" He pulled up her skirt, caressing each inch of skin he uncovered.

Lexi's breath caught when he rubbed his palm over her ass, where it still stung. He sneaked his thumb under the flimsy strap that separated her buttocks and slowly slid it downward, to graze her wet folds. "Yes, what, Xandra?"

"Yes, I want you. Okay?" She didn't sound half as nonchalant as she meant to, her words no more than a whisper.

Holding her thong away from her body with his thumb, Ric pushed two fingers inside her. They slipped in easily, doing little to alleviate the hunger consuming Lexi. She never remembered being so wet before. Never so out of control with lust.

He moved his fingers against a spot inside that made her feel she was going to die and at the same time like she was more alive than ever before. She prayed he never stop, that he keep fucking her with his hand until she got the exploding orgasm she'd read Xandra experience time and time again.

He withdrew his hand, and she almost cried.

She wanted to beg him for more, to please let her come the way she needed to. When she tried to raise her head and look at him, he held her in place by her hair.

"Don't move."

It was an order, and she obeyed, cursing herself for it. She managed not to move as he tugged sharply on her panties, though the elastic dug into her hips before it snapped. She held still when she heard his zipper slide down. She even stayed in place when she heard something tear. He must have opened the condom wrapper and put the thing on with one hand. She wished she could watch.

The blunt head of his cock brushed against her labia, and she couldn't help pushing back.

God, she wanted him.

He made no move to enter her, and she let out a whimper of frustration and need.

With a grunt, Ric grasped her hip and drove forward, burying his entire length inside her in one long smooth stroke.

He filled her. Stretched her. *God.* She gasped for air, tempted to fuck herself on him even as she strained to accommodate his girth. She'd hurt in the morning, but at that moment she cared about nothing but the pressure in her womb. Faced with the promise of pleasure more intense than she'd ever felt, she didn't give a damn about the office, her job, or the fact that she hated the man about to offer her that pleasure.

When he started moving, she lost herself. Every stroke, every plunge, drew sounds from her she didn't know she could make. He was long and thick and hard, and she wanted to see him. Wanted to lick the broad chest she knew hovered over her back. Wanted to rip off his T-shirt – the bastard hadn't even taken his jacket off — to feel his naked skin on hers as he drove her near the edge.

She writhed and whimpered, needing just a little more to push her over. As if he read the tension in her body, he let go of her hip and found her clit. Rubbed it. His thrusts turned faster. Deeper.

Things rattled on her desk. She didn't care if they fell over.

122

She was about to burst with something she had no name for. What was higher than satisfaction? More primal than pleasure? More engulfing than bliss?

"Who's fucking you? Who's making you come?"

Lexi's orgasm crushed against her in waves, her body tingling and shuddering with its force. *"Rex."*

*

The moment he'd felt how wet for him—for *him*—she'd been, he'd wanted nothing more than to fall to his knees and worship her with his mouth, taste her in her most intimate place, make her come against his face.

His girl wanted it rough, though. She wanted Rex, and that was what he give her, while deep inside he ached to do it all differently.

Lexi clenched and shuddered around him, and Ric pumped his hips harder, chasing his own release. It took no more than a few quick thrusts for him to follow her over the edge. It had been a while since he'd come with anyone other than himself, longer still since a woman's moans had urged him on. Feeling spent in more ways than one, he dug his fingers in Lexi's flesh to keep his footing.

He'd told her *Rex* would be the name she'd scream, but he hadn't expected it to hurt.

Next time would be different—and he'd have a next time with her, as God was his witness.

Next time she'd latch on to him, kiss him and touch him, and maybe even…

Yes, next time it might be *him* she screamed for.

Loath to leave her, but afraid cuddling her would earn him another stab through the heart, he pulled out, took off the condom, and knotted it. He tugged at the scrap of lace that lay in tatters under her and put it in his pocket. Without a word, he smoothed her skirt back down and went to the men's room to get rid of the evidence, semi erect cock still hanging out of his unzipped pants.

When the door was closed behind him, he slumped over the sink, gripped the cool surface with all he had, and took a long, hard look into the mirror.

He was Ric, and he was Rex, and he just had the best damned sex of his life. He needed to check himself and stop sweating the small stuff; a name was but a name, after all. When he was balls-deep inside her, *he* — not a fictional character — was the one fucking her. He wrapped the condom in paper and tossed it in the trash, then splashed some water on his face.

She wasn't there when he returned.

****

He'd left the room without a word.

Lexi's indignation threatened to kill her post-orgasmic bliss. She stubbornly ignored the small voice inside her that kept repeating she wouldn't have allowed him more intimacy anyway. She straightened, ran her fingers through her hair until it no longer looked like she'd just been screwed face-down on her desk, and did what she always did after one-night stands. She fled.

The only difference between now and all the other meaningless sex she'd had since she left Andrew was that

124

this time she'd had an earth-shattering orgasm. And there were tears running down her cheeks.

She spent the rest of the night loathing both herself and Ric for what had happened at the office.

At the office.

God, what if someone came back and saw them? And with Ric? *Ric?* How could she be so stupid? She hated him, and he hated her, and that was all that should ever be between them. What happened to be the best sexual experience of her entire life—she was still recovering from the mother of all orgasms—was something vile and degrading. The sex she and Ric had was something born of mutual hate. Nothing beautiful about it… though he was gorgeous.

But the ass couldn't even stomach sticking around after he came.

She once more chose to disregard the fact that she'd been the one to say there was no room for sweet talk. That they didn't do that.

Then again, she'd been talking about Xandra and Rex, hadn't she? And if Xandra and Rex were the ones who fucked on that desk, *she* had nothing to feel bad about.

The woman who moaned, asked for more, and screamed her enemy's name hadn't been Lexi; it had been a shifter.

What happened between her and Ric wasn't sex. It was just another chapter of an erotic romance novel.

Repeating that lie in her mind, she managed to drift off, not even bothering to wash off the traces of the tryst.

After all, it had never happened. She bit her pillow and buried a frustrated a groan. And it would never, *ever* happen again.

****

Ric didn't want to go home. He wanted to get lost in the fog that matched his mood. He wanted to get wasted. Wash down the bitter taste of rejection — the confirmation of his fear that, even though Rex was part of him, Lexi could never want all of him. She'd never want the part that dreamed of her green eyes. That wanted to hold her and protect her from anything that might make those eyes misty.

His feet led him through Chinatown and to a bar he'd noticed before but never been in. A scathed and battered sign outside read Willy's Dreams in light blue neon. It was a sleazy, dark place that didn't belong in that part of town.

Ric walked in, and the loud music assaulted his ears. He didn't mind. Loud music meant he didn't have to listen to his own inner whining. He headed toward the bar, pretending not to notice the glances the bar patrons — male and female — threw his way. They were appraising him, waiting to see why he'd invaded their turf. Most went back to their drinks when he met their gazes.

A small, olive skinned man looked up from the other side of the bar when Ric took a seat. He snapped a dishtowel in the air and hooked it over one shoulder. The dim overhead lighting made turned the puff of dust light blue. For a heartbeat, the specks looked like tiny jewels floating around the man's head. "What's your desire?" he asked.

The odd turn of phrase made Ric smile despite his shitty situation. "A blonde girl's heart. Guess you don't serve that, though, so I'll have a Jack. Straight."

"Does she have to be a virgin too?"

"Pardon?"

"The girl whose heart you want."

Ric did a double take before realizing the bartender had just made a joke. "Sorry, mate, my sense of humor's on leave."

"Bad day?"

"Let's just say my day redefined the term." He was about to spill his guts to a total stranger, and he didn't give a flying fuck.

"That bad?"

"Worse. Now where's my painkiller?"

The guy poured more than a measure of whiskey and pushed the glass Ric's way, along with a bowl of peanuts. "Who screwed up?" he asked.

The peanuts looked like they'd been around almost as long as the establishment. Ric still popped one in his mouth and chased down the stale taste with half of his drink. "Me. Her. Both." He sucked in some air through his teeth and raised the glass to his lips for more.

"And how's drowning your sorrows in booze gonna fix shit about it?"

Ric let out a shocked chuckle. "You realize you're in the wrong profession for that sort of advice, yes?"

The man shrugged. "I don't need your business. They"—he indicated just about everyone else in the room with a sweeping gesture—"practically live here. You… Well, I dunno if you'll be good for business."

Ric should be insulted, but didn't feel like taking offense. "I don't mean to run a tab here. I'm going to pay for what I drink."

"Not what I'm talking about, big guy." The bartender held up both palms.

Ric narrowed his eyes and waited for an explanation.

"I've seen my share of brokenhearted bad boys in my time. You drink enough, you start looking for trouble, or trouble finds you."

"She's all the trouble I'm looking for." Ric finished his drink and held the glass out for a refill.

The bartender shook his head. "You're not gonna find her in there. First one was on the house. Now go call your girl and patch things up. You have the right words in you. Just need to find them."

Ric didn't bother telling the man he had no girl— only a shag against a desk without so much as even a *see you later*. He stood and took out his wallet. "I said I'd pay."

The man shook his head. "On the house. And call her."

Ric didn't. He went home, caught up on alcohol consumption, and passed out on the sofa. Another thing he hadn't done in some time.

In the early morning hours, he had a dream. A memory-made-picture. The first few scenes between Xandra and Rex, as Ric read them through Lexi's screen, played out in his mind's eye. He woke up late for work and with a massive hangover, but not half as desolate as he'd been the night before. His subconscious had sent him a clear message — Xandra also hated Rex at first.

Ric had to drive that hatred out of Lexi.

Fuck it out, if need be.

Chapter Thirteen

Lexi had been at her desk for a couple of hours, by the time Ric got there. He had on his usual clothes and a jean jacket instead of the leather one he'd worn when they fucked, but with his hair still black and sleeked back, he was all Rex to her.

The bastard grinned. She shouldn't have given him the satisfaction. But then she wouldn't have felt it herself. Her pussy wouldn't still be tender from the pounding her gave her.

Her nipples strained against the lace of her bra at the memory of his skin against her back.

Gah.

She was driving herself crazy with embarrassment and anger—anger had to be there when the best sex of her life couldn't be repeated, even if she told herself she was only angry she gave into her baser instincts. Still, she had no intention of having people ask what was wrong. She focused on her screen and replaced the latest translation Edmund had asked for, which she'd already finished, with the next chapter of *Exotic Beast*.

She'd offered to do more once the translation was done, perhaps keep notes at the upcoming meeting, but Edmund turned her down. There was no real reason for her to miss out on her reading any longer, if there was no work for her to do.

Rex and Xandra were having an all-out fight, which couldn't have been more perfect for Lexi's mood. With every blow Xandra landed on her lover's ego, Lexi's spirits lifted a notch. By the end of the chapter, vampire and shifter patched things up and were laughing together, and Lexi felt chipper enough she decided to ping Angie on YIM and share what happened last night.

*

Ric's resolution not to give up faltered to the point of almost crumbling when he passed Lexi's desk on his way to his own. He gave her what he meant to be a friendly smile, only for her to ignore him. He managed not to flinch or miss a step and averted his gaze to hide the hurt he felt.

Whatever she played at, she wanted him. He saw it when she gave herself to him. He'd have her again soon, and he'd have her entirely. He knew what she wanted. She just needed to be reminded from time to time.

He kept his thoughts and his stride more confident than he felt, but if a good show would work on her, now was the time for one.

She didn't glance his way for what seemed like an eternity, but he knew she eventually would.

He studied her, searching for a sign she read something naughty. Something to indicate maybe she didn't regret what they did. That she might want more. The look on her face held none of the repressed lust he saw before. He had no doubt she wasn't working; she seemed captivated by whatever was on the screen, and wasn't typing but scrolling down from time to time. If he wanted, he could see what she was reading, but doing so without knowing for a fact she was reading *Exotic Beast* felt like an invasion of her privacy. It was stupid, and he knew it. He'd been invading her privacy since he first hacked into her PC.

Well, he had to draw the line somewhere.

He stepped over the line when Lexi giggled.

In a matter of seconds, he was on the same chapter she was, and decided he wanted to read more as soon as possible. Rex and Xandra weren't fucking or fighting, for a change. They were having fun, enjoying each other's company, and it was just... nice. Nice and normal.

He stopped thinking about Rex and Xandra when Lexi signed on her messenger and pinged that MagicA friend of hers.

Blondes_Rule: I got laid yesterday

The other girl couldn't be more shocked than Ric was. His chin almost hit his keyboard, at the suddenness of Lexi's confession.

MagicA: HUH? WHEN?
MagicA: No, not when. WHO?
MagicA: Ok, when too. And WHERE?
MagicA: Seriously, WHO?

Just as shocked, then. The lines appeared in quick succession, and Ric saw Lexi bite down on a smile at her friend's reaction.

132

Blondes_Rule: Last evening. Rex. On my desk.

MagicA: Ah, so sleep–laid then? Work still that boring?

Blondes_Rule: Not sleep-laid. Wide awake :-D

Ric saw her mouth *nope* and pop the *p* as she typed. She was so adorable, he wasn't even pissed off she said Rex had fucked her.

MagicA: Will you tell me what happened, or do I have to go all magic-y on you?

Blondes_Rule: can't turn me into a frog now. You'll never know about my hot passionate night if you do

Ric's grin threatened to split his face in half. His cheeks hurt, and he hoped she wouldn't look his way, because he'd be unable to hide his glee.

MagicA: I can make you mute till you write down everything that happened…

Blondes_Rule: I'm shaking in my brand new pumps. :-P

MagicA: Hey! Don't mock my powers missy. You do *not* want to mess with a pissed-off powerful witch.

Blondes_Rule: *is petrified*

MagicA: *sighs in resignation* Will you keep doubting my spell-casting abilities (which are totally real), or will you tell me about the sex?

Blondes_Rule: tell you about the sex *straight face* what more do you wanna know?

MagicA: Um… for starters, was there an actual male involved?

Blondes_Rule: I told you: Rex was here!!!

MagicA: Ok. *crosses arms* explain

Blondes_Rule: *whispers* IT-Richie *is* Rex. He came here afterhours, with the hair and the jacket and the boots and the swagger and the accent… *swoons*

MagicA: OMG, OMG, OMG! I KNEW you liked him!

Blondes_Rule: I don't, Angie. It was just sex. And it wasn't him. It was Rex.

MagicA: I didn't say whom I thought you liked, did I? And it's *never* just sex.

MagicA: Was it good?

Blondes_Rule: it was…

Blondes_Rule: …UNBELIEVABLE

This part of the conversation took place so fast, Ric didn't know whether he should be angry for being known as IT-Richie or bouncing up and down for being bloody unbelievable.

MagicA: See? Not just sex. *Unbelievable* sex. Good and to be repeated, yes?

Blondes_Rule: No

Ric glared at the screen. No? Why the fuck not?

MagicA: But why not, sweetie? It was great, and he's there.

Ric wanted to kiss MagicA — Angie. She could find out what held Lexi back. He clenched his fists and waited for the answer that would crush his hopes.

It took Lexi roughly a minute to reply. A minute during which one of Ric's hands found its way to his mouth, and he chewed on his thumbnail.

Blondes_Rule: several reasons, really
MagicA: name one.

*

Lexi rolled her eyes. Things were serious, if Angie didn't take the time to capitalize the first letter of a sentence, even while instant-messaging.

Blondes_Rule: he hates my guts

Her answer lacked something.

Blondes_Rule: and I hate his
MagicA: not enough to refrain from getting groiny with each other

Punctuation was gone now, too. Lexi scrunched up her nose. How much could she divulge while saving face? She decided to go with the whole truth. After all, this was her best friend. She typed, *when he came,* and then paused. The cursor blinked at her. She deleted the words and started over.

Blondes_Rule: when we were done, he just left. Angie, he wanted nothing more to do with me. It *was* just sex. Great, awesome, mind-blowing sex, and nothing more

MagicA: Aww, sweetie, did you show him you wanted more?

Blondes_Rule: of course not.

Blondes_Rule: who said I did, anyway? Did you miss my hating his guts? I'm just saying he was rude

MagicA: Sometimes I wish I could magic some sense into you, you know.

Blondes_Rule: well, first you have to manage to cast spells in front of other people ;-)

MagicA: You wouldn't have to be in the same room, for me to do it. I only have to find the right spell. Hahaha.

Blondes_Rule: again with the trembling in fear. lol

MagicA: *shakes head*

Lexi was about to lie and say she believed her friend could do magic — despite the utter lack of proof — when a new window popped up.

Rex_is_back: can't stop thinking about yesterday

Lexi couldn't believe the man's gall. Actually *that*, she could believe. It was her eyes she couldn't.

Rex_is_back: you shouldn't have left like that.

She threw him a murderous glare over her monitor, but he just smirked at her.

136

Blondes_Rule: you left first

Rex_is_back: had to clean up. I was right back, and you weren't here

He came back, hoping to find her waiting? This clashed with her world theory, and Lexi tried not to let it get to her. Flashbacks of the night before flooded her memory though, making heat rise inside her.

Blondes_Rule: why should I have stayed?

Rex_is_back: 'cause I wasn't half done with you

Blondes_Rule: maybe I was done with you!

Lexi had no idea why she kept answering him, but she promised Angie to meet her the next day and closed that chat window, so she could concentrate on messaging Ric.

Or Rex.

Yeah, it had to be Rex, because she'd never ditch her best and oldest friend for IT-Richie.

Rex_is_back: you weren't done. Trust me.

Blondes_Rule: I can always block you again, you know

Rex_is_back: you can, but you won't.

Blondes_Rule: and why is that, *Richie*?

Rex_is_back: call me that, if it makes you feel better about wanting me. You won't block me, 'cause you want to know what more I can do to your body.

Blondes_Rule: who said you have *any* effect on my body?

But he did. He made it hum with pleasure last night, and he now caused it to tighten with anticipation.

Rex_is_back: I can make you cum without even touching you, Xandra

Blondes_Rule: promises, promises

Okay, so she was taking things too far, flirting with him. At *work*. While people *worked* around them. The degree to which she didn't care amazed her. Despite playing it cool the entire previous night and this morning, the truth was she didn't want to be rejected by Ric. And she most definitely didn't want to deny herself the chance to experience again the level of pleasure she'd reached with him.

Rex_is_back: stay after work, and I'll prove it to you

Blondes_Rule: prove it to me now

He glanced at her, and Lexi arched a brow. When he leered, she knew he accepted her challenge.

Rex_is_back: what are you wearing?

So very original. Lexi decided she'd play dumb.

Blondes_Rule: what do you mean, what am I wearing? can't you see from there?

Rex_is_back: indulge me, *Xandra*. This is a fantasy. What are you wearing?

138

She spared a brief look at her jeans and white button-up shirt.

Blondes_Rule: I'm wearing a grey knee-length skirt, nude stockings, white blouse, and grey suit jacket

Rex_is_back: and underneath?

Blondes_Rule: a black panty set. And I have on my black stilettos.

She wanted to pat her own back at how he narrowed his eyes.

Rex_is_back: stilettos… Take the jacket off.

Blondes_Rule: it's off

Rex_is_back: take the blouse off too. Slowly, caress your stomach as you lift it

Blondes_Rule: mmm, feels good

It didn't really, but the way he gave her orders did. She tried to feel what he wanted her to. His right hand disappeared under his desk. Maybe experiencing the fantasy wasn't that hard.

Rex_is_back: now unzip your skirt and let it slide down. Stockings have to come off too, but leave the stilettos on.

Blondes_Rule: I'll have to take them off in order to lose the stockings. Is that ok?

Rex_is_back: has to be, unless you can magic them off!

Blondes_Rule: didn't I tell you I'm a magician?

Rex_is_back: you must be, making me imagine you in front of me in nothing but your knickers and heels

He turned away from his screen and met her eyes. She could feel his gaze glide over her like silk. She sucked in a breath.

Rex_is_back: I kiss you, nibble on your lower lip, feel your tongue play with mine, as you suck it into your mouth… It drives me crazy
Rex_is_back: Are you wearing a thong?

She was, but it didn't fit the look in her head.

Blondes_Rule: French lace panties
Rex_is_back: you sit, and I kneel before you, reaching up to lower the straps of your bra. I love the feel of your skin under my fingers
Blondes_Rule: I wanna take my bra off
Rex_is_back: not yet. I pull down one side of your bra, exposing the nipple. You arch towards my mouth
Blondes_Rule: mmm…

She had to type something, and 'mmm' was all she could come up with. She could almost feel his lips closing around her nipple, and had to bite back a moan.

Rex_is_back: want to lick that nipple, suckle it, feel it harden under my lips. I flatten my tongue against it, flick it, my teeth just barely grazing it
Rex_is_back: one of my hands is playing with your other nipple over the bra

Blondes_Rule: oh god…

Rex_is_back: is the bra lace too? Do you like the feel of lace scratching against your beautiful tit?

Blondes_Rule: fuck yes

Fantasy and reality merged. Her nipples were hard, stretching the lace of her bra, the scratchy fabric teasing them. Lexi's head felt light. She wanted to touch herself, trace the path Ric described. Knowing she wasn't allowed to made her need all the more intense.

Rex_is_back: my other hand takes over that precious mound my mouth has been playing with, so I can uncover your other tit. I pull down the lace with my teeth and lick that nipple while rolling the opposite one between my fingers… I love the feel of your tit in my mouth, could do that forever, but I want to taste your pussy too

Rex_is_back: I want you, but all in good time. I cup a breast in each palm. Knead them. You kiss me so hungrily, you make my head spin

Blondes_Rule: oh god, feels so good

Rex_is_back: I lick down your neck, your stomach. Trace your sides with my fingers and reach the top of your knickers, but I don't lower them

She needed him to cross the room, bend her over her desk, tear away her thong, and give it to her hard. She couldn't say that.

Blondes_Rule: please?

141

Rex_is_back: instead, I slide my fingers to your legs, all the way down to your knees and then up the inside of your thighs, until I reach your pussy. How wet are you for me, Lexi?

Lexi was too far gone to correct his slip of tongue.

Blondes_Rule: so wet. You feel so good
Rex_is_back: I nuzzle the inside of your thigh. Want to leave a hickey there. My mark. I run my thumb against your pussy over the lace
Rex_is_back: I think these have to come off too. Will you take them off for me?
Blondes_Rule: yes.

In her mind, the word was a sigh. She was breathing hard. Ric's words — no, it was Rex talking to her — turned her on more than she imagined possible.

Rex_is_back: good girl. Now I can spread your folds apart and, God, you're so fucking wet
Blondes_Rule: I am. Please, I need more…
Rex_is_back: I lick you, circle your clit. Do you want me to fuck you with my tongue or my fingers, Xandra?

She had her left hand in her lap, digging her fingers into her thigh to keep from inching just a little bit lower. She hadn't lied. She was wet. Uncomfortably so. She wanted to do something about it. Wanted *him* to do something about it.

142

Blondes_Rule: tongue

Rex_is_back: I flick your clit a couple of times, before plunging my tongue inside you. Fuck, I love how you taste

She was rocking in her chair. She crossed her legs. Rubbed her thighs together. The friction wasn't enough to alleviate the heat burning her.

Rex_is_back: I rub your clit with my thumb, as I push my tongue as far inside you as possible

Blondes_Rule: ...

Rex_is_back: you're so hot, pushing against my mouth, your fingers in my hair, pulling me closer. I want to get lost inside you. You taste like heaven

Rex_is_back: how does my tongue feel, sliding in and out of you? My thumb, pressing harder on that precious nub?

Lexi's mind objected to telling Ric how good he felt in her imagination. It would become too real. They wouldn't be Xandra and Rex, if she went there...

But he did have the jet-black hair. And the accent.

Blondes_Rule: feels so fucking good. I want you. Now.

She saw him look around and push back his chair. He wrapped his jacket around his waist and typed something, before disappearing around the corner.

He just left? In the middle of *this*?

With a frown, Lexi turned to her screen.

Rex_is_back: broom closet. Now.

143

Chapter Fourteen

It took Lexi all of thirty seconds to decide to follow Ric. The broom closet was located between the women's and men's restrooms, so no one would wonder why she walked in that direction. As long as they didn't see where she went, she'd be fine. Luckily, nobody raised their gazes while she passed by their desks.

Just as she reached for the doorknob, she felt a hand on her shoulder. She whirled around and saw Matt shaking his head at her.

Busted.

He must have seen Ric. He knew what she was about to do. How would he use that knowledge? What could she do, to save herself?

She opened her mouth, to sputter out something lame like *this isn't what you think*, but he tilted his head to the right, toward the ladies room.

"Unless you plan on mopping or something, I think this is what you're looking for."

"Right. Silly me. You'd think I'd know by now." Lexi rolled her eyes dramatically, praying Ric heard the conversation and stayed put. If he came out now, it'd be hard to explain how they were both lost while looking for the restroom.

"Nah. Happened to me a couple of times, too. In fact, I could swear John has actually… done his business there a time or two." He winked and nudged her with his elbow.

Lexi tried not to wince at the thought of having sex there after that piece of info. "You mean…"

"I'm kidding. That's what I do—I kid. Not that John isn't stupid enough to have done that." Another grin.

"Whew. Thanks." She returned his grin and entered the ladies room. Would Ric still be waiting for her after Matt returned to his desk? She chastised herself for the thought.

"Well… enjoy." Matt said, as the door closed between them.

"Oh, I'm sure I will," Lexi muttered to herself.

*

Five minutes after he'd gone in the bloody dark and cramped space, Lexi still wasn't there.

Ric was going berserk. Maybe he'd overestimated his sex-appeal, and she just wasn't coming.

No. She wanted him. She'd come.

Oh, she'd come all right. Again and again, if he had any say in it.

But maybe he should just take care of the throbbing in his pants and then return to his desk, like nothing happened. He paced as much as the four by four space allowed. Perhaps he should quit and save himself the embarrassment. He wasn't sure he could face the victorious smile he knew Lexi would sport, after leaving him high and dry.

145

The door opened, and she snuck in. A sliver of light entered the room with her, allowing him to see her. She chewed on her lower lip, her eyes hooded with lust even as she scrunched that adorable nose of hers with obvious doubt over what they were about to do.

He shouldn't have left. He gave her too much time to think. He remedied that the only way he could think of. He grabbed both of Lexi's arms, trapped her between his body and the door, and covered her mouth with his. He wondered at the part of his mind that was calm enough to think about locking the door, so it wouldn't open under their combined weight and spill them out in the corridor.

Lexi parted her lips with a sigh, giving his tongue free pass. Ric surprised himself when, instead of plundering her with hungry kisses, he traced her lower lip with his tongue and then pulled on it gently with his teeth. After their messaging, he knew she didn't expect tenderness. She might not even want it. This wasn't how Rex and Xandra would kiss when they were still enemies.

He didn't care. This was how he wanted to be kissing her. If she didn't like it, she could always tell him to stop.

She didn't. She drew her fingers down the front of his body, and Ric gasped. She hesitated for a moment when she reached the jacket that was still around his hips, and then she pulled on it and threw it to the floor. He moaned when she cupped and squeezed his erection over his jeans.

Lexi had already undone his belt, and was fumbling with his buttons, when Ric realized he stood there like an idiot, breathing inside her mouth, just holding onto her while she tried to free his erection. He

146

snapped back into action, unbuttoning her shirt. He took his time caressing her breasts through the thin lace, and loved the way her nipples rose to his touch. He wished he could see her, but it was dark, so touch had to replace sight.

At least that was the plan.

"We don't have much time…" Lexi wrapped one delicate hand around his length and shoved his pants down with the other.

Ric growled at the feel of her hand on his aching cock. He kissed her again, hard this time, popped the fly of her jeans and sneaked a hand inside. His fingers met her bare, wet flesh, and he groaned. "Thought you said you wore French lace panties."

"I also said I was wearing a skirt. Are you going to complain about my lying?"

"No, but I might punish you…" He felt more moisture against his fingers, and Lexi thrust her hips forward.

"Not now…" She pushed him back a bit, removing his hand.

He felt her try to turn her back to him, and he stilled her motions. "No. This time you'll be looking at me. Knowing who's fucking you."

"It's pitch black, so I can't see you anyway, and I'm wearing pants. Hard to do it face to face, Ric." Hope fluttered in his heart, but she corrected herself. "Sorry — Rex."

"Either's good, kitten" — he wedged one hand back between her thighs and pushed two fingers inside her — "and where there's a will, there's a way." With his free hand, he lowered the waistband of her pants until they

147

cleared her ass and bunched around her knees. He wrapped his free arm around her waist and raised her. Awkwardly, he managed to twist their bodies and perch her ass on the shelf at the back of the closet. Then he took a step back, withdrew his fingers, and bent her trapped legs between them, so he could raise them to his shoulders. Her pants stretched taut against his chest, not allowing her any movement.

*

Lexi tried to balance and hoped to God Ric's grasp on her thigh was enough to keep her from tumbling down. She barely had time to reach and grab onto the shelf behind her, when he thrust into her. The angle drove him straight to her G-spot and bowed her back with pleasure.

Her head thudded against the shelf, but she didn't mind.

Her moan echoed in the small space, reaching her own ears as the epitome of need, but she didn't mind.

Her body was folded in half, held in place by his hips and her precarious grip. Ric's dug one of his hands into the flesh of her buttock, covering her mouth with the other and stifling more moans as he plunged inside her, but she didn't mind.

All she cared about was his cock, stretching her, rubbing against the bundle of nerves inside her. She tried to meet his moves, pushing her ankles down on his shoulders as she rose her hips to his every thrust. He fucked her with such force, she couldn't breathe between thrusts, as she came closer to what she felt would be an

148

earth-shuttering orgasm. Ric brushed one of his fingers against her second hole, and she tensed for a moment before pushing into it, accepting the new sensation.

*

He'd have to remember this for next time. *Next time.* There was no doubt in his mind there would be more of this. More of him making her writhe. More of her body enclosing him. Burning him. Making him whole.

Just as he contemplated delving a bit further into this unexplored area of her body, she thrashed, squeezing him with her inner muscles. She lost purchase on the shelf and flailed her arm. The movement managed to bring down a couple of bottles from the shelf above, which by the sound they made, barely missed her on their way to the floor. Still, Ric didn't stop moving, pumping his hips even faster. Harder. She clenched around him, and he had to stave off his climax through sheer strength of will.

He wanted to tell her how much he wanted her, how *good* it felt being buried inside her. How desperately he wanted to be able to look in her eyes while he made her body quiver with pleasure. She wouldn't allow it, though. It wasn't what they were about. Not yet, anyway. So he did all he could do—he kept fucking her with all he had.

He didn't even stop when he heard Melody at the other side of the door, asking someone if the place had rats, because she heard something in the closet. Lexi shook her head frantically under his palm, and it wasn't in the throes of passion. He slid his hand to her cheek and then the back of her neck, and slowed his plunges. "What, love?"

149

"People," she breathed out. "What if they come in?" She didn't stop meeting his thrusts, despite the worry in her voice.

He pressed her legs closer to her body, thanking whoever listened for how flexible she was. "Guess we'll have to act like brooms if they do," he whispered and kissed her.

She giggled into the kiss, the laughter doing wonderful things to where his body was joined with hers. He loved her giggle. Loved being the cause of it.

He renewed the fervor of his thrusts and his kiss, and it didn't take long for her to climax. She kicked her feet in the air, as her body tensed and convulsed, almost driving him out of her pussy.

Ric swallowed the scream building in the back of her throat before it alerted the entire floor to what they were doing. Holding onto her for dear life, he impaled her on his cock a few more times.

He spasmed and spilled inside her, all the time devouring her mouth. He pulled back to breathe after what felt like an eternity and yet a fraction of a second at the same time. "Fuck. I love making you come." He nuzzled her cheek, wishing they were in his bed and not in a bloody closet, so he could just cuddle with her instead of going back to work and pretending this never happened.

"Fuck..." She sounded as breathless as he felt.

Ric turned for another kiss, but she planted both palms on his chest and pushed. "Fuck, Ric. You didn't wear a condom." She bucked, driving his softening cock out of her.

150

Ric took a step back and tried to lower her legs gently but dropped them when she kicked and thrashed in his arms. "I'm sorry. I didn't think—"

He heard her jump in place and then the sound of a zipper closing. "Seriously?" She poked him on the chest. Considering the darkness, her mark was good. "You didn't think to wear a condom? That should be on auto-pilot. You wanna stick your dick in someone? You wrap it up first." She tried to push past him.

Ric didn't move an inch, blocking her exit. "I wasn't the only one too horny to think. Was I? You were as eager to take it as I was to give it." He should be worried, but he was furious at her for belittling his intentions. Of course, for all she knew, he was just after a quick shag.

"Fine. My fault. I'm a slut," she hissed. "Couldn't wait to get fucked. Is that what you want to hear?"

There was a sob in her voice, and he couldn't resist reaching out to touch her. He got her hair, and she flipped it in annoyance.

"Hey. Hey, that's not what I meant." This time he managed to cup her cheek, but felt her jaw clench under his fingertips. She was waiting to hear what he had to say. He found it encouraging, until he realized her arms were crossed over her chest. Her posture was closed. He shouldn't have said what he did. Not after she'd thought he'd rejected her.

She didn't budge when he tried to pull her in for a hug. "I'm sorry," he said. "I'm a prick." She nodded against his palm. "I panicked, Lexi. I'm sorry. I felt like a right arse for not thinking about protection, and went on the defensive. You're not a slut. You and I want each other, and there's nothing wrong with that. If anything comes up, we'll handle it." He ran circles on her cheek with his thumb and leaned toward her, hoping to assuage her fears with a kiss.

She shoved him away violently. "There's nothing to handle, Ric. I'm on the pill. You can un-panic now. I'm just worried about where your dick has been before me."

He wanted to hit her, but he'd never laid a hand on a woman in his life—unless maybe during sex, if they asked him to—and he wouldn't start with someone he… someone he'd just had amazing sex with. It would be wrong.

Plus, he was maybe kinda falling in love with her.

He moved out of her way and opened the door just a fraction. The coast was clear, so he threw the door open wide and gestured for her to exit. "My dick's been nowhere but my palm for the last two years. I'll make sure to keep it that way now on, too."

*

Lexi didn't know why his words struck her as a threat, but she felt like crying. She had to brush past him on her way out and was careful not to look at him as light from the corridor windows showered over them both.

Of course he'd panicked. Thinking of how to cover his ass.

If something came up, they'd handle it… *Gallant.* He could have just apologized. Been different than the men she never stayed with till morning. Could have said he'd still be there, if things got screwy.

152

Still, he'd reacted better than most men would. He tried to calm her down and didn't take the easy out of blaming her.

She couldn't say why his words bothered her so much. It wasn't like starting a family, with *Ric* of all people, was anywhere on her agenda. But his reaction had hit her as another rejection. It stung too much, after what they just sha—

No. They shared nothing. It was a fuck in the dark. No sharing. Just fucking.

She rubbed the spot between her eyebrows, where a tension headache gathered momentum. Why was she giving him so much thought, damn it?

Chapter Fifteen

"We've been here for half an hour, and you've barely said two words." Angie's face was pinched with worry. "The bounciness you had the past few days is gone. Have you been sleeping well? Or maybe it's the lack of sleep?" She winked, but her effort at a joke earned her a half-hearted smile from Lexi. "Okay, what's wrong?"

"Nothing. Everything is just peachy."

"Now I know something's wrong. You never say *peachy*. Wanna tell me about it?"

Lexi shook her head.

"Let me rephrase. Tell me about it." Angie's understanding look was replaced by a resolved expression that brooked no argument.

Lexi sighed. "It's Ric." Her shoulders slumped.

"What did he do? Is he acting like the other evening didn't happen?"

"The other evening happened, all right. It even re-happened yesterday." Lexi felt the heat of a blush spread up her cheeks.

Angie gave her an incredulous look. "More X-rated fun after work? Wow. Go you."

"Um... not after. During."

"Huh?"

"During work." Lexi dropped her voice to an embarrassed whisper. "Broom closet."

"You had sex in the broom closet, during work?" Angie's voice was nowhere near whisper-level.

Lexi ducked her head. Could the earth open and swallow her whole?

"Don't be coy *now*. What went wrong? Wasn't it as good this time?"

"It was even better." At least until they'd finished.

"Why do I sense a big *but* there?"

"'Cause there is a big butt. A huge ass, to be more precise, and his name is Ric."

"Uh-oh. What did he do this time?"

"He didn't use a condom."

"Oh God. Is there— Are you..." Angie took a deep breath. "Should we be worried?"

"Nah-uh. Not for a pregnancy, at least. But like I told him, I don't know where his—well—where he has been." She narrowed her eyes at Angie. "Well? Aren't you gonna offer to turn him into a worm or something?"

"You told him that? Like in a chit-chatty *what-was-your-relationship-status-before-me* way? Please say it was in a chit-chatty *what-was-your-relationship-status-before-me* way."

"Nope. More like in a bitchy *no-idea-what-you've-been-fucking* kind of way." Lexi scowled at the shocked and disappointed look on Angie's face. "What? He deserved it. And why do you care?"

"Because you and he are meant to be—"

Lexi's cell phone rang, and she raised a finger for Angie to hold that thought. An old friend was on the other end of the line, and Lexi's spirits were lifted by the time

155

she hung up. Step by step, she was getting back the life she'd lost when she dropped everything for Andrew. "Remember Caitlin Taylor?" she asked Angie.

"From high school?"

Lexi nodded. "Ran into her the other day, and we exchanged phone numbers. She's married and has a kid on the way. Her husband is out of town, and she wants to go for dinner tonight. But you were saying Ric and I were meant to be doing something?"

Angie shook her head. "I just think you were kind of rough on him. Do you know if he's been with people from work in the past?"

Lexi wanted to laugh at how Angie never used the more vulgar words for sex — *sex* included — unless she had to, but now wasn't the time. "I don't think so. He doesn't seem too friendly with anyone else. Or too snarky." She fidgeted a little with the straw in her milkshake and lowered her gaze to the table. "Um, and he said he'd only been with himself for two years now, but I think he just said that out of spite."

"Hello? Earth to Lexi? Why would a man tell you he'd been with only you after two years of celibacy, to spite you?" Angie was talking fast, hardly breathing, the way she always did when she found something exciting or unbelievable.

"Maybe 'cause he said he'd go back to it?"

"To" — Angie gulped — "playing with himself?"

"Yeah. He said he'd been with no one but his own hand for two years and would make sure to keep doing so. Guess I can't even compare to a guy's fist, as far as sexual prowess goes." She tried to make light of it, but the words sliced her throat.

156

Without getting up from her chair, Angie wrapped an arm around Lexi's shoulders, and pulled her in for an awkward hug. "Aw, honey, that's not what he meant."

"What else could it be, Angie?" A tear ran down her cheek, and Lexi wiped at it furiously. When she raised her gaze, she felt her eyes blazing. "What else could it be?"

"It could be his way of saying he meant to keep away from anyone but you. And himself, of course. 'Cause you know, guys and themselves? Can't be apart that long." Angie shook her head. "He wouldn't risk having sex in the office, unless he wanted you, and he'd know if he wanted you or not after the first time. See? There'd be no need for a repeat performance."

"Oh." That was all Lexi could come up with. She didn't think she could handle this possibility either. Ric having sex with her and her alone? That was too close to... going steady. *Going steady?* Was she still in high school?

Relationship wasn't a concept she wanted to entertain. And with Ric? No way.

Only, he hadn't said he wanted a relationship anyway. How could he have? He'd been too busy being an ass.

Then again, she'd been an ass first.

The wheels turning in her head weren't enough to keep her from noticing a triumphant smirk on Angie's face. Lexi sighed. "You can stop hearing wedding bells in your head. Even if we keep screwing—"

Angie shook her head.

"Yes, Angie, it's screwing. No more than that. Even if we keep doing it, it doesn't change the fact that we don't like each other. He wants me out of there, for crying out loud."

157

"You're wrong. You don't get it. And Sarah won't let me—" She huffed.

"Sarah? What does she have to do with this?"

"She made me promise to stop interfering. Said I've done enough already, but it's not enough, because if you don't know, you can't believe. And if you can't believe, how can you be happy?" She spoke in a hushed tone, more to herself than to Lexi, which was fortunate, because Lexi had no clue what Angie was talking about.

"Know what? Believe what?"

"Never mind that." Angie waved her fingers in the air, and Lexi thought she saw thin strips of light extending from the fingertips toward her. It was the coffee high again, making her see things brighter.

Yeah, she wouldn't mind. If Angie said it wasn't important, it wasn't.

Angie went on. "The thing is, two weeks ago you seemed so down. Remember? You kept wishing something about your life would change. And sometimes wishes come true. Sure, you're not all happy now, but this is temporary. Before you discovered that novel, you were in a rut. Bored of everything. It was like you'd just given up. You weren't satisfied with your job, and you were lonely. So lonely."

Lexi opened her mouth to disagree, but Angie held up her palm. "You were. Even if you'd never admit to it. Now you don't have to be lonely any more, and I hate that your stubbornness keeps you from seeing that."

"Honey, Ric isn't the right cure for loneliness, and he's definitely not the answer to my wishes. There is no connection between us. No emotion. Just great sexy times." They were great, all right. And now they were over.

And she was done talking about the guy.

She asked Angie about Sarah, and then they talked about work and how Lexi still didn't find it exciting. She grudgingly admitted that despite Ric's selfish reasons for suggesting it, attending company meetings would be a step up. She felt bad getting paid full time, when she spent more than half of the working day online, reading *Exotic Beast*, but she'd tried talking to Edmund about it, and he'd told her to wait.

Mentioning the novel lead to speculation about who could be behind it, and then looped the discussion back to Ric.

"I don't wanna talk about it anymore. What's done is done, but there will be no more," Lexi said.

"Why are you so adamant?"

"Because I am. Now drop it." Lexi looked at her watch. "I need to do some shopping before I go home. You and Sarah wanna join us for dinner tonight?"

"Can't. Promised Sarah to watch some zombie movie with her. Have fun, and say hi to Caitlin for me."

"Sure."

They both stood. "I'm sorry I was a pain, Angie, it's just…"

"Hush." Angie pulled her in for a hug. "I know. You're always a pain, but you're my pain."

****

All in all, Friday was good, Ric told himself. Well, apart from how it all went belly up when he didn't use a sodding rubber. He ran his fingers through his hair. He wished he could take those last few moments back, along with his stupid admittance he wouldn't touch anyone but her. He wanted to stick with the memory of her coming, of her moans of release poured inside his own mouth, while her body shook with pleasure.

She'd called him Ric.

But even before her slip of tongue that made his heart lurch in his chest, she'd given him a glimmer of hope. Not just because she told her friend she'd had incredible sex with him, but because she followed him to the closet when he told her to. She wanted him as much as he wanted her, and she'd risk her job and her standing with Pedelty to have sex with him. With *him*.

She'd called him Ric, not Richie or Rex. She'd used his name, not that of a fictional character who looked like him. She'd known full well who fucked her, and this was the main reason she acted like a wench once they were done.

The thought that Lexi resented wanting him was a slap in the face. He lit a cigarette and pulled on it hard, to clear his mind of all doubt there could be a future between them.

She didn't resent wanting *him*. She resented wanting a man she thought hated her. He had to do something to fix this, and soon.

But what?

He remembered her reaction when he'd asked if the translation was giving her trouble. She'd been too defensive, as if trying to prove she was worth something. She shouldn't care what he thought.

Now what was wrong with that picture?

160

God, he was a moron. She'd told him, but he hadn't listened.

She thought he wanted her out of the company.

The first time she ever raised the subject was when she accused him of telling Pedelty to fire her. Ric thought she'd gotten the matter cleared up since, but she obviously hadn't. Just two days ago, there was that site debacle. She believed he was gathering proof to convince Pedelty to fire her.

Ric had to get Pedelty to explain. Get him to set things straight with Lexi, because she wasn't going to believe Ric.

He put out his forgotten smoke and lit another in its wake. It took all of three drags to come up with a plan, and three more cigarettes to build up the courage to do what he decided.

****

Lexi had a fun night reminiscing and reconnecting. She should try to locate more of her old friends. It was good to feel like she belonged again.

She was in her flannel pajamas, brushing her hair, when she heard the ringtone that usually cheered her up. This time she found it silly. She should change it.

She considered letting the call go to voicemail, but it was almost one in the morning. Only Angie would be calling this late, and she'd just keep trying until Lexi picked up.

She pressed the little green button and brought the phone to her ear. "Hello?"

"It's me."

161

A tingly feeling ran down her spine at the sound of Ric's voice, and her breath jammed in her lungs. "Why?"

"Why what?"

"Why is it you on my phone at this hour?" She didn't want to know. Angie had helped her feel a bit better about what he said yesterday, and whatever the reason behind this phone call was, Lexi feared it would result to another kick at her self-esteem.

"Wanted to talk to you." He sounded serious.

"Obviously, unless you have a habit of calling people to not talk to them. But I'm sure it can wait till Monday."

"No, Lexi. It can't."

"Okay. Talk." Her voice was harsh, but she felt about as tough as a marshmallow.

"What happened between us—"

"No." He wouldn't get to say how it was wrong. This was her line, damn it. No way would she be the dumpee.

"No, what? I didn't even get to finish the sentence, you silly bint."

Lexi lacked the strength to snap at him for calling her a bint again. "I don't need to hear the rest, to know what you wanna say. What happened was a mistake. It won't happen again. Feel all better, now we're on the same page?" Her spine was stiff, her shoulders slumped. He couldn't wait till Monday or act like nothing had happened. He had to spell things out for her. Eh, he got brownie points for honesty, at least.

"Oh, no. You're not pulling the it-was-a-mistake speech on me. If it were a mistake, you wouldn't have

162

done it a second time. What happened was bloody spectacular." He sounded angry, and Lexi was at a loss.

"Wasn't that what you called to say? I don't understand."

"Of course it wasn't, and if you heard me out instead of—" He took a deep breath. "Bollocks. I'm doing exactly what I want to stop doing," he muttered.

"Huh?"

"Listen, the reason I called was to offer a ceasefire."

"Ceasefire?" She felt stupid for echoing him, but she was confused.

"We can't change what's been done. I can't un-be a wanker, and you can't un-be a bitch."

"*Hey.*"

"I'm sorry, but both are true. And if we're to keep doing what we did, it'll be better if neither of us goes for the other's throat within seconds of the cum-shot."

She scrunched her nose at his vulgarity but stifled a surprised giggle. This was the last thing she'd expected to hear, and she wasn't sure how to react. "No strings attached?"

"None whatsoever."

"I'll have to think about it."

"About the truce?"

"No, whether we keep doing it." She bit her lower lip and waited for his response. She and Ric weren't arguing. Their exchange was almost… friendly. Was the world about to implode? And was her tone teasing? What was next? *Flirting?* She had to get a grip.

"Not much to think about, love. You either want this hot, tight body, or you don't."

163

"Yeah... I'll get back to you on that." She couldn't believe how easy this conversation turned out, after everything that happened between them. She still wasn't sure that deal came without a catch, but he sounded sincere.

"Truce is on, though?" he asked.

"The truce is on."

"Right. Goodnight, then."

"Goodnight."

She returned to brushing her hair, trying hard to convince herself the call didn't mean much. Her grinning face in the mirror indicated she wasn't exactly succeeding. Whichever way she analyzed Ric's suggestion, the only explanation was the obvious—he really offered truce, no strings attached, because he wanted to keep having sex with her. She was giddy at the prospect of amazing, drama-less sex, but couldn't avoid thinking there was one more guy who didn't view her as relationship material.

Despite her usual, self-deprecatory nature, she didn't linger on that. It didn't matter, because this time there was no room for falling. She knew what he wanted, and it wasn't like she'd ever want more with Ric.

All in all, the deal proposed sounded perfect.

Which was the main thing that worried her.

She wanted to call Angie, but it was late. Sharing the news would have to wait a day. Or two—there might even be more news to share by Monday afternoon. She let out a small laugh and got under the covers. She just got an offer for incredible sex, by a guy who would at least act like he didn't hate her. That was a definite go-Lexi situation.

164

Sleep claimed her almost as soon as her head hit the pillow.

Chapter Sixteen

When Lexi said she'd get back to him, Ric assumed it meant she'd sleep on it and call him in the morning. As the day went by and the phone didn't ring, his good mood from last night evaporated, leaving behind self doubt and worry.

But she'd sounded teasing on the phone and agreed to the truce almost instantly. It had to be a matter of time before she told him she wanted him again. When she did, all sorts of possibilities would be open for the two of them.

He groaned. He didn't care about *all sorts*. The single thing he was interested in was being with her. As in, hand-holding, spending nights watching silly movies, *with her*. As in, whispering… well, whatever cutesy couples whispered.

That kind of thinking kept him twisting and turning in bed on Sunday night. He chanced a glance at his bedside clock, to see how many more hours of fruitless efforts to sleep were ahead of him. He finally managed to drift off less than an hour before the annoying buzz of the alarm clock reverberated through his bedroom and inside his head.

He kicked off the covers and jumped out of bed, fully awake at the thought of seeing Lexi and gauging how she felt about continuing what they had.

He was a pillock. They had nothing, and he'd better get to fixing that.

****

Lexi put on her best, brightest smile and entered the office prepared to honor the truce. That smile cracked around the edges when she saw Ric by John's desk, barking at Melody to get her sorry *arse* out of his way and make herself useful.

What if being a jerk was his idea of foreplay?

Lexi hated the idea of there being — or ever having been — anything between Ric and Melody.

Her good mood returned full force, when Ric beamed at her. "Morning, pet. Bit late today, are we?" His tone was light, not chastising.

"Oh, I'm sorry. Will I be punished for it?"

She felt his gaze like a caress, gliding down the sleeveless white turtleneck she wore, and following each curve of her body down to the hem of her knee-length grey skirt. He took in her calves and cocked an eyebrow at her stiletto heels, and she smirked.

"What's that?" he asked, his gaze back to her face.

"I said I'm sorry. Will I have to be punished for my tardiness?" She gave him an innocent look and twirled a lock of hair gone astray from her ponytail. *God.* She had to get a grip. Openly flirting with him at work was one step too far.

Then again, she'd had sex with him at work...

She took her seat, without waiting for Ric's reply. She was already wet for him, but not to the point of losing control. "Um, I have work to do, so..." Her smile was

167

more restrained this time, but not forced. For some reason, the same face she wanted to punch on Friday made her grin on Monday. It had to be her hormones. *Yup.* Hormones. She congratulated the voice of reason in her head.

Ric stared at her.

"Guess I'll talk to you later?" She hoped he didn't think she brushed him off.

He nodded once, and then caught her gaze. "Later it is. Better catch up with all that work now."

Lexi tried. She did. But she was bored with a capital *B* before noon. Scratch that—with a capital everything.

"Lexi. Just the girl I was looking for." Edmund stopped in front of her desk and aligned her pen holder with her post-it notes and her stapler.

"I've been right here all day." She hoped he hadn't seen her yawning.

"Yes. Quite. Well, if you're not too busy, I would like you to attend a meeting at two."

This was new. She smiled. "Sure."

"Good. Two o'clock, conference room."

"I'll be there." She kept smiling while he walked away. Edmund was including her. This could be the change she needed.

She just had to finish some paperwork before that. Easy-peasy.

An hour later, she wasn't singing the same tune. Entering numbers in an Excel table, was no fun.

Although, while one did such menial work on the PC, one could also have a fun chat.

She signed in and grinned when she saw Rex_is_back was online.

168

*

Ric was trying to get one of the company's foreign associates to see there was nothing wrong with the software of the new CD-player the firm was launching. The darned thing just needed batteries. Unfortunately, the language barrier and stubbornness made communication via written speech difficult. He was about to take things from the top, when his messenger program let him know he had a new message. He clicked on the blinking icon, and a new window popped open.

Blondes_Rule: so… what does this truce entail?

Ric threw a glance Lexi's way and bit back a chuckle at how absorbed by her work she seemed to be. She was a natural-born actress. What else had she been faking? In his initial conversation window, he typed, "Sorry mate. You're right. I'll talk to the boss and get back to you." He didn't wait for a reply, before signing out of his company account and making himself invisible to all but Lexi.

Rex_is_back: thought that was clear, luv. No yelling or verbally abusing the other party
Blondes_Rule: so I can't call you an evil bloodsucker when you're all Rexed up? *bats eyelashes*

Lexi's question meant she wanted to keep things as they were, and that was all he needed to move them forward. At least he hoped so. He kept from hooting aloud

169

because he tried to play it cool. He didn't give a damn about anyone else at the office. They all seemed to expect him to act like a loon, and he didn't mind it one bit. It wasn't a coincidence that nobody on the floor commented on the sudden changes to his appearance. He knew his poor socializing skills kept people at bay, but he couldn't help himself. He wasn't the sharing type and hadn't been in a while, so he was polite but in a studiously cold way. After all, he wasn't there to make friends. He was there to work.

Mostly.

Rex_is_back: you can call me anything you want, as long as you're screaming it underneath me

Blondes_Rule: someone has a big ego :-P

Rex_is_back: not the only thing I got that's big, kitten…

Blondes_Rule: oh really?

Rex_is_back: if you don' remember, I'll be more than happy to remind you

Ric sucked in his lower lip and waited to see if she'd rise to his challenge.

Blondes_Rule: when?

He barely had time to see her reply, when Pedelty's voice sounded way too close. "Two o'clock, Richard. Shall we?" Edmund gestured toward his office. The door to the conference room was at the far end of it.

Ric kept his calm, although his heart raced. Edmund could have seen his screen. "Be right with you."

Remaining expressionless, he closed the conversation window and locked his computer.

Pedelty called out to Lexi to join them. She locked her PC too and then rushed to follow the two men through Edmund's office.

Ric took a step forward, to get the door to the meeting room. "After you, Eddie."

"I've told you not to call me that." Edmund walked briskly through the opening.

"You called me Richard first." Ric winked and gestured for Lexi to enter.

As she followed her stepdad, Ric leaned in and whispered, "Stay after work".

The only indication she heard him was a slight lifting of one corner of her mouth, but it was enough. The truce would be tested in just a few hours.

****

The meeting stretched interminably. Lexi felt stuck in the Twilight Zone, where time stood still, as she looked at the clock to find mere minutes had passed between one tedious topic and the next.

The heads of Marketing and Research had joined them—a jolly giant of a guy and a brilliant woman Lexi's age—and much as Lexi liked them both, she thought their suggestions were useless for the company. Not that anyone had asked her.

"Lexi, what do you think about all this?" Honest curiosity shone in Ric's his eyes.

Shit. He had to choose the one instance she wasn't paying attention? For a moment there, she believed his question was meant to show Edmund how useless she was.

"This is Alexandra's first time attending a meeting, Richard. She isn't required to actively participate. This is so she can be better informed, with respect to company matters," Edmund said.

"Girl has an opinion about everything, Ed. Listen to her. You may gain something."

To say Lexi was shocked would be an understatement. She must have done something right — thought not necessarily something work-related — if he was eager to hear her ideas. The problem was she had none of those for the time being. "I can't offer much of an opinion before I know what the rest of the departments think of the matter. Maybe after the follow-up meeting —"

Ric narrowed his eyes. "That one will take place *after* the results of this one are in effect." He sounded pissed off, and Lexi couldn't fathom why.

"Well it doesn't need to." She tried not to be intimidated by the four sets of eyes watching her. "It doesn't," she said again, in a more subdued voice. "We can have the second meeting the day after tomorrow and come up with more comprehensive results, so the changes can be better applicable. No use making half-informed decisions based on trial and error. Having the second meeting later on will mean we'll have to make a second round of adjustments to the processes. Why not make them all at once instead?" She was pleasantly surprised by herself.

Edmund just blinked. He'd never heard her use words such as *comprehensive* and *applicable* before.

172

The grin on Ric's face held a hint of pride. He was *so* getting a blow job for that look. Not that she'd ever tell him such a thing.

Larry, the Marketing Manager, clapped his hands. "Why, that's a magnificent idea." He turned to Edmund with a thousand-watt smile. "Will you arrange for all the kiddies to gather here on Wednesday, or should I?"

"I think Lexi should do it," Ric interjected.

Okay, no blow job for him. "Huh? Why? I've never said more than two words to them, and one of those was *hello*. I can't be calling meetings out of nowhere."

Edmund finally spoke. "Richard is right, Lexi. You should call the meeting. As a matter of fact, I think you should have some proposals ready for us. Nothing too detailed—just a few thoughts. Take tomorrow, and ask the managers for any assistance you may need."

Well, if she was in for it, she might as well gain something. "No reason to put off for tomorrow what can be done today. I'll just stay after work and see what I can come up with, so I'll have all day tomorrow to prepare."

"I can help out," Ric said. "Edmund, mind if we use this room?"

*

Ric spent the rest of the day looking at his watch. He hated waiting for everyone to leave before Lexi and he went back to the meeting room. Even his most adventurous part, however, knew the idea of shagging her while Pedelty was only a door away was way beyond risqué.

173

Still, he had to exercise every last ounce of self-control, to refrain from following her to the meeting room as soon as she went inside at five. There were still people on the floor, despite the hour. If Melody didn't get off the bloody phone, he'd rip the thing off the wall and drag her to the front door by the hair.

It took no more than a glare for her to say goodbye to her *winky-poo*—whoever the poor sod was—gather her stuff, and make a hasty retreat.

Chapter Seventeen

What kept Lexi from biting her nails was the money she'd paid for her perfect French manicure. Instead of coming up with ideas on improving interdepartmental communications and cooperation, she kept thinking of the two times she and Ric had been together. So far, her trysts with him had been hasty and spur-of-the-moment. This one was planned. They hadn't talked about it, but it was implied. Would they have to talk before? Or after? And could they talk, when talking didn't involve yelling and throwing accusations around?

Did she even want that?

There would be no biting off the very expensive nail polish… Her thumb was already in her mouth, and she was worrying the cuticle.

They didn't have to rush, this time around. There was a perfectly valid excuse for them to spend as many hours as they wished behind the locked doors of the meeting room.

But maybe he'd want to keep it quick and dirty. It could be just a session to get rid of the tension, before they got all worky.

She let her head drop on the meeting-room table. The reflection of a red light blinked on the shiny surface. When it didn't reappear, she thought of trying to locate its source. A knock on the door drew her attention from the light that might not have even been there. She bolted out of her chair and rushed to open the door, even though it wasn't locked.

The moment he entered the room, Ric grabbed her and spun her around. Her back hit the door and slammed it shut. Then his lips were on hers. His kiss was fervent and demanding as ever. His hands were in her hair, as if to keep her in place, while he pressed the hardness in his pants against her. There was such desperation in that kiss, such *need*, that all thoughts and doubts were erased from Lexi's mind. She just gave in and melted against him, trusting him and the door to keep her upright. Ric let go of her hair and glided his hands down her neck, to her collarbones, over her breasts, and around her back, to cup her ass.

He lifted her, and she wrapped her legs around his narrow hips, digging her fingers into his broad shoulders. She was intoxicated by his taste. His touch…

Ric's touch, not Rex's. This was Ric, and she knew it.

She'd withdrawn for the couple of seconds her internal debate lasted, but was back with a moan when Ric ground his pelvis against her. He smiled, turned with her still in his arms, and walked them to the huge oblong table. He carefully laid her down and unlocked her ankles from where they kept her anchored to him. With a quick peck on her lips, he placed his palm over her breasts. "Lie back, kitten."

It never occurred to her to say no or demand he hurry up. She was in a Ric — or Rex, or King of the Jedi;

176

she didn't give a fuck—induced haze. He was free to manipulate her body any way he saw fit.

He ran his fingers down her legs, feathering touches on her heated skin. He clasped her feet and planted them on the edge of the table, before pushing her skirt upward until it covered no more than her hips.

Lexi didn't care that her high heels could scar the dark surface. Every whispery glide of his fingertips traveled straight to her womb. Letting her eyes drift shut, she focused on the sensations his touches brought forth, but tensed when the hem of her skirt licked the top of her thighs on its way to uncovering her bare pussy.

He stopped touching her.

Lexi opened her eyes and tried to raise herself on her elbows. "Something wrong?"

"Don't move."

She surprised herself by obeying his order, until he dragged a chair right in front of her with a scraping sound. She half sat up, drawing her legs close to her.

With a look of determination in his eyes, Ric reached out and grabbed her ankles to pull her back into her original position. He wasn't looking at her face, but at her pussy. His hungry gaze made Lexi self-conscious. The overhead lights were on, and he studied her so openly. She tugged her skirt down, to cover herself from his lustful look, but a shake of his head stopped her as effectively as his hands would have.

"No. Let me see you, love. Never had the chance before."

She could give him one of half-a-dozen snarky responses at that point, but the amazing thing was she didn't want to. Instead, she spread her legs more but kept

177

her head lifted, not wanting to miss a second of his devouring gaze. She used the hands she'd meant to cover her nakedness with to bunch her skirt further up, allowing him to see all of her.

He wetted his lower lip with his tongue, and Lexi was astounded by how much she wanted to taste his mouth again. She whimpered.

*

Her whimper snapped Ric out of his trance, and he graced her with a leer, before leaning into the source of his wonderment. He'd wanted to taste her even before their first tryst, and he finally got to.

He'd savored the moment enough. Now was time to savor Lexi.

At the first touch of his tongue, her hips shot up. He planted his hands on her hips and kept her down, while he traced her labia with his tongue. He took his time kissing and licking her bare outer lips, nuzzling her thighs, and grazing his teeth over the soft golden flesh there. He loved the way she quivered against him. Loved the little mewling sounds that escaped her lips.

He parted her folds with his nose, running his tongue over her entrance on the way up, and she almost strangled him with her thighs. Prying her knees apart again with both hands, he slowly pushed the tip of his tongue inside her wet core. She bucked her hips, but he refused the urge to deepen the penetration, as she so obviously wanted. Instead, he withdrew from inside her to lick his way to her clit, then wrapped his lips around the swollen pearl and sucked on it gently.

When he heard her head thud on the desk, he pushed his tongue back inside her, this time as deep as it could go. He snaked the fingers of one hand up her thigh. He found her clit with his thumb, circled it, rubbed it, and…

"Oh, God. Just a little more. *Please*, Ric." Her voice broke at his name.

Ric increased the pressure to her clit and picked up the speed of his tongue's thrusts inside her.

Lexi rode his face and hand, until she crumbled against him. When she threw back her head and gasped a word, it was his real name. For the second time.

He waited until she turned her gaze to him.

Then he stood and peeled off his T-shirt.

*

Lexi felt as though ages had passed since she last saw his sculpted abs, the snaking muscles that rippled in his arms, and his pecs that seemed made of marble, but she hadn't forgotten how good his body looked. Still, she'd never seen the part of him that made her writhe with pleasure, and she had to dig her nails into her thighs to keep from reaching out and ripping the buttons he was languidly undoing. Her breathing had just returned to normal, but it sped up again while she took in the statuesque body in front of her.

He fished a condom from his pocket, and she remembered yelling at him the last time they'd had sex. She shook her head. "No need." They'd been over this. They were both clean, and she was on the pill.

"You sure?"

179

She was, and she was sorry she'd been a bitch about it last time, but an apology would ruin the mood. Plus, she maintained he'd acted like an ass. In lieu of an answer, she leaned in and tugged at his fly. When his cock was released from its denim confines, she couldn't control the widening of her eyes any more than she could refrain from licking her lips. She'd felt his length and girth inside her, but she never knew a cock could be beautiful. As pale as the rest of his body, it stood hard, a study in perfection. Veins running close to the surface added to the marble-like effect. A very live and pulsing piece of marble, jumping under her appraising gaze.

Lexi was torn between needing to feel it deep inside and wanting to run her tongue along its smoothness. Taste Ric like he'd tasted her and make him shudder with the same all-consuming pleasure he'd given her.

In the end, she was selfish.

*

She wanted him. Ric could see she wanted him as much as he wanted her.

He was seconds away from having her again, from being sheathed inside her heavenly heat, but this wasn't what the smile on his face was about.

This time they weren't playing someone else's part, and they both knew it. This was them, Ric and Lexi, and he didn't know if it was the truce or how long it would last, but he felt like laughing and crying and thanking the Powers-that-Be and whoever wrote that wonderfully wicked book, for allowing him to have this.

180

She spread her legs wider and opened her arms to him, and it was like Heaven calling. She didn't order him to fuck her or to hurry up. She opened herself to him, beckoned him to her, and he intended to take full advantage of that openness, short-lived though he feared it would be.

Even if it hurt more, when she ended it all.

He sank inside her slowly, with a sigh that was equal parts relief and longing. He wouldn't be hurried. He raised the hem of her top and took his time laving her perfect creamy breasts and teasing the rosy peaks, before returning to her lips.

He let her hair loose from her ponytail and buried his face in it, inhaling her unique scent and delighting in the silky feel of it against his cheek. Her nails dug furrows in the flesh of his back when he changed the angle of his thrusts. The way she clutched at him, more like holding on than being consumed by passion, shook him to the core.

He was watching Lexi's face when she came. He saw her eyes widen and roll back, before she squeezed them shut. Her mouth fell open, and a tremor shot down her body. When she bucked her hips, he came too, biting his lip to keep from baring his soul to her.

He held her close as he turned to his side, never wanting to stop touching her.

She didn't pull away, and Ric knew better than to second guess this gift he was given. He feathered fleeting touches on her face, her arms, her sides—wherever he could reach—afraid she might just disappear if he lingered on any one place longer than fractions of a second. Her heat around him sent new jolts of life to his softening cock,

181

and he loathed the thought of withdrawing from inside her.

*

Lexi didn't know what changed from their previous encounters, but it scared her as much as it elated her. Ric's body once more lit a fire all over hers, but this time it didn't feel like a blaze. More like a deep burning. The kind that leaves scars. For a moment, when she caught his gaze, she wanted to shove him off her and run before it was too late.

She wanted him closer. Deeper.

And then he swiveled his hips and thrust again, and she was lost...

She lay in his arms, one hand toying with the golden down on his forearms. She should go. She wanted to stay there forever. She wasn't very consistent these days.

"So..." She chewed on the inside of her cheek.

"So..." Ric's tone was careful.

"So this truce is working out." Her giggle was genuine, and she stifled it with her palm.

Ric tangled his fingers with hers, pulled her hand out of the way, and kissed her. "Your laugh is doing amazing things to my nether regions." He waggled his eyebrows. "You up for another round?"

"Are you?" She batted her eyelashes.

A rocking of his hips was all the answer she got. Not that she required further clarification.

Chapter Eighteen

This time there was no post-coital snuggle.

Lexi said they had some work to do, but she said so with a grin, and just before giving him a quick peck on the lips.

Ric's own grin began to hurt the muscles in his cheeks, but he couldn't drop it.

Her hair was pulled back again, allowing him to study her profile. He couldn't pry his gaze from her lips, wrapped around her pen as she considered where to start making the suggestions Pedelty had asked for. Well, he could, but it was to watch her fingers play with an errant lock.

She gave him a questioning look.

"What's that, love?"

"I said, if you didn't write the book, who could have? And why?"

"What do you mean?"

"*Exotic Beast.* Someone has to be behind it all. I mean, who'd know Mom calls me Xandra, and would have enough free time to do something like that? And what would they gain by my finding it?"

"You're saying someone uploaded it for you to see?" This never occurred to him.

"Yes, Ric. I don't know how much you believe in coincidences, but a novel that can only be read *on my office computer*, and features me and you, is too much of one for me."

"They had to know I was Rex too..." Ric mumbled.

"You were Rex? Like how? Fangs popping out and eyes going yellow?" She giggled and a tiny snort escaped. Adorable.

"No. Like with the hair." He pointed at his head. "And the attitude." He leered and then asked, "Only reached from your PC?" just as Lexi said, "You were really Rex?"

Ric took a deep breath. "I called myself that. A rebel phase, that was. Ended when I started working here. Edmund knows." He saw no reason to elaborate further. "Now you. You can't access the novel anywhere else?" He raised both eyebrows.

"It's the weirdest thing..." Lexi explained how she first stumbled upon the site, as well as all efforts she'd made to reach it from other PCs. "Nothing works."

"Nothing works."

"Nope."

Ric watched her lips form the word and indulged in the fantasy of her rosy lips wrapped around his—

She snapped her fingers in front of his face. "Earth to Ric. You still with me?"

"Yeah. I tried to access it from my PC too, and no page would load, but I thought I got the address wrong." He was glad she still hadn't asked how he knew about it in the first place, and hoped to keep it that way. "You do realize the only person who knows about your being Xandra and my being Rex is Edmund, right?"

184

"Yeah... *Somehow*, I seriously doubt he'd go through all the trouble of writing an entire erotic romance novel—eww to his possibly writing those sex scenes, by the way—just to get the two of us together."

Ric chuckled when she scrunched her face in that charming way of hers, but when her point sank in, his eyebrows shot for his hairline. "Get the two of us together?"

Lexi shrugged. "With all the Rex-loves-Xandra, Xandra-loves-Rex, they-seem-incompatible-but-aren't-really, and the meant-to-be-togetherness... it's like whoever wrote it wants to get us together."

"Whoever wrote it..."

"Will you stop repeating what I say?"

She glared daggers at him, and he was half tempted to repeat her last question, to see if her gaze could become any fiercer. Fierce was a good look on her.

Pissing her off more wouldn't be wise, though, especially since they seemed to be getting along so well tonight. "I'm sorry, love. Was just thinking... what if nobody wrote it for us? What if it's not Pedelty, and it *is* the mother of all coincidences? Then it's all about you and me in an alternate universe, doing the nasty and then—" He tried to come up with the best phrasing possible. "It could be a sign." Subtlety wasn't within his spectrum of approaches, but he didn't want to scare her away by saying they might be meant to be together.

Lexi laughed. "Oh, come on, Ric. This is a little fatalistic, coming from a techno-geek, don't you think? So what? It was kismet that we'd fuck?" Her words squashed his hopes, ripped out his heart, threw it on the wall-to-wall carpeted floor, and stomped on it with her sexy spiked heels.

The sound of her laugh would have expanded Ric's heart under different circumstances. Now it hurt like a motherfucker. "I didn't say that, did I? I distinctly remember not using the word *kismet* or anything of the sort."

"I didn't mean to make you pout," Lexi said with a smile. "Besides, I'm not denying it's the utter pinnacle of fucking. There's just nothing more to it. I mean we had to *try* for a truce. That's not typical of people who get along."

Her glibness drove the knife deeper in his heart. He wouldn't give up on her, though it would take longer than he'd thought to make her see she was made for him. For now, he'd play along. "No argument there. Just thought…" He shook his head. "Bugger it. Let's finish what Pedelty asked for, and I'll look into the bloody site myself. I'll ask an old mate or two to help, if need be."

They managed to come up with a handful of ideas, before Ric decided it was time to shag her senseless — it seemed to be the way to her heart. He'd show her the difference between himself and Rex. Make her realize what they did on that table was so much more than just a fuck.

He hoped she'd catch on quickly. He doubted he'd manage to keep up the selfish-vampire persona for long, when he touched her.

He took her on all fours, landing more than a couple of slaps on her glorious bum, although he made sure not to hurt her. He made a point of calling her *Shifter* and used the palm of his hand to stifle the name she cried out as she came under him. He didn't want to hear it. If all

186

she was after was a fuck, that's what he'd give her, but there was no reason to have it rubbed in his face.

Lexi wanted him, not Rex, but she refused to see it and wouldn't appreciate him talking to her about his desires and dreams. Not giving in to the frustration choking him at her stubbornness, he disentangled himself from the heap their bodies formed, adjusted his clothes, and went to get her a glass of water. Once she'd quenched her thirst, he gave her a lingering kiss and helped her up. He watched as she straightened her clothing, and then he held the door for her, before locking it behind them and leading the way down the stairs.

Lexi passed him when they reached the lobby. He was tempted to pinch her delectable bum, but it wouldn't do, in front of the security guy.

Lexi waved at the man. "Goodnight, Chad. 'Night, Ric."

Chad gave a nasty smirk and looked from her to Ric, to the huge screens in front of him.

"'Night, Lexi." Ric turned to the guard. "The lady said goodnight."

"I'm sorry." Chad didn't meet his gaze. "My mind was elsewhere."

So he had a mind? He didn't look it. Ric made a mental note to check the man's internet usage. He wouldn't be surprised if Chad spent his shifts watching porn. His station had the screens for it.

****

Lexi's mind was like a nest of live wires when she got into bed.

187

Just like after their phone conversation last night, she was amazed at how easy being with Ric had felt.

She sighed.

His strong arms around her felt so good, even if he didn't really like her. But then, why had he held her?

Good bedside manner. That was all. He didn't like her as a person, but he enjoyed having sex with her, so he was polite about it.

Despite really not liking her.

Ric could be charming and witty, but if she let him get close, he could hurt her.

Like Andrew had.

Because Ric didn't like her.

And Andrew was supposed to love her.

Still, something had happened between her and Ric. Something big. And it affected him too, because that last round — oh, *God*, that last round — was nothing like the first one. Both times had been filled with passion, but when he took her on the meeting room table, she felt like he wanted to touch her soul. The connection and intimacy made it so much more than the rough sex that followed.

She glanced at the carpet burns on her knees.

She preferred the latter. It was familiar and set her mind at ease. And she didn't have to see his blue-blue eyes filling with wonder when she fell apart beneath him. She wouldn't have to put an end to things between them, if all times were like the last one. They'd each be safe in their solitude and share nothing beyond their naked bodies. The way things should be.

The safe way.

Ric was an amazing lover, but Rex was the man Lexi needed. She couldn't contain her relief when Ric got

188

into character and called her *Shifter*. She was just glad he covered her mouth when he did, because she lost control, and some stupid part of her made her call out his real name.

God, she was a mess. And that stupid book and whoever wrote it were to blame.

Whoever wrote it.

Someone who *wasn't* Ric.

But then...

She huffed and ran downstairs, to find Edmund.

Back in her room a few minutes later, she rolled on her stomach and dialed Ric's number.

"Hello?" He sounded groggy.

"Hey. It's me. Did I wake you?"

"What clued you in?" His tone was light, despite the sarcasm.

"It's nine o'clock, grandpa. You shouldn't be sleeping anyway. Told Edmund I forgot to get your opinion on something, so he gave me your number."

"And what was the real reason, kitten?"

The pet-name no longer bothered her. When did that happen? "Ummm... The part about wanting to ask you something was true."

"And what would that be?" His voice slipped into a deep purr, and Lexi had to try hard, not to think of him naked.

"How did you know about the site?" she asked.

The silence on the other end of the line was deafening. Lexi thought of repeating the question. She should demand an answer before he had time to come up with a lie.

What Ric said next made no sense. "Tomorrow afternoon."

"Huh?"

"I'll tell you all about it, tomorrow afternoon. After work. We'll go get us a cup of coffee, and I'll tell you."

"So you have time to come up with an elaborate lie?"

"No, love. So I can get some sleep. It's a bloody long story, and I'm sleepless and severely dehydrated, due to repetitive shagging."

Eh, he did have every reason to be exhausted. "Tomorrow it is, then. But you better not try to weasel your way out of it."

"Or what? You'll spank me?"

"I just might." She squeezed her eyes shut. Why did he always bring out this sultry side of her? How did he do it?

"I'll be looking forward to it. Five okay with you?"

"It's a da—deal." It was so *not* a date. "Meet you outside the front door?"

"It's a deal. Good night, blondie."

"Good night, Ric."

190

Chapter Nineteen

Lexi awoke a whole hour earlier than usual, to get ready for work. She jumped out of bed at the first beep of the alarm clock, instead of setting the snoozer for ten minutes later. Why was she so jittery this morning? Today wasn't a big deal. Just coffee after work with a coworker.

Who was hot as hell and made her body sing.

She rummaged through her underwear drawer, grabbed a pair of nude panties, and slammed it shut again.

She took a quick shower and rolled her hair, to dry in ringlets while she put on her makeup. She carefully applied base. Maybe she should straighten her hair instead. She let it loose and put a light, shimmery eyeshadow on her left eyelid. In the mirror, her hair looked nice and summery. She'd let it dry freely. She put on some mousse and went back to her makeup. She made quick work of her cheeks and lips, but something was wrong with the end result.

She narrowed her eyes and studied her reflection.

Forehead — not shiny.

Complexion — clear.

Cheekbones — contoured.

Lips — glossed.

Eyes...

191

Shit. She hadn't done her second eyelid.

She hurried to fix that and gave herself an approving smile in the mirror. Her patent-leather briefcase lay by her desk, unused since her mom gave it to her as a gift when she started working for Edmund. Lexi snatched it, shoved in her lip gloss, wallet, and a couple of empty folders, and left her bedroom.

She didn't run into her mom or Edmund on the way out, so it was a good thing she caught her reflection in the hallway mirror.

She was heading to work in her bathrobe.

Okay, she had to get a grip.

The second time she came down the stairs, she was dressed in a white pencil skirt and a black sleeveless shirt. The third time, in a pair of jeans and baby-pink turtleneck.

The fourth and final time, she was back in her skirt but with the pink turtleneck, and almost happy with how she looked. Though her hair was a mess from changing tops. The inventor of turtlenecks needed to be tortured.

She smiled at her reflection. She'd pull her hair up, after all.

She got to work twenty minutes late, hair cascading down her shoulders.

With the whole day and most of Wednesday to polish up her suggestions, she could read a couple more chapters of *Exotic Beast*.

The next chapter ended in a cliff-hanger, and so did the one after that. And the one after that. She couldn't help but feel both pity and exasperation for Rex. The vampire came to terms with his feeling for Xandra but self-doubt made him fence himself in and not allow hope to enter the barriers he'd set for his existence.

192

Why was he so stubborn? He wanted her; he should claim her, for fuck's sake. Lexi rolled her eyes as chapter after chapter the two got closer and still he waited for the other shoe to drop.

All the while, a pesky thought tried to get to the forefront of her brain. Who did he remind her of?

Not Ric. Right?

Lexi was relieved when, a little before four, Edmund told her he'd like to see her in his office for a brief chat. Nothing else could make her pry her gaze from the screen. She terminated the browser and locked her PC. A quick trip to the ladies room, to check her appearance, and she returned to her desk, to pick up her neat pile of notes.

She was on her way to Edmund's office, when she saw Ric setting his laptop on his desk. He looked up and winked at her, and Lexi felt breathless. He looked like he had the first time he'd taken her atop her desk — tight T-shirt and combat boots included.

She wasn't the only one slack-jawed at his makeover. Edmund strode to Ric's desk and asked something Lexi didn't catch. Ric shook his head a couple of times and said something else she couldn't hear.

Edmund nodded and gestured for her to approach. "I hope you don't mind Ric joining us," he said when she reached them. "I felt his presence was needed, and since he was back in time..." He turned and walked toward his office

"No, not at all," she said to his back. "Know what this is about?" she asked Ric.

He shrugged. "No idea."

193

"Didn't he tell you just now?" She came to a halt outside her stepdad's door and studied Ric's face.

He took another couple of steps, before he turned to look at her. "He asked if I reverted to Rex." He chuckled.

"And have you?"

"No, love. God, no. I wanted the bloke I met with to feel comfortable with me again. I'll tell you about it later." He leaned in closer. "Now move that sexy bum of yours, and let's get this over with."

People were watching—not many, but a couple were enough to start a rumor—so Lexi pretended to check something on the top sheet of paper in her arms, nodded, and walked inside.

Already behind his large desk, Edmund motioned for them to sit in the leather armchairs facing him. "The reason I called you both in here was for a preliminary discussion on your ideas to be presented tomorrow. I'm certain that, with Richard on your side, you must have come up with brilliant suggestions. However—"

With Richard on her side.

Lexi winced. Of course. Heaven forbid she come up with anything all by her little lonesome. She was particularly proud of herself, for not rolling her eyes despite the intense urge to do so. "However, you still had to check. It's cool. I get it."

"Indeed. I still have to check."

Ric turned to her. "Show him what you came up with."

What *she* came up with. Lexi didn't like that. Maybe Ric hated her ideas from the start and was setting her up. Her ideas, her screw-up. If he hadn't winked at her just

194

then, she'd have freaked. Instead, she laid down her notes and began presenting her thoughts on possible solutions.

Since the most important problem was the lack of coordination between departments, due to miscommunications, her plan consisted of tracing every order throughout the system, so each department would know what was expected at any point. As she explained to Edmund, *order* wasn't limited to outside clients, but could be anything a department asked of another. By combining her proposal with a couple of forecasting tools that considered more than end sales, "—there would be elimination of slack time and a subsequent increase in efficiency."

While making her brief presentation, she'd forgotten she was being tested, and relaxed. The moment the last word left her mouth and she took in Edmund's thoughtful frown, her confidence faltered. "What?" she asked.

"I believe Richard is at the moment tempted to rub my face in something. It seems I have made a mistake with you." The frown was still there, and Lexi turned to Ric, who smiled triumphantly.

"More than tempted, old man." Ric cleared his throat. "I told you so." He punctuated each word separately, voice booming, then leaned back in his chair with a self-satisfied expression.

"You did, but I suggest you remember to whom you're talking. I'm your bloody boss." The smile forming on Edmund's lips belied his chastising words, as did his use of *bloody*.

"Yes, Sir." Ric mock-saluted.

Lexi was looking from one to the other, as if watching a tennis match. Her gut twisted as her fears came to life. Ric set her up, to prove to Edmund she shouldn't be there. And to add insult to injury, he'd fucked her. Her eyes felt hot, the betrayal cutting so deep, all her sense of self-worth vanished. All her focus went to keeping back the tears that threatened to roll down her cheeks. If she could, she'd spring from her seat and flee the building, but her strength had seeped out of her while the two men gloated in her failure.

She was about to try to bolt anyway, when Ric grabbed her wrist. "Ed, you'd better tell Lexi what you mean. I think she understood something completely different."

"What?" The man seemed at a loss for words. "Dear, what—what's wrong? Do you need me to—"

"She needs you to tell her what you thought of her presentation, Edmund. Now, please."

"I—I was astounded by it, of course." Pedelty removed his glasses and began polishing them. "Alexandra, your ideas were good and very well supported. I should have heeded Richard here, when he said you were being wasted at your current position, but I was too eager to protect my little girl from the pressure of responsibility. It was selfish of me to try to keep you from growing up, and for that I apologize. I'm going to ensure you are more involved in the company affairs now on. We shall start by filling you in more next week, after I'm back from my business trip."

Lexi had to try to form words. It never occurred to her that what she'd proposed was good. "You" —she took

196

a deep breath—"liked them? And Ric said I was being wasted? When did he say that?"

"I told you he thought I made a mistake with you, but you insisted you were happy where you were."

She couldn't believe how stupid she'd been. All that animosity toward Ric had been for no reason at all. Well, not *no* reason. He'd acted like an ass at first. But still... She chanced a glance at him, and he leered.

Lexi stifled a giggle.

She wanted to apologize.

She wanted to kiss him.

She settled for beaming her brightest smile his way. She'd make their not-a-date worth his while.

After Edmund, Ric, and Lexi agreed on dates for subsequent meetings to get her all caught up, she and Ric were free to go. A glance at the clock showed the workday was over.

"Well, I'm off," Ric said to nobody in particular. He left in an apparent hurry.

"Yup. I'm going too," Lexi said to the exact same nobody, but took her time collecting her stuff before making her own exit. She was jittery again.

But it was *not* a big deal.

So not a date, she repeated in her mind, as she passed by the front desk. And if that asshole Chad leered at her one more time, she'd have him fired, even if it meant she'd wear a sign reading PEDELTY'S BRAT around her neck for the rest of her life.

As soon as she was out of the glass doors, Ric pushed away from the wall he leaned against and offered her his arm.

Lexi couldn't take it. She just couldn't.

197

It would be like they were going somewhere together, which was what they were doing, but not in the *together* sense of together. She pretended to look for something in her briefcase.

He smirked. "Suit yourself, kitten. Without my shoulder to lean on, walking where I have in mind won't be easy in those heels of yours."

Lexi considered his words for a moment, and then touched her fingertips to his elbow, holding her head up high. Saving face was less important than saving her pumps.

Chapter Twenty

All they talked about on the way was the meeting with Pedelty. Lexi tried to get Ric to share what he'd told her stepdad about her, but he wouldn't.

"Your noggin's big enough without me giving you more positive feedback," he said.

The comment made her grin and drop the subject.

That and sheer force of will kept her from grumbling about walking six blocks, while both her car and Ric's were parked right outside the company. Her heels were killing her, and she caught herself leaning on Ric on more than one occasion. By the time they reached the small café he had in mind, she was too relieved she'd be taking some pressure off her poor toes, to protest when he chose a table at the back and pulled out a chair for her.

"Thank you," she said.

He smiled and took a seat facing her.

Lexi looked around, as Ric went through the coffee shop's menu. The day was clear, and the street outside buzzed with life, but only two more of the café tables were occupied. No sound penetrated the large window panes. It was like she watched a very private silent movie, in full color.

She itched to ask Ric about *Exotic Beast* again. She accepted he had nothing to do with it, but he knew about it, and not from her. Lexi chewed on the inside of her cheek. It would be impolite to go for it without letting him get a cup of coffee first. And maybe she didn't want to know the answer. She and Ric had reached a place where they could talk and jest and take walks with her holding his arm and…

She did *not* just think that. They hadn't taken a walk. They'd moved pedestrian-y, to where he could answer her question. End of story.

"How did you know about the site?" she blurted.

"Can we at least order first? I'll have an herbal tea."

"You'll have herbal tea?" So much for the She felt every bit like the incredulous round-eyed, gaping messenger smiley that shook its head from side to side.

Ric left the menu on the table, sat back, and raised both palms. "I'll tell you now, on three conditions. Yeah?"

That killed her mirth on the spot. "No." She squinted at him, the suspicion Edmund's explanations had dispelled rushing back, to flood her mind. "You already had a condition. *One.* And we're here. Are you trying to get out of this?"

"No, I'm not." He seemed hurt the idea crossed her mind. "Listen to the conditions first?" At her nod, he fisted his left hand with the thumb sticking out. "One, we order."

"Done."

He popped out his index finger. "Two, you hear me out. No interrupting." She opened her mouth to protest, but he didn't let her. "No interruptions. You hear the whole thing out."

"And the third one?"

"No matter what, we finish our coffee."

200

"Don't you mean your herbal tea?" She snorted. His conditions were nothing sinister, and she was in too good a mood to second-guess his good intentions.

"Right. Knew I should have said four conditions." He sucked in both cheeks, and the accentuated hard lines of his face added to his beauty.

No, not beauty.

He was hot-*ish*. Could be hot. Okay, *was* hot. Not beautiful, though.

Crap. He was beautiful, and Lexi had noticed when she first saw him.

Before he'd spoken and ruined it for her.

"I'll have a green tea, and the lady wants a coffee. Strong, sweet, and hold the cream, please."

His words snapped her back to the here and now, and Lexi didn't know if she was more surprised she hadn't noticed the waitress approach or that he knew how she liked her coffee.

Ric looked into Lexi's eyes with such intensity, she flinched. Was he hoping to see something, or praying not to?

"Keep in mind whatever I tell you happened before the truce. Right?"

Lexi nodded, amused by his unease. She got a bit more comfortable in her seat and motioned for him to go on.

"I saw you working long hours and — well — I knew your workload didn't justify it." She glowered at him, and he slammed one hand on the table. "Bloody hell, Lexi, you know the shit they have you do is too easy for you."

*

201

She tilted her head to the side and wrinkled her nose, but she didn't speak. She took the no-interrupting stipulation to heart. He'd chuckle if he weren't sure she'd forget all about his conditions and ditch him the moment he told her he'd spied on her.

"So one night, when you must have thought you were alone…" The words wouldn't come. He couldn't say he'd watched her masturbate and then hacked into her PC.

But Lexi looked at him so pleadingly, he had to. "I watched you. I watched you" — he struggled to find an inoffensive word, to make what he had to say less bad — "*touch* yourself. You were captivated by something on your screen." A blush crept up her face. She opened and closed her mouth, and Ric knew he had to tell her the rest fast. "I had to know what got you that way. I hacked into your computer, saw *Exotic Beast*, and was hooked."

The silence seemed to draw out too long, and he realized she was waiting for him to finish. "End of story," he said.

Lexi pushed her chair back.

He panicked. "I wanted you." As if that made it all better. He'd been an ass, and there was no excuse for it.

She stood, shaking her head.

"Lexi, please. Your coffee isn't even here yet. You said —" He stopped there. Whatever she might have agreed to, she was well within her rights to leave and never talk to him again. "It was before the truce," he whispered.

"I'm going to the ladies room. When I come back, we're going to have our coffee and never mention my pleasuring myself in the office ever again. Clear?"

It was his turn to nod. He was so thankful she wasn't fleeing, he didn't even have the presence of mind to turn and watch her bum swish away.

****

When he admitted to watching her get off, Lexi was more than tempted to make a run for it and never show her face at work again. Then she remembered Ric was the one who'd had sex with her in a broom closet, during work hours, and she decided indignant outrage wouldn't fly as a response.

Plus he had those puppy eyes.

She sighed and splashed enough water on her face for her color to almost return to normal. She swabbed off and then wiped the mascara that had run down her cheeks. Yup, now she looked cool as a cucumber.

On her way to the table, she could see Ric was all but bursting with nervousness. Their drinks had been served, and he held his cup in a hand balanced on his knee.

"I'm back," she said in as cheery a voice as she could muster.

He set his cup on the table, not meeting her gaze. "I'm sorry."

"That I'm back? I can go."

He raised a face so stricken with remorse, she felt bad for him. "It's okay," she said. "I mean, it's not okay, and you have to promise to never invade my privacy like that again, but" — she shrugged — "it was before the truce."

"Never again, Lexi. I promise."

"Good. With that out of the way, what will we talk about while we sit here?" She licked her lips and arched an eyebrow at him. Sex talk wouldn't be half bad. They'd be on familiar territory, and she might get fantasy material for her alone-time.

"Meant to tell you about the guy I met with. The one I had to be in character for?" He plucked at the lapels of his leather jacket with both hands.

"Oh, that. Right." She grinned. "Well, why are you in your Rex gear?"

"He was an associate of mine from the old days." He winked. "I wanted to see if he'd suss out anything about the site. He didn't. Couldn't trace a single thing about it, and he's the best there is." He seemed to think for a second. "This side of the jail bars, that is."

"Why doesn't it surprise me IT-Richie hangs with such a crowd?"

Ric glowered. "Not hanging with them. Used to. Before..."

She could tell the subject made him uncomfortable. "We have a truce. Remember?" she asked. "I promise not to use anything you say today against you."

He nodded. "My third year of uni — college for you — I fell in love with the wrong woman. She was wild and unpredictable, and seemed drawn to darkness. I came from a loving family, wanted to be an artist, and was too much of a ponce. Too soft, for her to notice me. So I dyed my hair, purchased every leather piece of clothing I could, and played at being a badass. I still went to my classes, though. Studied hard. I was going to ask her to be my wife."

"She didn't feel the same?" Lexi could tell where this was going. Like her, Ric had placed his hopes for a future on the wrong person.

He thrummed his fingers on the table, not looking at her. "She wasn't made for the shackles of conventional relationships. She said so when I caught her making out with some stoner she brought to my graduation party. I must've drunk my weight in alcohol that night. When I got home, my dad got in my face. I pushed him, and he pushed back. I was out of control. Blinded by my pain." He met Lexi's gaze now. "I threw a punch at him. Didn't mean to hurt him. I was just lashing out. It caught him in the chin. I'll never forget the look in his eyes. There was no anger, just sorrow. At what I'd become."

His voice broke, and Lexi felt a tug at her heart at seeing him so vulnerable. "Ric…"

"He didn't deserve that, Lexi. He never laid a hand on me, was always on my side, and I… I couldn't handle the guilt. I mumbled an apology and ran out. Withdrew what I had in the bank, and jumped on the first plane here. I no longer played at being bad. I became bad. I got into fights, worked as a bouncer, changed my name to Rex, and ended up doing some not-so-legal computer-related work.

"Edmund came to my place one day, out of nowhere. I was hungover and didn't remember him at first. Hadn't seen him since I was eight or so. He smashed my nose with my own front door, then said my mom had suffered a heart attack and needed to see me."

The anguish in his voice cut Lexi to the core. "Did your mom —"

"No, no. She's fine now."

She huffed a sigh. "Good. I mean, that's great. I'm glad."

"Yeah." Ric smiled. "Anyway, when Edmund saw the condition my life was in, he offered me a job, provided I reformed. And this is me — a reformed man with a shady past."

*

Lexi didn't even frown when he told her the worst of it, and Ric was grateful.

"Everybody has a past," she said now. "Where did the name Rex come from, though? I know it's Latin for *king*, but to me, it's a dog's name."

He groaned.

"You chose to have a dog's name? Why?"

"It was chosen for me. While I worked as a bouncer, I had a reputation for being a dog."

Lexi widened her eyes. "Oh." Still no recrimination in her gaze. Just surprise.

"Your turn," he said. "Why come back here? Rather, why leave in the first place?"

She grimaced. "My story is eerily similar, except Andrew didn't give me the anti-monogamy spiel until after we were engaged. We hooked up right after college. He was charming, funny, handsome, and way into me." She shook her head. "I *thought* he was way into me. He was done with his MBA, and when he got a job in New York, he proposed. My mom wasn't half as psyched as I

206

expected when I told her the news. I assumed it was because I'd be moving so far away." She looked somewhere above his head, her face pinched.

Ric wanted to hold and soothe her, but held back. "Mothers have a radar for bad seeds." It wasn't the most inspired comment, but it made her smile.

"For all the times Mom has been vocal about her opinion, she chose this one to keep it to herself. Not that I blame her. I was head over heels, and anything she said against Andrew would just drive a wedge between me and her. I applied for a Master's in New York, got in, and followed Andrew across the States. As soon as he started work, I stopped seeing him. Late hours at the office. Dinners with clients. Briefings. He always had an excuse, and I always bought it."

Ric nodded. There had been signs Bridget wasn't faithful too, but he'd turned a blind eye.

"He worked late again on our one year anniversary. He'd said he'd be alone at the office, so I packed a mini-picnic and went to surprise him. Found him sprawled on his boss's couch, with her sucking him off. I had a bottle of wine in my right hand. I threw it at him and left. He didn't even run after me. Just called me half an hour later, berated me for making a scene, and told me he did what was best for us. He promised it was one-time thing. That it meant nothing. He said I had to forgive him. People made mistakes."

"You didn't." He hoped she didn't sell herself short like that.

"I thought about it. I considered staying, playing house, and trying to forget my future husband cheated on me." Her face was drawn in anger.

At herself.

"I didn't want the hassle of moving again," she said. "Didn't want to have to tell my mom I'd fallen for a man like my dad. I called my best friend—she's here in San Francisco—and she told me not to dare think about it. She walked me through packing Andrew's stuff and leaving it outside our apartment, and two days later, she flew in to get me. If it weren't for Angie..."

"You'd still have done the right thing. Eventually. You wouldn't have married him."

"No?" She met his gaze and held it. "How do you know?"

"Because the kick-ass woman in front of me wouldn't put up with that shit." That woman was smart and funny and independent and had stolen his heart.

Her smile didn't reach her eyes. "Sometimes I think maybe I wanted to. Maybe I stayed in New York another year, looking for a job, because subconsciously I was hoping for a reconciliation. Not that Andrew tried that hard. He sent a couple of gift baskets. A new ring. Bigger. Instead of sincere apologies, there was more passive-aggressive crap on the cards—he thought I was more open minded than the average housewife, who measured love by fidelity; he expected me to care more about a solid future with him, than about something as trivial as a tiny, little slip; he believed I was his soul mate, but I was not cut out for a mature relationship." She listed Andrew's covert accusations as if she believed them.

"He was a wanker, and you're better off without him." The way she talked about her ex, Ric had the impression she was over him, but not over blaming herself.

208

"I know. Better off alone."

"Not what I said."

She didn't give him time to clarify. "Edmund wanted to pay Andrew a visit, but I stopped him."

Ric remembered the pain of his nose breaking when Pedelty shoved his door into his face. "You should have let him. Pedelty could fuck him up. In fact, give me the wanker's address, and I'll fuck him up. I have some business on the East Coast."

Lexi stifled a giggle with her hand. "Ric, you growled."

*

Discussion flowed. Lexi loved hearing about London, and how Ric was brought up to be a proper gentleman. She spoke about her childhood, her absentee father, and how Edmund filled the void in her and her mother's lives.

"He's been more than amazing," she said. "I don't call him *Dad*, just because I've associated the word with someone worthless. But you said Edmund could fuck Andrew up? And he hit you with your door? It doesn't sound like the man I know."

"I was blocking the entrance to my apartment. He shouldered his way in, and the door busted my nose and bruised my ribs. He sort of carried me to the bathroom, shoved me in the tub, and hosed me down until I was sober."

"Edmund did that?" Lexi couldn't believe what she was hearing. Was that the same man who'd treated her scrapes and scratches when she tripped and fell? The man who'd stayed up all night for a week when her mom developed pneumonia and ran a fever? She shook her head.

"You haven't seen the other side of him. My dad hinted at stories, but I saw it for myself. Edmund can be scary."

"I still can't believe it. He's always been so gentle and soft-spoken."

"I grew up hearing how he rocked when he was young. He was my childhood hero of sorts." His face broke into a boyish smile. "Nudged me towards painting and called me *Richard of the Brush*."

She laughed. "*Richard of the Brush?* That's disturbingly cute."

"I wouldn't talk about disturbing, love. I wasn't the one who wanted to dye a Capuchin monkey pink."

She let out a squeal of mock protest. "Oh, my God. Edmund told you that? I'll kill him. He won't survive dinner." *Dinner.* "What time is it?"

Ric looked at the screen of his cell phone. "Eight thirty. Why?"

Lexi jumped up. "I have to go. Thanks for the coffee." She didn't really care about dinner, but she'd been having fun. With Ric. They'd been talking — *talking* — for more than three hours. She hadn't been interested enough in a guy to want to know him since Andrew, and that had ended in pain and tears. She grew since then. Learned to protect her heart. Even if it meant running away from a man who called to every fiber of her being.

She weaved her way toward the exit. She couldn't breathe. Had to get out of there. Ric said something, as

210

Lexi reached the glass door, but she didn't pause. She threw the door open and walked outside.

Into the rain.

It was one of those sudden storms that give no warning. No gradual gathering of clouds. Nothing. They break out when you least expect them, soaking you to the core and leaving you with two choices — either return to the safety of indoors, or run and play in the water.

Lexi's choice was made for her when Ric grabbed her arm. "Tried to tell you it was raining." He took off in a light jog toward the office, dragging her with him.

She tried to shake off his hold, but he didn't let go. His face was turned to the sky, and he was grinning. The knot in her stomach eased. He wasn't out to hurt her. *He wasn't Andrew.*

Ric's giddiness was infectious, and Lexi allowed him to lead her to the end of the block and around the corner, into an alley. The rain was loud — so loud, she could barely hear herself laugh. She hadn't done anything like this since high school, when she'd tried to coax Angie into following her but always ended up the only one having to explain her drippy clothes.

She didn't care about her clothes then, and she didn't care now, as Ric turned and pulled her against his body.

He was laughing with such unabashed glee, she had to kiss him.

*

He was happy. Fucking unbelievably happy.

Lexi was there, with him. Living it up. *Feeling* alongside him. Her pink-and-white outfit was sodden, outlining her lithe body. Her makeup was smudged, and her hair plastered to her cheeks, but she'd never looked more beautiful. She was a vision.

He inhaled deeply. Lexi and rain. No better scent on earth.

He turned them so her back was against the wall. She didn't seem to mind the dirty bricks scraping her white skirt, as she clung to him and he clung to her. Rain poured into his mouth, making their kiss more urgent. He fought for breath but never drew back from her lips for more than fractions of a second.

She clawed at his jacket, while he roamed his hands down her back, trying to raise her top. Unzip her skirt. Feel more of her. They both moved frantically, but the wet clothes resisted. Lexi was the first to give up trying to work her zipper. She raised her skirt with one hand and used the other and her thighs to climb up his body. She locked her wrists at the back of his neck, steadied her shoulders against the wall behind her, and lifted her hips.

Ric sneaked his hand between their bodies. He had to fumble with his belt and buttons for a second, before his cock was free. Making sure to peel the soaked jeans down, so he wouldn't hurt her, he grabbed her hips and lowered her to him slowly, until he was as deeply buried inside her as possible.

Only then did he break the kiss, to look deep into her eyes.

"You feel so good, Lexi. So right." He began moving inside her, and now it was their gazes that were

212

locked in as intense and soul-searching a union as their lips had been.

She didn't answer, just moved her body to his rhythm, the pelting rain around them failing to hurry their coupling.

"Right. You're so right. Made for me."

*

His voice was gruff and no more than a whisper, yet it carried to her with all the force of thunder, despite the whoosh of the rain. His words travelled through her body, making her quiver, reaching her womb at the same time they made her heart constrict.

With fear.

She squished that fear until it was small enough to hide behind the lust and the need and the sense of completion that threatened to take her over and turn her into nothing more than flesh.

No mind. No rules. No boundaries.

For the first time in her life, for the briefest of moments, Lexi let go. The waves she feared would drown her if she dared lower her walls rushed and filled the space inside that had been hollow since Andrew's betrayal. She floated on top of the waves, toward Ric. Toward his voice that demanded more from her.

"Tell me who's making love to you, Lexi. Who your body responds to. Tell me, love."

"You." She panted for breath, rain and desire stealing her voice. "You, Ric."

*

He closed his eyes, to relish her words, and leaned in for another kiss. This one lasted an eternity, melding them both into one and driving them even further — deeper — inside one another, until they found their release in unison.

They stayed there, getting showered by the rain long after he started softening inside her. Their lips were still locked, but they weren't kissing as much as drawing breath from each other.

Ric couldn't hold back any longer. "Go out with me, Lexi. On a real date."

She averted her face, but made no more effort to pull away. "No."

He almost didn't hear her answer. He wished he hadn't. "You're constantly on my mind. Your scent. Your taste. How your breath hitches when I enter you. How you flutter around me when you come. I can't stop thinking about you, Lexi. Be with me."

"No." She lowered her legs, letting him slip out, and fought to lower her skirt. Cover herself. Do anything but meet his gaze.

He didn't give her an inch. Didn't move back, to facilitate what he knew was a retreat from him and what they could have. "We can be good together. Give me a chance to show you."

She pushed him. When she looked up, her eyes were bloodshot. "This can't happen. I can't have this. I don't *do* this." She tried to sidestep him.

Her voice broke into a sob, and he wanted nothing more than to hold her. He ached to wrap his arms around her and never let go.

214

He reached out to her, and when she fought off his hand, he blocked her way by planting his fist against the wall. His throat felt raw, and his eyes burned. "Why? What's so fucking wrong with going out with someone you have fun with? Who you have great sex with? Who wants you so fucking much?"

Her lips moved, as she wiped at her eyes with the backs of her hands. He couldn't be sure but she might have said, "I'm sorry, Richard." He didn't care. What mattered was that she was gone.

He clenched his jaw and turned his face to the attacking skies, hoping the heavy droplets cooled his pain and fury into something more manageable. He remained there, hunched, while the cold engulfed his body. He'd touched heaven, only to be ripped out from it. If he hadn't promised Pedelty to never give into self-destruction again, he'd go drown the pain in alcohol until the numbness once more became a permanent part of him.

"Now is the time for a bloody sign," he hollered at the clouds above. "Should I give up?" He was tucking himself in, aware of the pitiful sight he made, muddy and wet and disheveled, when something vibrated in his pocket.

Chapter Twenty-One

Lexi didn't doubt Ric's intentions. She simply didn't believe what he wanted existed. That she could have it. Fairy tale romances were made for movies and television shows and romance writers who needed something to hold on to. Not real life. Ric knew her breath and scent now, but if he woke up next to her enough mornings, he'd start looking for something new. Fresh. More exciting. Men weren't built for monogamy, and she knew better than to think she could change them.

But Edmund…

No. He was the exception. Lexi remembered how destroyed her mother had been after Lexi's dad left them. She herself had felt so little, so insignificant, when she discovered Andrew's infidelity. It was like her insides had been torn, her heart ripped out of her at the casual manner he'd dealt with her hurt. A wound still gaped where her hopes and dreams used to be.

She would never let another man close enough to hurt her.

But her mom had allowed herself a second chance…

No chances. Lexi knew better. There was nothing to hold on to but herself. And even herself could betray her, once she gave someone more than her body. Lexi did that before and lived to tell the tale, but she'd been younger then. Naive. She couldn't do it again. Wouldn't. She was only up for casual encounters and could give nothing more. Take nothing more.

She needed nothing more.

Besides, who could love her?

One of her heels broke off on the way to her car, so she limped for the last couple of blocks, driven forward by adrenaline and the fear Ric would catch up with her and force her to own up to feelings she'd long denied herself.

A different kind of fear and worry started eating at her once she was safely inside her car.

Ric should be there too by now. Where was he? What if something happened to him?

She pulled out her cell and called him. No answer. She typed a text.

Where are you? Your car is still here. Please tell me you're ok. I'm worried. I'm sorry. It's me.

Something was missing.

I can't be what you want.

She hit *Send* and waited.

Ric didn't reply, call, or show up for the hour or so Lexi waited in her car.

The cold water that had cleansed her soul when she'd run with him in the rain now made her clothes cling to her, numbing her skin. The pain deep inside — the gut-wrenching ache stifling her, squeezing her heart, and

217

keeping her lungs from expanding with her panted breaths — got stronger by the minute.

What if something happened? What if…?

Nothing happened. He was pissed off and ignoring her calls and texts.

She could go look for him, but she'd miss him if he came for his car from a different route.

Lexi was torn between driving back to where she'd left him, to make sure he was all right; staying there and waiting for him; or going home and washing the rain, the mud, and his memory off her sore and tired body.

Going after him or waiting would show she cared. It'd give him the wrong picture.

Or maybe the right one.

She disregarded that last thought. She didn't care for him, except in a humanitarian way. He was a fellow human being. Her coworker. Her lover.

Not her lover any more.

The idea of not being touched by him again hurt. But there was no reason for that. They could touch. People touched. Touching was all the two of them could have.

He gut clenched. They could no longer have that either. After today, nothing would be the same. They'd reached a crossroads, and she'd taken the wrong turn. Lexi threw back her head. He was a guy, and no guy turned down casual sex. She had been engaged to the living proof.

She lowered the visor and studied her image in the tiny mirror. Her eyes were red rimmed and smudged with mascara. "No guy could say no to this," she told her raccoon-like reflection. She let out a sob. Ric had liked *this*.

218

He'd wanted *this*. He'd wanted her, and she'd screwed it all up.

She composed herself. Ric was fine. Sulky but fine. Tomorrow she'd screw the sulk out of him, and all would be right as rain.

Why did people say that? Rain wasn't always right. Sometimes it soaked you through to the bone and made you feel cold and dazed and empty, and there was nothing to be done about it unless you found shelter and something — *someone* — to warm you up.

Had she lost that?

She never had it.

Shaking her head to drive away the thought sent water spraying the windshield and mirror. Stray strands of hair got in her eyes. Good. She could blame them for the tears that ran down her face during the drive home.

She was out of excuses when the tears didn't stop flowing after she'd taken a hot shower and snuggled into bed.

She woke up with puffy eyes and a newfound determination to make things work.

Her way.

He was just a guy, after all.

****

When Ric saw the missed calls and text, he thought maybe they were his sign that he shouldn't give up. But that would make him — how had Lexi phrased it? — a little fatalistic, for a techno-geek.

He threw his cell against the wall with all the force he could muster, and had a moment of savage joy at the

219

crunching noise it made, before bits and pieces flew all over the place. He was a fool for love and always had been, but he wouldn't be Lexi's fool. If she was worried, she could come find him and apologize for treating both him and herself so harshly.

She wouldn't. She'd already be on her way home.

For a handful of moments, they'd been at the same place. He'd felt her open up, and he couldn't forgive her for allowing her past and her issues and her bloody fears get in the way of what they could have. All that kept her from seeing how great they were together was her stupid stubbornness.

He should get home.

Instead, he headed to Willy's Dreams on foot. If he didn't get something to soothe the pain and blur the memory of Lexi walking away, he'd lose himself in mourning what might have been.

The bartender frowned when Ric sat at the bar, and Ric couldn't blame him. The man had been wary of him when Ric showed up looking half-decent. He ought to be downright scared now that Ric looked like a madman — drenched, messy, and scowling.

"Guess things didn't work out, huh?" The bartender poured him a glass of Jack before Ric could ask for one.

"Nope." Ric downed the drink in one large gulp. "If anything, they're more fucked up than ever."

"Give up." He refilled the glass.

"Pardon?" Ric stopped watching the amber liquid level rise, to glare at the man.

"Give up. She doesn't want you — you give up. That's how it goes."

220

"She bloody well *does* want me." Ric shot upright, toppling over the stool he sat on.

The bartender took to wiping glasses clean behind the bar. "Then maybe she's scared, and you should give up either way. Can't make people see what they don't want to." He shrugged. "And you might wanna watch it. You sound like a stalker."

Fuck. He did. Still… He leaned over the bar and grabbed the guy by his T-shirt that had seen better days. "Listen here, shorty."

"It's Willy."

"Whatever. You have no idea what it's like, so maybe you shouldn't be voicing opinions."

Willy got a surprisingly strong grip on Ric's wrist. "I know more than you do, buddy," he said. His voice boomed, as if inside Ric's head. Had the alcohol gotten to him already? "Give up on half-measures. They ain't for you. You're an all-or-nothing man. If she wants you, she'll come back. If not, good riddance to her. Now put that stool right and walk out, while your arm is still attached."

Ric wanted to refuse. Pick up a fight. Funnel his resentment over Lexi's rejection into trashing the place. Instead, he did exactly what he was told, the minute Willy let go of him. His legs led him to the exit, as if he were in a trance.

He half ran to where he'd left his car, sure his heart had stopped beating. The talk with Willy had been his sign. He'd give up trying to get Lexi. No half-measures. If she wanted him, she knew where to find him.

****

221

Lexi acted absorbed by her work while at the same time keeping an eye on the door.

When Ric showed up lacking visible wounds, she all but sighed with relief. Then she noticed his hair — or lack thereof. He'd cut his honey-colored locks when he first appeared to her as Rex, but his hair was now shorn so close to the head, she could see his skin. He hadn't been attacked or involved in a freak accident. For all she knew, he'd been at the barber the whole hour she waited in her car.

Why did he cut his hair so short? Nobody else seemed shocked at the makeover, just like they had no reaction when he dyed it black. Maybe his makeover wasn't as surprising as she thought, or maybe she was the only one who paid him this much attention.

He glanced her way, and Lexi managed a shaky smile, but the coldness in his eyes froze her all the way to her heart. He regarded her with the same look of scornful disinterest he did everyone else in the company but Edmund.

She bit back the cheerful greeting she'd been practicing all the way to the office and returned her focus to her monitor.

Her eyes stung. Had to be because she'd looked at the screen for too long.

God, she'd screwed up.

She had to do something.

There was nothing she could do.

There was always something.

Sex.

Yup. That would fix everything, but not just yet. She opened *Exotic Beast* and went back to reading. The

222

vampire laid out his heart, hoping not to be rejected by the woman he loved. How could the shifter say no to him? Was she made of stone?

Lexi spent the hours until the meeting reading and sneaking glances at Ric. She tried to catch his eye, but he never once looked at her direction. Not even when she elbowed a heap of manuals and guidelines to the floor by accident. She might not exist, as far as he was concerned. The upside of that was she got to examine how the new look suited him, and the verdict was that he looked hotter and more dangerous, his features striking.

When it was time for the meeting, she was equal parts relieved and nervous. He'd have to talk to her there, but would he still be on her side?

Of course he would be. He wasn't petty, and this was work.

She wondered since when she thought of Ric as anything more than a jerk. The answer was simple. Since the previous afternoon. He was nothing like she'd imagined. The small voice she usually ignored told her he was so much more — *worth-a-chance* more — but she silenced it with more denial, the sort book-Xandra would be proud of.

Lexi gathered everything she needed and walked to the meeting room, where the others waited. Ric still had the key, so he stepped forward to open the door. As soon as the room came into view, he grabbed Lexi's pack of notes, rushed inside, and slammed them on the conference table. He took the seat right in front of the pile and folded his arms over his chest. So much for gallantry.

Lexi followed, planted herself on the seat to Ric's left without a word, and pulled the stack of papers in front

223

of her. She gasped. The lacquered black surface under the papers was marred by a large stain.

Edmund, who sat on Ric's other side, noticed the mark. "You'd think people would know to use coasters by now," he said. He took out his handkerchief and scrubbed the spot.

Ric blanched and at the same time seemed to try to fit his entire fist into his mouth. When Lexi's stepdad brought the hanky to his nose, to examine what had been spilled on the table, Ric guffawed, and Lexi understood why.

Edmund was rubbing at the dried-up wet spot from the night before.

Ew.

Lexi choked, reached out, and grabbed the hankie. "Shouldn't we be getting started?"

Edmund opened his mouth as if to protest, but nodded and waved for her to proceed.

Things went smoothly, considering Lexi was focused on Ric while trying to sell her creative ideas to people set in their ways for years. She kept track of the times Ric agreed with her and the times he looked at her while doing so. Sadly, by the time the meeting was over, the score was seventeen to one.

"I think that covers everything," Ric said in his most professional and least Rex-like accent, once everyone's agreement had been established. "I will email all of you the results and pass around hard copies, so you can go through them with your people."

"Good thinking, Richard. What say you all we reconvene in about a month's time to see how things worked out? In the meantime, try to get feedback from your departments. Alexandra, can you stay and help Ric?"

"How exactly would she do that, Ed?" Ric raised an eyebrow, the rest of his face a mask of boredom.

Lexi smiled. "I'm sure I'll find a way. After all, you did so much for me these days. Have to return the favor." She hoped he'd catch on and leer at her or something.

"Whatever floats your boat," he said drily.

God, the man was oblivious.

Chapter Twenty-Two

Lexi watched Ric type, a deep vertical line between his eyebrows. His fingers flew on the keyboard. As the department emptied, she got excited, thinking of how she'd make him forgive her. The sense of warmth in her belly, combined with the nervousness over the confrontation that would precede what she had in mind, made for a very jittery Lexi. At least angry sex was good sex.

When she was sure everyone was gone, she waited for Ric to take the printouts he collected from the printer to the photocopy room, and then followed him inside.

"You didn't reply to my text." She shut the glass door behind her and closed the blinds.

His back tensed, muscles stretching the cotton of his shirt, but he didn't turn to look at her. "My mobile doesn't work."

"You didn't ask what text, so you saw it." She sauntered around him, and insinuated herself between him and the copier. He still pretended to be too busy to talk to her, so she placed a hand over the feeder of the machine. "I called, too. You could have let me know you were okay."

He finally faced her, and it was the same ice-cold gaze he'd spared her that morning. "Didn't think you cared."

"I said I was worried. In the text." She tilted her head and let her tongue run what she hoped was a seductive path along her lower lip.

He didn't seem enticed. "Well now you know I'm fine." He removed her hand from the copier none too gently and turned away, to resume with the next stack of pages.

Lexi wouldn't give up so easily. She caressed his back, and when he swiveled on his heel toward her, knelt in front of him.

"What the bleeding hell are you doing?" Rex wasn't out of his system, then.

She looked up at him with a saucy grin and reached for his belt buckle. "Nothing." She'd never done this for him before and was excited to now. The outline of his cock pressed against the buttons of his jeans. Pride rushed through her veins at having that effect on him even before touching him.

But it couldn't be because of her. If she were that irresistible, Andrew would have kept it in his pants around other women. Ric was excited because he was about to get a blow job, not because *she* was about to give him one.

She popped his buttons and pulled him out. Encircling his shaft with her palm, she marveled at how small her fingers seemed against his girth. She felt him pulsate in her hand, felt a little jerk and twitch when her parted lips were close enough for her breath to wash over the head. Her mouth watered at the expectation of tasting

227

the strength and smoothness she held in her grasp, of using the tip of her tongue to trace the small veins that had her entranced…

*

When Lexi entered the room, Ric entertained some crazy notion that she was there to tell him she'd been an idiot and wanted to be with him. Such hope weakened his resolve to give up on her, but he didn't care, if weakness meant he could have her.

The seductive sway of her hips dispelled his daydreams. Her heart was still out of the equation.

Ric hated his treacherous body for responding to her proximity the way it did. Her scent was enough to send his blood rushing to his lower extremities—and no, that didn't mean his feet. He wanted her to leave. Wanted to be away from her before he forgot he couldn't settle for less than everything.

He froze when she knelt in front of him. The fantasies he'd entertained when he first realized he wanted her flashed through his mind. God help him, he wasn't strong enough to resist when she took his cock out of his jeans and gave it an experimental lick.

She hummed, and Ric squeezed his eyes shut. It was all he could do not to grab the back of her head and push past her full lips, all the way to her throat.

She wrapped those lips around the head and seemed to suck all memories of the previous day out of him with the first pull. All that remained was the scorching heat surrounding him, as she grazed his inner thighs with her fingernails and kneaded his ass with her

228

other hand. He opened his eyes and looked down, wanting to see himself disappear inside her. Hoping her gaze was trained on his face.

It was, but her look of triumph slammed reality into him with a force that made him lose his footing and almost crash into the copier behind him. Lexi kept licking and sucking at him with gusto, rolling his balls in her palm as she tried to take him down her throat. Luckily, the position they were in wasn't ideal for that, which allowed him some semblance of reason.

He grabbed a fistful of the golden mane and only hesitated a second — one more second to feel her tongue against the underside — before pulling her off him. He kept tugging upward, so she had to stand for his hold not to be painful.

The victorious expression was still on her face, as she leaned forward to kiss him. It turned to one of puzzlement when he held her a hairsbreadth away from his lips. "Is this what you want?" he asked. "Is it what you do?"

"Yes." Again, she sought his lips, but he drew her head further back, stretching her neck.

He looked deep into her green eyes, searching for any indication of a lie in her words. He found none. She meant it. This was all she'd allow herself. All she'd allow him.

It wasn't enough.

"Well, you're no longer doing it with me. I'm done." He pushed her aside and stormed out of the room, buttoning his jeans on the way out.

*

229

The door banged shut, but Lexi didn't react. She was too stunned.

Ric didn't just stop her in the middle of a blow job. He did *not*.

Wasn't she good enough? Did she do something wrong, while she had him in her mouth?

No, he enjoyed that.

Shit. Maybe her entire approach was wrong. Maybe she'd *been* wrong all along, starting with the moment she decided to box Ric into her preconceived notions of his gender.

Tears welled up in her eyes. She couldn't be wrong about Ric. If she was, perhaps she'd been cheating herself out of true love, by insisting there were no Prince Charmings out there. That all men were like her father and Andrew.

Ric might cherish her heart, not break it.

She couldn't have been so wrong.

Letting herself believe this meant admitting she'd chosen the sterile safety of loneliness over the real reward of letting someone in, not over the heartbreak that came with false promises. If she lost her certainty of who she was and what she wanted—what she could expect—she was left with nothing.

A sound of pure despair ripped from her throat and reached her ears. Her voice was unrecognizable. She opened the door with trembling fingers and leaned against the jamb. "What do you want from me?" The words stumbled over a sob. She hugged herself, feeling small and weak.

Hunched over his desk, Ric turned to look at her. Even in the dim light, Lexi saw his eyes were bloodshot. "Thought I'd made that clear," he said, his voice harsh. "I want *you*. All of you."

She shook her head and tried to sound calm despite the tears gliding down her cheeks. "I can't... What we had was fine. Why change it?"

"What we had?" He snorted. "We had nothing. I was just another notch on your belt. Just a good fuck, is all."

He was right, but it hurt to hear him say it. "And what's wrong with that? Why does it have to be more?"

"It has to be more. *All*. Or nothing. Can't keep doing this."

"Why can't you?" She ached to reach out to him. Touch him. Remind him how they both felt whenever he was inside her. "Why not?"

"'Cause you only let me inside your body, and bodies I can find at prices lower than my heart. 'Cause I'm falling in love with you. Might already be there." His tone was harsh, his gaze challenging.

The words lingered in the air between them that was so thick with tension, Lexi couldn't breathe. If she could take a deep enough breath, she'd be able to answer. Able to tell him...

What? That he couldn't be falling for her? That she wasn't worth it? That there was no love?

What if love existed, and it was staring her in the eye? What if Ric was the one? *The* one?

She shook her head. Was she able to take this leap with him? She let herself love a man before, and her feelings had been thrown back in her face, together with her dreams of forever. She'd spent the past year or so convincing herself there was no happy-ever-after.

Steeling herself against what Ric asked of her now.

This hurt she felt inside when he wasn't touching her — the void — was it love?

No. It couldn't be.

Could it?

She pushed away from the doorframe, fiddling with her hands, trying to keep from holding them out to him. Her entire body tensed. She was torn between asking him to make her love him and walking away.

The wall she'd spent years of building around herself — the one Andrew first pushed through and then reinforced — won the debate between her mind and heart once more.

Lexi ran.

She ran down the stairs, heedless of the tears blurring her vision and making her hasty descent dangerous.

Her escape was halted when she crashed into what felt like a boulder. She raised her gaze from the thick chest she'd collided with and saw Chad's round, sweaty face above her.

"What's the hurry, Ms. Adams?" He closed his meaty paws on her shoulders.

Lexi pushed free from his grasp. She never liked him, but now he seemed menacing. His posture, the look in his eyes scared her. It was a stupid fear, she decided. "None of your business," she said and tried to sidestep him.

Chad moved with her, blocking her path. "Oh, I think it is my business. You see, as a security guard here, I have to keep an eye on all after-hours activities." He stole a glance in the direction of the monitor console. "And of course, report everything to Mr. Pedelty."

There was a definite threat there. Lexi narrowed her eyes and took a step back, careful not to trip on the stairs behind her. "What would you have to report?"

"Nothing. At least, not if someone was willing to ensure my silence." He reached for her, but she climbed up the bottom step.

"Don't touch me."

"Why shouldn't I? You seemed so eager to be touched just moments ago. You were gagging for it."

Lexi felt faint. Chad had seen her and Ric? "Not by you." Her whispered words still carried all the disdain she felt. Edmund would never believe Chad over her.

"So I'm too lowly for you? The princess won't put out for the hired help? He's an employee here too. It didn't stop you."

"It was different with Ric." God, that was as good as a confession. "It's *you* I have a problem with, not your status. You make me sick."

Hatred radiated from Chad's expression, but he said nothing. He turned his back to her and returned to his station.

Lexi was surprised by his apparent surrender, but took the opportunity to flee before Ric caught up to her and she had to face him and her fears once more.

She resisted the urge to run to her car. She wanted to seem as self-composed as possible. In case Ric was looking out the window.

No. It was to show Chad she wasn't afraid of him.

233

Lexi slid in the driver's seat of her car, buckled the safety belt, and slumped forward, to rest her head on the wheel. Part of her hoped Ric came after her and forced her to admit that she wanted more too. That she was afraid and hurt and aching to be proven wrong.

She silenced that part. Ric meant nothing. He was just a great lay, and she could find that anywhere.

Something caught her eye in the rearview mirror. A movement. No, a... spray? Could be glitter. Cornflower-blue and shiny, it looked like a cloud of sparkly dust hovering over her back seat. She turned to take a better look. There was nothing there, but the air smelled like leather and smoke and home. Like Ric. He'd never been inside her car, yet his scent surrounded her like an embrace. How was that possible? Was her subconscious telling her something?

The blue cloud was still apparent in her mirror when she sat back in her seat and put the car into gear. Had to be a smudge — one that swayed and moved, and pulsated like a heart. The smell lingered as she peeled off the curb. It made her ache inside and at the same time tugged the corners of her lips into a smile. This wasn't something she could deal with alone. She needed to talk to someone. *Two* someones.

****

Ric was proud of how he handled the situation.

He wanted to smash his head against his desk, but he was proud nonetheless.

His self-restraint had been stressed to its limits, yet he managed to stand his ground.

234

And he'd lost her entirely. *Great job.* Now he had nothing. No chance of opening her eyes to the reality of his feelings.

He shouldn't think this way. There was the glimmer of hope Lexi would realize he wasn't what she thought and change her mind about being with him.

Nah. She was too set in her ways. By rejecting her sexual advances, he severed the only connection she'd allowed him. Was he going to survive the loss?

He had to. Settling for less than what he wanted would eat away at him, until he was as hollow inside as she was. He'd hoped to fill that hollowness of hers—that she'd let him try. Her eyes betrayed her inner struggle, and he'd remained optimistic until the last moment. Part of her wanted to give into whatever the future had to offer.

In the end, however, she didn't. She ran, from him and from herself.

There was no hope.

Not giving a shit about the law or company policy, Ric lit a cigarette and smoked it at his desk. He needed his heart to settle in his chest.

He didn't want to go back to his empty, lonely apartment, but staying in a place suffused with her memory wasn't an option. He had to figure a solution for that too. He didn't want to leave his position with Pedelty, but he might ask to be moved elsewhere. When he made his way downstairs, it was with feet made of lead.

The security guard stood with his back to the corridor, a wireless phone cradled between his head and shoulder. "Something has come to my attention, and I would like to discuss it with you as soon as possible," he said into the receiver.

Ric was too exhausted, mentally and emotionally, to berate the man for his lack of vigilance, so he just passed him by.

Chapter Twenty-Three

Lexi rang the doorbell a second time. The girls were probably out, enjoying the things couples did in the evenings. Or maybe they were having sex. She should have called first, damn it.

The moment the door was open, she flew into Angie's arms. Sarah looked startled, and Lexi gave her a bear hug too. "I'm so glad you guys are home. I need to talk to you."

"Sure." Angie wrapped an arm around Lexi's shoulders and led her toward the living room. "What's up? You look... Huh. I can't think of a positive way to finish this sentence."

"I don't know how to handle him, Angie."

Sarah and Angie exchanged a look.

"What?" Lexi asked. "Is this a bad time? I should go."

"No, no. Stay. I'll go make some herbal tea," Sarah said. She must have had some ready, because she was back in no time, a steaming mug in hand.

"Is this about Ric?" Angie asked.

Lexi nodded and focused her attention on the cup in her hands. "Herbal tea. He likes herbal tea." She took a tentative sip and scrunched her nose when the liquid burned the tip of her tongue. She was prepared to chug it all down, if it would save her from having to explain. She needed to talk but the girls would take his side. They'd found true love, so they believed in all that romantic crap.

"Ric likes herbal tea?" Angie asked.

Lexi nodded.

"Well, it's cleansing, and the one Sarah makes helps settle the nerves," Angie said. "You have to get the mix of herbs right, of course, and she's much better at that than I am. We get the herbs from a small shop on the other side of town. It's got all sorts of —"

"Baby, I doubt Lexi is here to talk about tea." Sarah turned to Lexi. "What's wrong?"

"Everything." The words spilled out, reluctantly at first, but soon Lexi found herself telling them about the sex and the truce and what she saw as the beginning of the end — the not-a-date.

When she and Ric got to know each other better.

When she caught glimpses of what they could be like together.

"And then he asked me to be with him. *Be* with him." Lexi sniffled, tears streaming down her cheeks and soaking the neckline of her shirt. "I can't fucking be with him. I'm not lovey-dovey girlfriend material. I'm not. You know I'm not." Andrew sure knew it. "Right?" She waited for even a nod of confirmation from her friends. They just looked at each other. And the blue cloud had to be in her eye, because now it surrounding them. She rubbed her eyes, and when she looked again, the sparkles were gone.

"What did you tell him?" Sarah asked, after a heartbeat.

Lexi wiped her nose with the back of her hand. She wasn't crying now, but her eyes still burned. "I told him I

238

couldn't, and I left." She'd been honest up to that point, but couldn't find it in herself to relay the entire conversation or how she'd been a mess when she walked away.

"And what did he do?"

"What does it matter? He tried to stop me. Insisted I give us a chance. What does it matter?"

"So let me get this straight," Sarah said. "He tells you he wants to be with you, after amazing lovemak—*sex*, and you run away?"

"Well, yeah. I felt pressured."

"So you needed time?"

"I needed him to see there can't be more between us. And then he went broody on me, ignoring me at work and not taking my calls." She sniffled. Her cheeks felt sticky with dried tears.

Angie spoke up. "That makes sense, sweetie. Your rejection hurt him. Can't you see?"

Lexi was getting pissed off. "I was hurt too, when I got on my knees to suck his dick and he pushed me away, so I guess we're even."

Angie and Sarah looked at her, mouths agape.

"What? Like you've never..." They both shook their heads. Lexi rolled her eyes. "Never mind that. The thing is I tried to patch things up, and he didn't let me. And then he started spouting that nonsense about love."

Once again, the reactions Lexi got weren't exactly understanding. From the dreamy look in Angie's eyes, she'd only focused on *love* and was about to start picking china.

Sarah glared at Lexi, the stern expression almost alien on her face. "You don't know me well enough, but you're Angie's best friend and that makes you my friend too. I'm sorry in advance for what I'm about to say, but you tried to patch things up with a guy who didn't just want to fuck you by *blowing* him, and you expected that to go down well?"

Lexi gaped. Sarah said *fuck*?

And more importantly, why would nobody see things her way?

The nagging feeling she might have kicked away the best thing that ever happened to her, made her rationalize her actions. "He just wanted to humiliate me, anyway. He said what he had to, to get under my skin, so I'd fall for him and hurt more. He lied about his feelings, like he lied about the site. He has to be the one behind the book, after all. He wrote it and created the site it was hosted on, and I was right not to trust him from the beginning. He's only playing nice so he has a better case against me." She didn't care that her arguments held no water.

"We've been through this already, Lexi. And not just once." Sarah glanced at Angie—who averted her gaze—and huffed. "There's no way Ric could have written *Exotic Beast*. It would take months of preparation, if not years, and he couldn't even be sure you'd find it."

"He's in IT. He could've planted the link in somehow. I'm telling you, he's been playing me from the start. If you heard him… He said he might be in love with me. *Love*. It's probably some obsession he had since before he met me." She was negating conclusions she'd reached a minute ago and going out on a limb. And she didn't care. She just needed the girls to agree that Ric was a jerk, so she could start the long process of getting over him.

240

"There were much easier ways for him to approach you. He didn't have to go through the trouble of acting like he didn't like you," Sarah said.

Especially the way she ogled him the first time they spoke. Lexi shook her head. "He wanted to lull me into a false sense of safety."

"But for what? He's not even vying for your position, and he's built you up to your stepdad."

"I don't know, okay? I just know he's a fake. He can't love me, and this whole mess is his fault."

"You're wrong." Angie wrung her hands together, her voice barely above a whisper.

"I'm not. Whose side are you on, anyway?"

"Ric isn't the one behind the site." Angie sounded certain.

"How do you know? Did you find something out? Why didn't you tell me?"

"Ummm... I know, because"—she squeezed her eyes shut—"I kind of think I'm behind it."

The words tumbled out in a jumble, and it took Lexi a moment to make sense of them. When she did, she couldn't control her voice. "What? *You* are behind it? How? Why didn't you tell me? Why did you pretend to help me figure it out? *How?*"

"I didn't know it was me. I'm sorry." Angie ducked her head, and her chestnut hair hid most of her face. "I didn't know."

Lexi was too shocked to move. "How could you not know?" she spat out through gritted teeth, trying to contain her frustration. She wanted to grab Angie by the shoulders, and shake the story out of her. "Did you write an entire novel in your sleep or something?" The best-friend code might not allow shaking or slapping, but it allowed snark.

"No." Angie looked up imploringly. "I didn't know I made it appear with what I did."

"You're making no sense. What did you do?"

"I made a wish for you."

Lexi rolled her eyes. There went the magic crap again. "You made a wish. You realize a wish doesn't write six-hundred-something pages?" For the first time, she worried for her friend's sanity. Why didn't Sarah discourage Angie's hocus-pocus delusions?

As if she heard her name in Lexi's thoughts, Sarah glanced her way. She shrugged and then stood and left the room.

Angie followed her with her gaze, worry flashing in her eyes for a split second. She turned back to Lexi. "Just hear me out, please. Remember our last coffee-date before you found the book?"

Lexi nodded, going over all the red flags Angie had given her through the years. Lexi should arrange for her to see a therapist, and talk to Sarah, who was obviously in denial.

"You had me really worried that day." Angie's voice snapped her out of her thoughts. "I was recovering from a cold, had a persistent cough and watery eyes, and you *still* were in worse shape. You sat curled into yourself, arms folded like you wanted to keep the world outside. I'd never seen you so miserable. And you insisted you were fine."

Lexi remembered. She'd lied. Nothing had been fine. Work was boring, she had no social life, and she was

242

lonely. Angie had picked up on that and kept asking, until Lexi cracked and told her how she really felt.

"I was numb," Lexi said now.

"You were. I couldn't stand back and watch the life get sucked out of you. I needed to do something. When you started saying how you didn't believe in love—that the whole Andrew thing had convinced you it didn't exist—I had to show you how wrong you were. You had to see. You deserved to be happy."

Did she? She didn't even know how.

Angie went on. "When I got home, I did some research on benevolent deities—"

"As you do." Lexi might as well play along with the insanity until she got Angie professional help.

"—and I decided on Xochipilli."

"Who?" Lexi asked despite herself.

"Xochipilli. Prince of Flowers. Our coven has worked with him before." Sarah reentered the living room and left a pencil on the table in front of Angie. "Some believe it's another name for the Greek god Apollo. He's the Aztec god of flowers, love, games, beauty, song, dance, and—oddly—maize."

"As in corn?" She wouldn't touch the *coven* thing.

Angie nodded. "Some call him the Corn-Flower prince."

Cornflower. The cornflower-blue lights...

Lexi shook her head. She'd play along, but she wouldn't be pulled into this craziness. "So he's who you wished at?"

"I didn't want to invoke a more powerful being, since—you know—things could go wrong and stuff."

243

Of course. They wouldn't want things to go *wrong*, when they were going so well, what with Angie—and apparently Sarah too—being nuts. "And what exactly was the wish for?" Lexi asked.

Sarah sat on the armrest of the lounger Angie was in, and Angie burrowed in her arms. "I had no idea how the wish would be fulfilled. I swear I didn't know the book had something to do with it. When we couldn't find its origins, I talked to Sarah, and we did a tracing spell. It led back to me."

Lexi let her irritation seep into her tone. "What was the wish?"

"I asked for you to find your soul mate." A sigh accompanied Angie's words. "Oh, and for your worth to be recognized at work. I'm so sorry I butted in, but I'm not sorry my meddling led Ric to you. You two are meant to be together."

Lexi's worry over her friend's delusions overcame everything else. "Angie, I was recognized at work because Edmund gave me a chance. Ric and I aren't meant to be together. Your wish wasn't what created the site or wrote *Exotic Beast.*" She softened her voice, to cushion the blow of what she said next. "You're not a witch, hon." She turned to Sarah, whose gaze was glued to the coffee table. "Neither of you are. Magic isn't real."

Sarah pointed to what she was looking at.

Lexi glanced that way and gasped. The pencil swerved slightly from left to right and back again. "Is it an earthquake?" Not unheard of in San Francisco.

"It's her." Sarah tilted her head toward Angie.

Lexi's stomach lurched when she saw her best friend's irises were white. She grasped Angie's hand.

244

"Ang? What's happening? Sarah, she's having a seizure. We must call a doctor."

More movement caught her eye.

The pencil floated.

On air.

It drew an invisible circle over the table.

Lexi jolted upright, unable to stop looking at it.

"We really are witches," Sarah said softly. "Angie is a better spell caster than me. I'm more of a potions kind of girl."

Angie smiled, her face aglow with the same cornflower-blue specks of light Lexi had seen in her car. The color matched the stone on her ring. "When you first told me about the story, I didn't know it was the answer to my wish, but it is. You and Ric are destined to be together. He's your soul mate."

The pencil fell on the table, and the sound spurred Lexi into action. She ran for the door.

Angie called out her name, but Sarah said, "Let her go, baby. She'll deal and come back."

Lexi wasn't all that sure about either.

Chapter Twenty-Four

Despite the short distance, the drive to Lexi's place seemed more like a crawl. She kept rehashing things in her head. Ric telling her she should be with him. That he was falling for her. And Angie's magic...

Magic? How could it be?

How could Lexi not know her best friend could cast spells? How could she accept Angie used magic to find Lexi's soul mate—or that the one meant for her was Ric?

What if he was?

The *what-if*s haunted her. Despite her fears and her wounds and her fuckups, Ric might really love her. If she accepted the possibility, she gave up on all her prior beliefs. She'd done it before, and had sworn to never again open herself up to the searing pain of betrayal. Could she give into love again? And would it end differently? The attraction between her and Ric was irrefutable. He'd admitted he had feelings for her, and she'd gone crazy at the thought of something happening to him the other night.

"If magic and soul mates are real," she said aloud, "I want a sign."

As she expected, none was forthcoming.

Her mom's and Edmund's cars were parked outside the house when Lexi pulled up the driveway. She

246

blotted her puffy eyes and blew her nose, composing herself as best she could before going inside. Fortunately, she ran into nobody on the way to her bedroom. "If he's my soul mate give me a sign," she chanted under her breath over and over. Her need grew deeper with every iteration of the words.

A compact disc couldn't be called *a sign*, but it was what greeted her when she threw open her door. It lay on her bed and had a post-it note on it. Lexi snatched the yellow square and read the message.

I didn't watch it, but maybe you should.
Love, Edmund

Welcoming the distraction, she switched on her PC and slipped the disk into the drive. It contained a single video. She pressed *Play* and saw herself pacing. Her heart skipped a beat. Ric entered the room and gave her a kiss of the non-PG variety, pressing her against the door. Slack-jawed and sickened, she fast-forwarded the video. How much of their conference-room indiscretion was on here?

Way too much.

The sight of their naked bodies, intimately joined, filled her with horror, but something else caught her attention. Barely controlling her fingers, she clicked on *Pause*. The screen showed her, head thrown back in the throes of passion. On top of her, Ric faced the camera, his expression one of pure bliss.

Not ecstasy. *Bliss.* Like he was absolutely, completely, perfectly happy.

Could it be love?

Lexi didn't linger on it. She resumed watching, and by the time the video was over, what she'd seen on his face was no longer her main concern. She felt as if all the blood had been drained from her body, leaving her weak and cold.

Who recorded the video, and how did it get to Edmund?

Stupid, *stupid* question. The angle was from high up. A security camera. *That sick fuck, Chad.* She'd noticed the stupid light. Why did she put it off her mind?

Because… Ric. And amazing sex.

Had Chad recorded their other trysts? Should she expect more such CDs? And why did he give this one to Edmund?

Fuck. It was retaliation for her turning him down.

She had to call Ric. He was involved in this too. It was his job on the line as much as hers, let alone both their relationships with her stepdad. She tried his number repeatedly, but her call wouldn't go through.

She steeled herself for combat. She'd face Edmund alone and hope to convince him to at least not fire Ric.

There was a soft knock on the door. "Alexandra? It's me."

Was it too late to think of facing a million dollars? Maybe they'd also materialize outside her room. "Come in, Edmund." She sat on her bed, ready to accept the consequences of her actions.

He entered, closed the door behind him, and leaned against it. Lexi was prepared to do some major groveling, but his expression was concerned.

"I'm sorry," was all she could utter.

"Are you all right?"

248

"How can I be? I hate myself. I'm so sorry, Edmund. You said you didn't watch it, right?"

"Went no further than the kiss, though I imagine the two of you did." He removed his glasses and wiped them studiously, avoiding her gaze. "Let me say my piece, and then I'm all ears."

Lexi nodded, expecting the worse.

"While I do not by any means condone the choice of venue for your... activities, I believe you and Richard are quite fond of each other. I mean, the two of you wouldn't find yourselves in such a compromising position just for *kicks*, right?"

"No. I like him. A lot." She was amazed by how easily the lie slipped out from her lips, but then it hit her.

It wasn't a lie at all.

If anything, the lie had been her insistence that what she felt for Ric was purely physical.

"In this case," Edmund said, "and though I cannot stress my disapproval enough—"

"I know, and you're right, and I'm so sorry. But there's nothing to worry about any more." Lexi's voice broke into a sob. "I screwed up."

As if her own misery wasn't enough, she felt sorry for Edmund too. The poor man never knew what to do when faced with a damsel in distress, but he set aside his discomfort. He pulled her closer and wrapped her in his arms. "There-there, now. It can't be that bad."

"It is." She inadvertently wiped her nose on his shirt, as she spoke against his shoulder. "I can't even get him on the phone."

"You could always find him at his place. In fact, I'm positive that's a much better rendezvous spot than the company premises. Don't you think?" He pulled back, brushed the tears from her cheeks with his thumbs, and winked.

Edmund *winked.* If that wasn't a sign, nothing was.

Lexi hated the idea of explaining to her stepfather how she'd screwed things up with Ric, but because Edmund was who he was, he didn't ask.

"Thank you. I know I'm not your favorite person right now, but I'll make it up to you. I'll work twice as hard, till I convince you to trust me again. And please don't blame Ric for this. He needs his job, and it's more my fault than his," she said.

"If you'd let me finish in the first place, I'd have told you I plan on putting this entire thing behind us. As far as I'm concerned, this disc never existed." He patted her back and stood.

Lexi felt a fresh bout of tears threaten to choke her. "Why are you so wonderful?"

"It's a curse, my dear, but I've learned to live with it." He jotted something on a post-it note he took from her desk. "This is his address. Do you want to call him first? I can write down his home number for you."

"I doubt he wants to see me or talk to me. If I go by there, he'll have to," she said. "About the CD?"

"I will destroy it."

"Thank you. But how—"

"It's all settled now."

"Was it Chad? I know this doesn't change anything, but he tried to blackmail me into—"

"If you finish that sentence, I may have to kill him. As is, he will not be bothering us again. I told him I know where he lives." Edmund smirked, but his eyes hardened.

250

Ric had been right; Edmund could be scary. "I'm sorry I didn't do a better job protecting you from the likes of him. From anything and anyone that could hurt you." Edmund was once again the gentle, caring man who'd patiently taught her how to ride a bicycle. "Go fix things with Ric."

"Thank you. I will." She went to him for one more hug. "I love you."

He beamed at her. "I love you too, Lexi, and I'm proud of the woman you've become. You do realize you'll eventually have to fill me in on the... non-X-rated parts."

"I will." She'd tell him everything he wanted to know, as soon as she worked things out with Ric.

Chapter Twenty-Five

The day had taken its toll on Ric, and he'd drifted off while watching television. He heard the timid knock and forced himself to roll off the couch.

The apartment was dark. Good. He wasn't feeling very sunny either.

He shuffled his feet to the door and threw it open, expecting to see one of his neighbors. The corridor light blinded him temporarily. He rubbed his eyes and looked at his visitor.

Lexi.

Every nerve in his body ached to touch her. Hold her. Have her.

His brain took over. "What now? Going to get on your knees again? When a bloke says no, he means—"

He didn't get to finish his sentence. He got an armful of crying Lexi. She clung to him as if for dear life, her frame was wracked by sobs, her cheek hot in the crook of his neck, her tears burning paths down his skin.

Pissed off though he might be, he was a man in love—one who couldn't help but wrap both arms around her and bury his face in her hair. "Shhh. Hush, love. Whatever it is, it'll be all right." He walked backward, pulling her into the apartment, shut the door with his foot, and pawed the wall for the light switch.

252

She was still crying, twisting his insides into knots every time she drew a shuddering breath to let out another sob. It had to be something bad. "Is it your mom? Edmund? You can tell me. We'll figure it out."

"I'm sorry," she whispered.

If he hadn't been studying her so intently, trying to gauge what was wrong, he would have missed it. "Come again, pet?"

"I'm sorry. I'm so sorry. I screwed up." She pulled back and made a visible effort to compose herself. "I was scared."

He tightened his grip on her arms — it felt like his grip on sanity. Was he awake? Was she really there, telling him what he'd dreamed of hearing?

"Did you hear me? I'm sorry. Please say it's not too late." She hung her head, to look up at him through wet, lowered eyelashes. "It's not, is it?"

Ric crushed her against him and slanted his lips over hers. He couldn't believe what he'd heard, but refused to give it a second thought. Lexi wanted another chance. She wanted him.

Words failed him. No matter how he tried, the right sentences wouldn't form on his lips, to let her know he'd have waited forever if he had to. So he kissed her, pouring all his love, his need, his hope into the kiss they shared. He devoured her lips and tasted her tongue with all the fervor of feelings he could express no other way at that moment.

When he pulled back from the kiss, his head had cleared. "It's not. Never too late for you to come to me."

"Oh, thank God." She buried her face into his chest and slipped her arms under his, to wrap them around his waist. "Oh, thank God," she said again, squeezing him. "I was so worried. I was sure I screwed up. That you'd hate me forever. And then Edmund said I should come over here and—"

"You told Edmund about us?" It was the last thing he'd expected to hear. If she'd told Pedelty, then that was it. She wanted to be with him. But what if the old man hated the idea? "What did he say? Do I still have a job?" He tried to make light of the situation, but he'd hate to lose the trust and friendship of the man who'd saved him from himself.

"I didn't tell him." She took a deep breath and blurted out everything in one long hurried sentence. "I think Chad did, and then I was asking the Aztec guy for a sign and wasn't getting one, so I got home, and there was this CD on my bed, and Edmund hadn't watched it, but he came in after I saw what was on it, and I was shocked, and he didn't yell but said I should come here. And I'm here, and I'm so sorry for everything."

She sniffled and turned her face up to him for another kiss, the matter settled, as far as she was concerned.

Ric wanted to ask her a million more questions, but had to start somewhere. "A CD?"

"Can we sit down for this?"

He disentangled his body from hers, took her by the hand, and led her to the sofa. "You sit. I'll fetch us something to drink."

"Do you have diet soda?"

He chuckled at how even in her current state— distraught, puffy eyed, and thoroughly kissed—she was still the Lexi he knew and loved. "I don't do poofy drinks

254

in here as a rule, but stop by more often, and I'll get you a fridge-full of the stuff. For now, you'll have to make do with water."

By the time he returned with two large glasses of water, she was curled up into a little ball at one end of the couch. They had their drinks, and Ric sat on the opposite end and gathered her close. "Want to tell me about it, or do I have to shag it out of you?"

She threw him a cheeky grin, despite still sniffling a bit. "I'm not sure how forthcoming I'd be with the information, following a proper *shag*." The last was said in a Pedelty-like manner, complete with the wiping of nonexistent glasses.

"That imitation killed any chance you had for one." Truth be told, he had no intention of making love to her at the moment. He was too interested in finding out what had changed her mind about the two of them. Maybe it would clue him in on how long this resolution of hers would last. He wanted her to feel relaxed and comfortable enough to open up, since this was the first time he'd seen her the mood to share anything not involving bodily fluids.

*

"Oh, okay." She heaved an exaggerated sigh. "What do you wanna know?" She glided forward on her seat and rested her head in the crook of his shoulder, not wanting to face him while she talked about stuff that made her uncomfortable.

"Everything, but start with who the fuck Chad is."

255

"He's the security guard who's been on almost every night lately?" She phrased it as a question.

"Right. That overgrown arse of an army puppet." Ric nodded, fury blazing in his eyes. "What did he tell Pedelty?"

"He saw us. He said he'd talk unless I was... friendly. I thought it was an empty threat and brushed him off, but he gave Edmund a disc with—" She motioned her index finger from her to him and back, still unable to look at him. "You know... on the conference-room table. Edmund could have seen us have sex." She covered her face with her hands.

"But he didn't?"

She shook her head and heard him let out a whoosh of air. He kissed the top of her head. "Go on."

"He knew what was in it, 'cause he said he didn't condom, er... *condone* the place we chose, but he's cool with us together and all, as long as it's not just something casual." She waited for his response, her gaze trained to the glasses on the table in front of her.

"And is it or isn't it?"

She didn't blame him for wanting to hear the words. She'd been giving him mixed signals for a while. "I thought it was. I tried hard for it to be. I mean, *love*? Pfft." She was no longer talking to him, so much as thinking aloud. "Life isn't a fairy tale. It's mean, and you get hurt. When you said you loved me, it felt like a bucket of ice down my spine." His body went tense against her. "Not because it was you. That's not what I mean. *Shit.* I'm not good with words." She tried to pull away, but he clutched her tight.

256

"Tell me what you mean, then. I won't say a thing till you shape it all into what you really want to say. We've done this with me doing the talking. Remember?"

"Okay. What I wanted to say was that I—" She cleared her throat. "That nobody loves me. Well, except for my family. Though not my dad. But Mom and Edmund do. And my friends." She was digressing. "The thing is, I'm not the girl men fall in love with. I'm stubborn, and I'm bitchy, and I'm whiny and weird, and I don't believe in love. When you said what you said, it was like I'd either been wrong for a long while, or you were lying. I didn't want either to be true. Make more sense now?"

"It does. Your dad and that other wanker have messed with your head, but it's *because* you're stubborn and bitchy and whiny and weird that I'm in love with you." There were no maybes this time.

Her heart lurched in her chest, and her stomach felt funny but in a good way. "You like them damaged, huh?"

"I like *you*." His voice was heavy with unexpressed emotion. "What made you change your mind?"

"Angie."

*

Ric wanted to press her for more, but she might clam up, so he waited. When she spoke again, her voice was so hushed, he didn't catch her words. "What was that, kitten?"

"My best friend. She cast a spell." He heard her this time, though just barely. It sounded barmy, so he waited for her to elaborate.

257

"She made a wish for me, to a god called something-Billy. No, wait. *Xochipilli*."

"What was the wish?"

"For me to find my soul mate. And he sent me you. We're meant to be together. You were right all along." She sniffled again. "I was so stupid. I should have seen you meant what you said. It was there, in your touch. In your kisses." She shifted in his arms and leaned upward, but Ric wasn't going to oblige her.

"A spell? Your friend cast a spell to send me your way? Are you pulling my leg?"

"No, it's true. She and her girlfriend are real-life witches. I swear. I didn't believe it either, till they floated a penc—"

"I don't give a flying fuck if they're Magica De Spell and Witch Hazel. You found it easier to believe your friends are witches and that a spell brought us together, than that I love you."

"I didn't realize you could be telling the truth. I was afraid you were just trying to get to something. I couldn't get hurt again. Please forgive me, Ric. I didn't think—"

"Oh, but you did think. That's your bloody problem—you think too much. Feel, Lexi."

"I am feeling now. I'm feeling that you love me, and I need you in my life."

She tried to get closer, but he held her at arm's length so he had a clear view of her face. "So what do you want now?"

"I want us to be together."

"Why?"

"'Cause it's how it's supposed to be. I told you, Angie said—"

258

"Wrong answer." He pushed her away softly and got up from the couch. Head down, he walked to the door and opened it.

"How can it be the wrong answer? You said I should be with you. Isn't that what you want?" She glared. "Or was it just a game? Wanted to see if you could get the boss's daughter to fall for your stupid British charms?"

He could tell the exact moment she reverted to her guarded, hostile self, but he had no fight left in him. Only pain and sorrow. "But you didn't."

"Huh? Didn't what?"

"Didn't fall for me. See, you could've said you want to be with me because you want me. Hell, because you may be returning my feelings. But you didn't. 'Cause you're not."

"But Angie said—"

"*I don't fucking care.*" He slammed his open palm on the doorframe hard enough to hurt. "I want you. I choose my life, and I chose to let myself love you, knowing how much it could hurt. I waited, and I hoped, but I chose to stick around and to let you walk all over me. I can accept that you don't feel the same way, but I won't let my life be dictated by wishes and spells. There's nothing I want more than to be with you, but I can't do it. Not if there's a chance of you waking up to a new spell a year from now, and deciding your fate is in bloody Tibet. Without me." He pushed the door open even wider. "Now please get out, while I'm still in control of myself."

Chapter Twenty-Six

There was nothing for Lexi to do but respect Ric's wishes. At this point, saying she returned his feelings would seem forced or fake, never mind not entirely honest. She cared for him, but she still needed time to come to terms with everything.

She used the backs of her hands to dry her eyes, and mumbled she was sorry one last time, before brushing past him and out of the apartment.

The door slid closed behind her, but it might as well have been slammed shut. Lexi turned and ran her fingers down the wooden surface. "I don't know if I love you yet, but I think I can," she whispered. "So I'll give both of us the chance to find out if it's true. Whatever it takes."

She'd get her man—kicking and screaming, if she had to. And no, she wasn't above groveling.

She got in her car and gripped the wheel. Focusing on regulating her breath, she tried to clear her mind. Step one was no more tears. She was never a crier, but this whole situation had pushed her to her limits.

Now about step two...

Going home meant facing her mother, who was nothing like her discreet husband when it came to Lexi's private life. Returning to Angie and Sarah's wasn't Lexi's favorite option either; she still didn't know how to handle the shitload of information they dumped on her. She had half a mind to keep driving around in circles until she ran out of gas or it got late enough for her mom to go to bed, when something dawned on her. She'd spend the night at Pedelty Electronics. Edmund's office would be locked, but her chair wasn't all that uncomfortable.

When Lexi reached the company's entrance, a new security guard stood behind the reception desk. Refraining from doing a happy dance for being Chad-free, she approached the man. "Hello," she said. "I'm—"

"I know who you are, Ms. Adams." His smile was friendly. "Anything I can do for you?"

She liked him already. "No, but thank you"—she looked at his name-tag, embarrassed she didn't know his name—"Mr. Weald. I'm fine. I just have some stuff to do, and I don't know how long I'll be."

"No worries. Just call me if there's anything you need. Until then, have a nice evening." The man got extra brownie points for discretion.

Lexi made her way upstairs and to her desk. She'd need a couple of chapters, to get sleepy. She switched on her computer, before even sitting down, she set the alarm on her cell-phone for seven. She'd hurry home for a shower and fresh clothes in the morning, and then get back to the office before Mom had time to grill her.

It didn't take long for her to settle down and find the last page she was on.

Within a few paragraphs, Xandra faced a dilemma similar to Lexi's own. A vampire—a creature she'd been brought up to distrust but ended up sleeping with— professed his love. Xandra couldn't return his feelings.

Could she? And then there was the big reveal. A prophecy that foretold wolf and undead would share a path of love and save all worlds. Xandra didn't believe in fate, though. She wanted to make her own destiny and choose her own path. If it lead her back to Rex, so be it, but no prophecy would force her to make a choice.

The shifter's reasoning made Lexi appreciate Ric's reaction. If he were to give her another chance, she had to let him know how she felt about him—and soon. But that meant she first had to know for sure.

She didn't realize she was drifting off, until she saw herself lying on her back, in the center of an enormous bed.

Her arms are stretched above her head. Her legs apart. Her wrists and ankles chained to the bed. The bonds allow no leeway. She's spread out. Defenseless.

She's not worried. Neither is observer-Lexi.

Ric approaches, and both of her tense. He's naked. He's magnificent. The look he spares the naked body on the bed is cold. Lexi shudders. This isn't the Ric she knows. He's fierce. Uncaring.

She's wet and wanting.

Ric swaggers toward naked-Lexi. He crawls on the bed. He straddles dream-Lexi's hips and rubs his erection on her mons. "What should I do with you tonight, hmmm?"

Dream-Lexi lowers her eyes. "Whatever you deem appropriate."

Cruel fingers pinch a tender nipple. Dream-Lexi arches her back.

262

"You forgot something, pet. Do you want to be punished?" His voice is full of promise and threat. "Do you like it? Do you, Xandra?" It's Xandra on the bed. Xandra and Rex.

"No. No, Sir." It's a lie. Xandra is as wet as Lexi.

"I think you do, you little slut. And you're lying, on top of being disobedient and wanton. I know just the treatment for dirty little liars." He flips Xandra on her stomach, the movement almost too fast to follow.

How do the chains accommodate the move? Right. It's a dream. A very hot, incredibly vivid, God-please-let-him-take-her-next erotic dream, and nothing more.

A slap lands on Xandra's ass, and Lexi yelps at the sting. She wriggles under the hand grabbing Xandra's reddened flesh. It's beyond weird watching as an outsider and feeling the silken sheets against her bare skin at the same time.

"You know you love it, my little slut. Look how you arch into my hand." Rex trails the fingers of one hand down Xandra's spine, and she melts into his touch. As she relaxes, the touch turns into a hold that presses her flat on the mattress. He starts raining slaps with his free hand. One after the other, he delivers the blows on her ass and upper thighs. There's no specific rhythm or pattern. Each crack of his palm against her flesh pulls out a cry of surprise more than pain.

Her skin glows red, and he smiles. Satisfied. "If you could only see what I see, pet..." Neither Xandra nor Lexi can do anything but moan. Lexi's skin hums with desire. She wedges her hand between her legs, but there's no friction. She's spectral, but for the Xandra version of her.

Xandra bows her back. Tries to move. Struggles against the chains and his palm that keeps her immobilized. "Please, Rex, fuck me."

A loud slap lands across the back of Xandra's thighs. "It's not Rex. *It's* Sir. *How hard is that for you to remember? Or isn't it? Do you remember and ignore my wishes anyway? Is that it?"*

She shakes her head. Lexi doesn't blame her for her inability to formulate words. She shares Xandra's desperation. Her need.

"Well, either you want me to keep punishing you, or you're stupid. Which one is it, Shifter?" Rex squeezes her ass. His cool fingers soothe the burn of the slaps, but his grip keeps her uncomfortable. "Are you daft, or are you a wanton harlot, begging for more? Are you my harlot?" His touch changes to a gentle caress. "Are you mine, Xandra?"

The blonde on the bed grits her teeth. Lexi knows without seeing her face. She also knows Xandra doesn't want to reply. Doesn't want to give him the satisfaction of saying she's his.

"Stubborn little thing, aren't you?" He smirks right at Lexi, not Xandra. Lexi gasps. Even though it's her dream, she feels like an intruder. "We'll try another way of breaking you, then," Rex says.

Xandra tenses with the expectation of more harsh treatment, but Rex leans over her and places cool kisses on the heated skin. He uses his lips and tongue to lavish every inch his hands marked. The pleasure is too much yet not enough. Xandra keeps trying to push back. Trying for more. No sound escapes her lips. She chokes down the whimpers and pleas building in her throat. She already said please. *She won't stroke his ego further.*

Or so Lexi thinks.

Letting go of her back, the vampire places both hands on her ass and spreads her. Without warning, he runs his tongue down the valley between her buttocks, down to her puckered second entrance. She flinches, but her restraints and his hands won't allow her to pull away. "Relax, and you'll like it. All dirty girls do." He licks around her hole, his agile tongue massaging the tight ring of muscle.

Lexi is fascinated. She watches herself engage in anal play – something she's never done in her real life – and it turns her on more than she considered possible. Plus, she feels the wicked tongue against her own ass, and the sensation is surprisingly not unpleasant.

Rex licks his thumb and inches the tip around Xandra's uncharted territory. At the same time, he shoves two fingers in her pussy, and Lexi can't stifle a moan of desire. More. She wants more. She wants those fingers in her ass while Ric –

Rex. This is Rex.

She doesn't care. She wants Ric

– pistons inside her pussy.

As if reading her thoughts, Rex withdraws slick fingers from Xandra's pussy and circles her virgin hole with them. He graces Lexi with a leer and presses them to Xandra's asshole. Lexi watches Xandra's flesh – her own flesh – whiten with resistance before it yields. His fingers push inside her up to the second knuckle.

Xandra groans. Lexi's body is torn between pulling away and pushing back into the burning sensation. Rex solves the dilemma for her with plug that appears in his free hand. He pumps it inside Xandra's pussy, and then pulls it out to run it along her slit and closer to her second hole. He withdraws his fingers, and using them to keep her spread, slowly pushes in the plug. She's not stretched enough, and the burning is intense, but he doesn't relent until all of it is inside her.

The pressure is near-intolerable. So is the pleasure of being so completely filled.

265

Lexi feels like she's dying. It hurts in such a delicious way, she'll come if he touches Xandra's clit.

Why won't he touch Xandra's clit?

Placing the heel of his hand on the plug to keep it in place, he slides two fingers from the other hand inside her pussy again. Moves them in and out of her. The way his hand is positioned moves the plug in sync to his fingers. He fucks both Xandra's holes, and Lexi pants.

"Please. Please. Please." Her own voice reaches her ears, but Xandra still makes no sound. She remains silent, biting the pillow beneath her head, while her body thrashes to the limits of the chains.

Rex's hand doesn't provide the friction she needs to reach her climax, and he knows it — the same way he knows she'll reach the breaking point and beg for him to bring her off. He thrusts inside her with his fingers and the toy, adding to the fire building in her belly but not letting it erupt.

Lexi lets out a frustrated sob, and Xandra echoes her.

The self-satisfied smirk on Rex's sensual lips grows wider. He turns his wrist so his fingers rub the bundle of nerves inside her, and then takes hold of the plug's end with his other hand. He twirls and pushes it from side to side, stretching her more. Another finger is shoved inside her pussy, and each thrust in her ass is harder than the last.

Now Lexi's glad she's incorporeal. Her legs couldn't hold her otherwise. She is ready to burst and not above pleading for her orgasm.

"Tell me you're mine, pet. Beg me to fuck you."

"Tell him, for God's sake," Lexi yells, aware of the futility of talking to her dream self. "You belong together. Don't you see?"

266

A blinding light fills Lexi's vision, and she shuts her eyes. When she opens them again, there aren't two of her anymore. She is the girl on the bed – and just in time.

Rex slides the toy out of her ass and replaces it with the tip of his cock, still fucking her with his fingers. She wants to cry out that she isn't prepared enough, but her body welcomes every inch of him that pushes inside with the rocking of his hips. The burning is there, but it adds to the pleasure of having him fill her.

Once he's seated inside her, he stops, and she can't keep from whimpering. "Why did you stop?" She tries to catch her breath.

"Still didn't say you're mine, Shifter. Are you?"

"Yes." She knows it's true the moment she says it. "I'm yours. I love you."

He freezes over her, and she realizes the impact her words have on him after all the rejection he's received.

"I mean it," she says.

That brings him back to his senses. He starts moving inside her in deep, long strokes, kissing her neck. "Well, that works out swimmingly" – he chuckles, but his voice is heavy with emotion – "because I love you too."

In that magical way dreams have of twisting things around, Lexi's on her back, with him still buried inside her.

He massages her clit with his thumb, his gaze locked with hers. "Say it again."

"I love you."

His expression serious, as if this is the most serious piece of information he's ever been given, he nods and swoops down for a kiss that leaves her breathless. "Don't change your tune when you wake up," he says. A sway of his hips and a pinch on her clit send her spiraling into an all-consuming burst of

267

absolute pleasure. A wave of sensation and bliss carries her to heaven and then brings her swirling back down to bed and Rex's arms.

The air feels alive against her skin. A caress. Her heart pounds in her ears. Her blood rushes through her veins, and her head is light with unprecedented euphoria. She clenches around him, and he drops his head to the hollow of her shoulder, to bite the base of her neck. His movements turn jerky. A tattoo of short, hard thrusts. It's not long before he roars his release, following her over the edge.

They stay locked together until Lexi once again feels in control of her limbs. Rex gives her another languid kiss and unlocks the manacles from her wrists. "You're free, love."

It's true. She's never felt as free before in her life. She stretches and closes her eyes. Rubbing her wrists to get the blood flow back into them, she relishes the feel of him softening inside her.

Then his cock is gone, as is his weight on top of her. She lifts drowsy eyelids and focuses on the bowl of peanuts in front of her. She's on a barstool, in a sparsely lit joint.

"Gimme something sweet, Willy," she tells the short guy behind the bar. She's never seen him before in her life.

"Rough night?"

"Just had a kinky sex dream. The bondage kind." She's still in the dream. No way she'd share something like that and not die of embarrassment in real life. And her mouth keeps working without consulting her brain. "Think my subconscious is telling me I need more sex, or that I need to spice it up a bit?"

"It's not about sex. It's about control. When you're in love, you give it up."

His reply makes no sense to her and yet she doesn't find that weird. "And how do you know you're in love?" she asks.

"You're willing to give up control."

268

Lexi didn't drift out of the dream, as much as snap out of it, her mind instantly alert.

Why did she always want to be in control of everything?

Because she was afraid of being hurt again.

But she never sought control when she and Ric had sex, though she called the shots with all other lovers since Andrew. She always gave Ric the upper hand, and believed she maintained the power by guarding her heart. *Wrong.* Her heart wasn't guarded. He was already in it, and she'd hurt both him and herself by refusing to embrace her feelings for him.

She had to push her ego aside and let herself fall into the arms of the man she loved and who loved her back.

The alarm clock sounded, and Lexi turned it off. She smoothed the wrinkles off her clothes with her hands, and grabbed a cup of coffee. She wouldn't go home to change. She'd read more, and when Edmund got to work, she'd talk to him.

Chapter Twenty-Seven

Lexi was on the last sentence of *Exotic Beast*, when Edmund came in.

Ric followed closely, and the two locked themselves in Edmund's office.

As Lexi pondered whether or not she should knock and interrupt them, she heard her stepfather's door slam shut. Soon after, Ric stomped into view. He was mumbling to himself and making wild gestures with his hands, a deep frown etched into his forehead.

She didn't spare a moment's thought on how they last parted, before springing from her seat and all but running to him. "Ric? What happened? Did Edmund —"

"He didn't. That's the bloody problem." He all but growled the words at her without breaking his stride.

This was *so* the wrong time and place to make a scene. Lexi resisted the urge to press on the subject, and instead just headed to Edmund's office more determined than ever.

"I have to talk to you." She closed the door, not waiting for an answer.

Edmund showed no surprise that she'd just barged in. If anything, his next words surprised her. "Ah, there you are. I've been expecting you. Please make it brief. I have a headache."

Damn. She didn't call home to let them know she wouldn't be back for the night. "I'm sorry, I fell asleep and —"

"No more apologies. What have you done to the boy, to make him want to move to any other branch of the company?"

"Okay... *Huh?*" So it wasn't her disappearance all night that caused his headache. Ric wanted to leave? And Edmund obviously thought she spent the night with him. Heat crept up her cheeks at how wrong that must have seemed, after the video of her extracurricular activities.

"You didn't know?" He left her no time to reply. "He came by the house this morning and practically stalked me here, giving me perfectly bad reasons to relocate him."

The blood drained from Lexi's head, and her body froze at the thought of losing Ric just when she realized she needed him. That should teach her not to be so stupid. "What did you tell him? You didn't —" She couldn't voice the possibility. "Please tell me you didn't. Please."

"Of course I didn't. He is my most valued employee, for goodness's sake. Besides," he said, with a cheeky grin, "I can't let the man your mother wants you to date go away if I hope to maintain a happy marriage for myself."

"Oh, thank God. But you may have to let me go."

"I was hoping Ric would change his mind once he got the chance to calm down. Don't tell me the two of you had such a fight that you cannot stand each other's presence."

Lexi avoided looking him in the eye.

271

"If that is the case, you'll have to work things out. You are both adults, and this is a place of business, Alexandra, not—"

Lexi didn't let him finish his sentence. "No. I mean yes, we had a fight, but no, I don't want to not see him." She paused and went over her last sentence. "I'm making no sense, huh?"

Her stepfather stared at her as though she were a peculiar species of a parrot that just did a cartwheel in high heels. He shook his head.

"From the top, then," she said. "I want to see him. Want to *be seeing* him. For a long time, if possible." She wondered if she should tell Edmund she was in love, but decided against it. Ric should be the first to know.

"Then why, pray tell, would I have to let you go?"

"'Cause I'm about to go out there and do some not work-safe stuff, to make me and Ric happen."

Edmund sputtered, and Lexi had to try not to giggle. He removed his glasses to rub the bridge of his nose and put them back in place. With visible effort, he collected himself. When he spoke, his voice was defeated. "Please tell me *not work-safe* isn't on grounds of nudity."

Lexi laughed. "No, but I may need to make a spectacle of myself. Ric put himself out there, and I was an idiot and turned him down. Now I have to convince him I mean it. Public ridicule is a possibility."

"Makes sense. You should follow your heart."

"If I go overboard… I'll leave the company, if I have to."

He stood and gave her a hug, before nudging her toward the door. "Leave damage control to me. Until then, the stage is yours."

272

And she'd have to give the performance of a lifetime.

****

She exited the office with a spring in her step and walked straight to Ric.

He scowled and whispered, "Now what do you want?"

"You."

"Next option, blondie. Already told you — I'm not interested."

"Yes, you are," she said. He didn't pursue her for this long, only to decide he didn't want her.

"Why? Why am I? Why should I be? Because it's written in the stars?" He hissed the last sentence. "I don't give a bloody fuck about them. I wanted you. You weren't available. End of story."

"But I was. I am. Available." When he turned to his computer screen, Lexi grasped his chin and forced him to face her. "Will you look at me? I want you. *I* want *you*." She didn't bother keeping her voice low. The single person on the floor she cared about, other than Ric, had given her carte blanche to do what she felt like.

"Well boo-fucking-hoo. It's too late."

"I finished the book." Her voice didn't waver. This wasn't going to be easy, but she'd be damned if she gave up on her plan. Or on him.

*

Ric was thrown by the randomness of her last statement. "What are you on about? Are you off your rocker?"

"*Exotic Beast*. I read it all. Xandra and Rex end up together."

"Talking about fantasy land again, are we? Get a grip, little girl. Better yet, get a life. This is reality, and you and I have to live in it, make our choices, and deal with the consequences." Why wouldn't she just give up? All this time she acted as if they had nothing, yet he'd believed she felt something for him, despite being vocal about the opposite. Now she admitted she wanted him, and all he heard was a plea for someone to save her from her loneliness.

"But Xandra and Rex are all about consequences," she said. "They loved each other and were torn apart out of fear of consequences. Their story shows a way of fixing things, because things are fixable."

Just his luck that he was in love with a crazy woman. "What does that have to do with—?"

"Rex and Xandra are star-crossed lovers. They don't exist, but the setting of their relationship does. They're an improbable couple in an impossible situation. They both had their issues, and reality—*their* reality—tore them apart. Then the writer, or a god with a silly name, found the millions of things they had working for them. He threw hurdles their way but wrote them a path that ultimately brought them together, despite everything, because being a vampire and a shifter wasn't reason enough for them not to work." She paused and looked at him expectantly.

274

"Do you have a point in there somewhere?" Ric cocked his head to the side and arched an eyebrow. He was intrigued by the analysis but refused to show it.

"Just shut up and hear me out, will you?"

He faked a yawn and stretched, taking in the rest of the room. Everybody was looking at them. No matter how pissed he was at Lexi, he didn't want her getting in trouble with her stepfather. "Pet, leave it be," he said in a hushed voice. "You won't change my mind, and we have onlookers."

"I don't care. Like, at all. As I was saying—"

"You don't care?"

"Not about changing your mind—I care about that. The onlookers? Not so much. Will you stop interrupting me? As I was saying…" Her gaze challenged him to cut in again. When he didn't, she said, "Think about it. A story about love conquering all." He could help the widening of his eyes at the l-word, and Lexi blushed. "Their love, I mean."

Of course.

*

"Rex and Xandra despised each other at first, but they were drawn together anyway." She stopped talking, to make sure he was still with her. He was. His arms were folded, and he tapped his foot impatiently. He wanted to see what her rant was leading to.

Lexi took a deep breath and went on. "Xandra has every reason to hate him, and he should resent her, but they fall in love. You know? Against the odds, against reason, they end up together."

275

"And…?"

That was all he had to say? If she didn't know she deserved this treatment, she'd be fuming. "And we're the real Rex and Xandra. The obstacles their natures posed, the way Xandra and Rex found love, were there to show me that. Regardless of who wrote the book and made sure I'd find it, or how they did so, it accomplished its goal." Her turn to fold her arms over her chest and wait.

Ric said nothing. He pushed back his chair and stood. Without even a glance her way, he circled the other side of his desk and started down the corridor in long strides.

Lexi rushed after him as soon as she snapped out of the stupor his abrupt departure caused. Right before he entered the men's room, she grabbed him by the arm. "Where are you going?"

He looked at her like she was a moron. "To take a leak," he said slowly, freeing his arm from her grasp.

She followed him inside.

"And where are you going?" he asked.

"We're not done yet."

"Yes, Lexi, we are. Have been since the beginning, really."

Nope. Not an acceptable answer.

He entered a stall and bolted the door, while she contemplated what to do. What was it Willy said in her dream?

And who the fuck was Willy?

Give up control. Lose it.

"Give me a chance," she called out to him from outside the lavatory.

"For fuck's sake, I'm taking a piss. Sod off."

276

"No. I want a chance."

The stall door slammed against the wall behind it, and Ric stormed out and headed out of the room.

Lexi ran after him. "Aren't you going to wash your hands?"

"Didn't get to do my business, did I?" He took his seat at his desk again, a tortured look on his face.

When she perched on the corner of his desk, he stood and went to the kitchen.

She followed him there, but had to back down when his cell phone rang.

He waved the phone at her. "Client," he said and accepted the call.

She'd get him later.

*

Lexi returned to her desk, and Ric was glad to hang up on the telemarketing call he pretended was work-related. He was on his way back to his desk, when he heard shuffling sounds and then the noise a stack of paper makes when it's dropped to the floor.

"Ric Ackart, will you please go out with me?" Lexi's voice was loud and clear in the silence that suddenly reigned in the office.

Ric turned as if in slow motion, noticing the open-mouthed faces around him before his eyes locked on Lexi's calves.

She stood on her desk. *On* her desk.

"One date is all I ask for, you stubborn man. Give me a chance."

277

She was out of her mind, and this was the sexiest thing a woman had ever done for him. He closed his gaping mouth and strode to the sales department. After what seemed like ages of walking, Ric stopped in front of the woman he loved and looked up at her. "When?"

"Saturday. Pick me up at seven?"

He nodded, not trusting his own voice. She'd asked him out, in front of all their coworkers. It was more than he ever thought she'd do.

He shouldn't get his hopes up, but he was already daydreaming of where he'd take her, what he'd show her, how he'd kiss her, when she said, "I'm planning the date."

"Right." He'd make do.

"And, Ric?"

"Yes, love?"

"Can you help me down?"

Chapter Twenty-Eight

Following the show she gave the entire floor, Lexi slipped her notice of resignation on Edmund's desk. It'd save him the embarrassment of having to fire his stepdaughter. She left the building before he returned to his office and while Ric was away from his desk.

She drove to Sarah and Angie's, determined to work things out with her best friend.

Sarah got the door, a look of cautious optimism on her face when she saw Lexi at the opening. "Should I hide the china?" she asked.

"Nah. I'm not gonna make a mess. I'll just shoot her. One bullet. Right to the head. Don't try to stop me."

They both giggled.

"Was that the doorbell?" Angie called out from somewhere inside the house.

Sarah looked at Lexi questioningly. Lexi smiled and took a step forward, and Sarah moved to the side. "It's Lexi, baby."

Things were heard tumbling to the floor, followed by quick stomping, and Angie appeared in the living room. Hair disheveled and eyes puffy, she came to a screeching halt a few feet away from Sarah and Lexi. "Did you come to tell me I'm an awful person and a horrible friend?"

Lexi spread her arms, and Angie ran to her, and the world tilted back into place.

Lexi told the girls how she'd come clean to Ric about everything except for her actual feelings for him. Angie acted like a puppy during the talk, bouncy and excited. She got Lexi water and cookies, and anticipated her every need. Her behavior was out of guilt, and Lexi took advantage of it by getting a foot-rub out of her while Sarah made dinner for the three of them.

When Lexi mentioned a craving for cheesecake, and Angie offered to whip one up, Lexi couldn't help but burst into laughter.

"Oh. *Oh*, you're so mean." Angie didn't sound all that outraged.

Sarah all but rolled on the floor laughing.

Lexi fought to catch her breath. "I couldn't help myself. You were so eager to please." A fresh bout of chuckles.

"I guess I overdid it, huh?"

Lexi nodded.

"So, am I forgiven?"

Lexi pretended to give the idea some serious thought. "On one condition."

"Anything. You can have my leather jacket. I never wear it anyway."

"Nope, that won't do it. You have to come shopping with me tomorrow. And I know what you did was out of concern for me, but you never ever do magic that will affect me again."

"I promise."

****

By the time Lexi got home, dinner was served, and Edmund had apparently filled her mother in on Lexi's attempts to get Ric to go out with her.

"Shame on you, Lexi. You embarrassed Edmund in front of everyone." Her mom's voice was stern, but her eyes held something else.

"Actually—" Edmund tried to cut in but was stopped by twin glares.

"I didn't embarrass *him*, Mom. I embarrassed myself."

"You made him fire you. And for what? Did you get anything out of it?"

Ah. This was what she was getting at. "I got what I wanted." Lexi grinned.

All reproach left her mom's face, and the smile that blossomed on her lips made her look ten years younger. "Which means?"

"I got me a date for Saturday." Lexi smirked smugly. "And Edmund didn't fire me. I quit." Yup. She was totally victorious.

Edmund slammed his hand on the table. "All right. Neither of you interrupt me this time. I didn't fire her, and I did not accept her resignation," he told her mom, before turning to Lexi. "I did, however, grant you a two-week leave. Make the most of your time off while today's incident fizzles out, and we'll discuss options once your mother and I are back from Italy."

Lexi gaped at him.

"I almost forgot." Edmund fished a credit card out of his wallet. "You can charge a dress…" He kept it out of

Lexi's grasp when she reached for it. "*One* dress and dinner on this. Anything extra, I have to authorize."

"Any dress I want?"

Her mother laughed, and Edmund raised an eyebrow. "One that won't bankrupt us or make me upset."

"Yes, Sir." Lexi mock-saluted. She snatched the card and proceeded to squish the air out of his lungs. "Now, where to make reservations?" she mumbled to herself, when she allowed him to draw breath.

"Ahem, that's been taken care of, too."

****

If Lexi had been stressed when she and Ric went on what was so *not* a date, this time she was driven to paranoia, trying to anticipate and prevent anything that might go wrong.

She double-checked the straps of her dress for loose threads that could lead to the unimaginable catastrophe of a nip slip. She stowed a second pair of silk stockings in her purse, in case she got a snag in the ones she wore, and she spent about a quarter of an hour trying to calculate the probability of one of her high metallic heels breaking off. Should she just pack another pair of shoes? A rucksack that fit her boots in wasn't the best accessory for a classy date. She'd have to mind her steps.

Deciding on makeup wasn't any easier. Luckily, she'd foreseen this and started putting it on about three hours before Ric was to pick her up. The first try was smoky eyes and red-lacquered lips. Nope. Too eager and vampy. She took out the makeup-removal tissues and

282

started over. The second try wasn't eager enough—sticking to mascara and lip gloss was too little effort for a first date that needed to leave a lasting impression. She went for a mix-and-match and liked the outcome. She enhanced her green eyes with a thin line of eyeliner and put the red lipstick back on. There. Simple, clean, and with a touch of sexy.

She ran first one hand and then the other along the line of her cleavage to adjust her breasts. They looked full and enticing but, not overly so. She was lucky to find the perfect date-dress yesterday. Short but not too revealing, it hugged and accentuated her curves in black satin, and the square neckline showed just the tops of her breasts. It took her and Angie hours to spot it, but Angie's promise meant she didn't complain once during the hunt for the perfect outfit.

Unfortunately, it also meant Lexi couldn't call her now and ask for a spell or charm, to ensure her date went smoothly. Lexi toyed with the idea of begging for one nonetheless.

No. No need. She'd make it work. She'd get her guy and her happy ever after on her own."

She removed the curlers from her hair, twisting each blonde lock around her finger so it kept its form, while she went over the details once more, to make sure she wasn't forgetting anything. She was loosening the tight ringlets so they showed their length, when her phone rang. Ric could be calling to cancel. Her heart leaped up her throat, as she rushed to get it. Still running the fingers of one hand through her tresses, she looked at the little screen.

283

Not him. "Mom. How nice of you to call. *Again.* For the fifth time today. What can I do for you now?" Her light, playful tone didn't match the abruptness of her words.

"Careful how you talk to your mother, young lady," her mom replied in the exact same manner.

"Yes, yes. How is Milan? Want to pay some attention to it and leave me alone for tonight?"

"I will, as soon as you tell me how you're wearing your hair."

The woman had a radar. No other explanation. "It's down. Bye now." She started to press the little red button, but her mom's drawn out plea to wait made her bring the phone back to her ear. "What?"

"Pull your hair up. You appear more serious when you do. Richard has to realize you're serious about the two of you. It also makes you look taller."

"Bye, Mom." Lexi hung up. She turned to leave her phone on her dresser, and caught her reflection in the mirror. She loosely pulled up her hair on the visible side of her head. Not bad. Not bad at all.

Once her hair was done, she had reservations at the classiest restaurant in town, wore a little black dress to kill for, sported the perfect coif, and was waiting for the most awesome guy in the universe.

And she had cold feet.

She glanced at her tiny, bejeweled wristwatch. Twenty minutes till he showed up. Too late for her to freak out over whether he'd like what she had in store for him.

The doorbell rang ten minutes too soon, and Lexi made her way down the stairs on wobbly legs that balanced on higher-than-high heels.

She took a deep breath, put on her brightest smile, and opened the door.

Her brain shut down, and her heart missed a beat, at the sight that greeted her.

Ric grinned and offered her an armful of daisies. "Sorry I'm early. Thought a fourth walk around the block would make me sweaty and ruin the outfit."

"My favorite. How did you know?"

"Edmund mentioned it at some point." Did he blush?

Lexi kept stealing glances at him, as she scouted the house for a vase. She'd hoped he would wear a suit but didn't expect him to, even after he called this morning to ask if they were going somewhere *fancy*. And he cleaned up nicely. He was dressed all in black, matching her perfectly, the color and fabric of the suit adding a feline quality to his movements. He looked like a panther as he prowled the living room, while she figured out where the flowers would look best displayed.

Afraid she'd lose it and jump him, Lexi wanted to leave immediately, so they arrived early at the restaurant. Not that being at a public place made it easy on her. It didn't help that said public place didn't exactly qualify as public. Edmund had made a reservation at a very exclusive restaurant, and she and Ric had their own booth.

Lexi was grateful for the waiter hovering and fussing over them, as well as for the wine that flowed freely, making her feel less self-conscious and allowing her carefree self to surface. The conversation didn't focus on

285

their relationship at any point. Instead, she kept discovering more things she liked about Ric, or interests they had in common. They shared an intense dislike for okra and were willing to kill for chocolate. So maybe these examples weren't very unique, but they managed to keep talking about them for a good half hour and laugh the entire time.

By the time the main course was over, Lexi couldn't believe she'd resisted his charm this long. Other than gorgeous and a sex-god, Ric was smart, funny, caring, proficient at snark, and easy to talk to.

She let him choose desserts for both of them from the cart the waiter wheeled to them, and was delighted to see him place a steaming triple-chocolate soufflé in front of her. She cut into it with her spoon, and melted chocolatey goodness poured out. Momentarily forgetting everything but the sweet in front of her, she took her time assembling the perfect spoonful. Spongy cake and gooey chocolate lava topped with Madagascar-vanilla ice cream. As soon as the rich combination of flavors touched her taste buds, she couldn't hold back a moan.

"Good, huh?"

"*Mmm...*" She swallowed and licked her lips. "Oh, my God. This may be the best thing I've ever had in my mouth." She winced, but it was too late to hold back the innuendo.

Ric's eyes darkened. "Truth be told, kitten, I didn't give you enough time to have something to compare it to." He tilted his head to the side and waggled his eyebrows.

Should she reply in the same tone or ignore his comment altogether? He helped her out of that

286

conundrum by chuckling. "You're adorable when you're frazzled."

"You're such a jerk." She scrunched her nose, in an effort to keep a straight face.

"You should have seen your face." Tiny laughter lines formed around his eyes. She wanted to kiss them one by one.

They laughed and teased one another until the waiter cleared his throat. One look at her watch showed it was well after the establishment's closing time.

*

Ric's heart had been racing in his chest since she opened her front door. She was a vision in black, which screwed his plans of playing it cool and aloof. The only thing that kept him from skipping the small talk during dinner, granting Lexi forgiveness, and having her on the spot was the very proper waiter, who was never more than a few feet away from their table.

Their waiter signaled it was time for them to go, and Ric stood and pulled out Lexi's chair. He wasn't ready for the night to be over, but he hoped there would be more. He helped her up and was elated when she didn't let go of his hand while they walked to his car in silence.

When they were both seated and buckled up, he couldn't help but ask the question that had been at the tip of his tongue since she asked him on this date. "What changed your mind?"

"A talk with a friend." She gave him a cryptic little smile.

Ric groaned. "Not about omens and spells again."

287

"About us" — she hung her head, averting her gaze from him — "and feelings. I realized I really, *really* like you."

It wasn't a declaration of love, but it was more than he dreamed of just a few days ago. He nodded and closed his palm over hers. He brushed his thumb over her knuckles, before bringing her hand to his lips and laying the gentlest of kisses on her fingertips. "And you want us to be together?"

"Do I have to get you a ring or something?" She turned to look at him, her misty eyes belying the lightness of her question.

Instead of answering, Ric cupped her face with his free hand and leaned in to answer with a kiss that had nothing to do with lust, and everything to do with tenderness and love and the promise of a future.

As much as he hated letting her go when they reached her doorstep, he felt as bouncy as a teenager on his first date. In a couple of seconds, he'd be kissing her goodnight.

And maybe this kiss would be mostly about lust.

"So…" He couldn't come up with a wittier intro to a goodnight kiss.

"I had a great time," she said.

Ric wanted to slap his forehead. He could have said that. "Me too, and I can't wait for our second date. Till then, goodnight, kitten." He smiled and leaned closer, lips already parted.

She stopped him with one palm on his chest. "Um, we don't have to say goodnight yet. You could come in."

There she went, nibbling that bloody lip again. It was so sexy, it should be illegal.

288

"There's something I… Just come in for a drink?"

He should say no. The first date should be chaste and romantic. His mind had to be clear of thoughts of wild, passionate sex, if he wanted a fresh start.

"Lead the way," he said finally. He'd trust her not to make their date a prelude to more of the same.

Trust her with his heart.

She left him in the living room and said she'd go take off her shoes because the heels were killing her. Nothing in her voice indicating a sexual invitation. As much as his body ached for her, Ric was happy for that.

"Ric?" Her voice came from upstairs, lined with urgency.

"Is everything all right, love?" He was already on his feet and flying up the stairs. "You hurt?" He ran to the direction of her voice, and entered a room at the end of the corridor.

The sight that greeted him stopped him in his tracks as effectively as a punch to the gut. Lexi was buck naked in bed, on her back. Her legs were spread, and her wrists secured to the headboard with handcuffs.

Ric hated his cock for stirring to life. He hated Lexi for cheapening everything he felt, pummeling everything they could have into a pulp, until there was no room left for hope anymore. Sex was a vital part of every relationship, but it couldn't be all said relationship consisted of.

He was an idiot for believing things had changed. She just wanted him to keep fucking her, and played the romance angle to get her way. He said nothing — what could he say? Shoulders slumped, he turned to leave. He

289

hated himself for worrying she might not be able to free her hands on her own.

"Ric, wait. It's not what you think."

He wanted to rip his ears off, for hearing the plea in her voice. Rip his heart out, for making him pause to hear her excuse. To give her another chance. "What is it then?"

"Please look at me."

He wouldn't face her. She could say her piece to his back.

"This is not about sex, Ric. It's about control. I'm giving control to you. I've never consciously handed it to anyone before. I couldn't. Not even..." She took a deep breath, and when she spoke again, she sounded composed. "I didn't love him this much."

And he ran to her.

Chapter Twenty-Nine

He fell to the bed on one knee and brought her to him with an arm around her shoulders. "My love," he whispered over and over again, kissing her lips, her nose, her cheeks... With his free hand, he fumbled with the handcuffs, thinking they were the kind with the safety latch.

"The key is on the dresser," she told him between kisses.

He stood, to get it.

"No. This is me giving myself to you. You better take what's offered, mister."

He could see the fear of rejection in her eyes even as she joked, and he did what he could to reassure her. He sought her lips and claimed them, losing himself in her taste. He needed her to alleviate his fear, too. Needed to hear her say the words. He let her need come first, as he plundered her mouth. Afraid he wouldn't hold back if he touched her body, he cupped her cheeks in both palms and held her to him.

Lips pressed to hers, he found her wrists again and gently massaged them, before he trailed his fingers down her forearms. He took the time to stroke the inside of her elbows with his thumbs, before tracing his way to her shoulders. Pulling back from the kiss, he looked into her eyes. "Do you think you can turn on your stomach?"

She nodded and squirmed, trying to roll over. Both wrists were constrained by the same set of cuffs and wouldn't strain her much if she managed it, but it was hard to get into the position he wanted without the use of her arms.

As tantalizing as her jiggling breasts were, he didn't want her to hurt herself while trying to flip her body over. "Here. Let me help you." Once she was face down, he stood to take in the sight of her body. He'd felt it more than once, but had never been allowed to look at it to his heart's content.

She was on edge, her toned muscles tense beneath her smooth skin. There was little doubt in Ric's mind that she'd try to flee if she weren't bound.

"Um, are you still there?" She turned to look at him over her shoulder. "I know I said I'm giving myself to you, and I'm not taking it back or anything, just… please, be gentle. 'Kay?"

He smiled, kneeled on the bed, and crawled up her body. When her thighs were trapped between his, he leaned down and nuzzled her neck. "Not taking you yet, love. I want to see you. Feel you. Map every centimeter of your body. And when I'm inside you, it won't be me taking you. It will be us taking each other. For good. You will be mine, and I will be yours, and you will start telling me what's in that pretty noggin from now on. Yeah?"

"But what if I can't?"

He sat back, trying not to let her feel his erection. "Can't or won't?"

292

"Can't. I mean, what if I don't know how to share and be all open. And you think my head's pretty?"

"Yes, I do." Her head was beautiful. She was beautiful. And he tried hard to stay civil. "But you want to try?"

"I don't do my best trussed-up-Christmas-turkey impersonation for just anyone, you know."

"Then we'll figure everything out together. I'm here for the long haul, if you'll let me."

"I want to let you. Just promise not to let me push you away without a fight?"

"Cross my heart and hope to die. Now hush and let me take care of you." He leaned forward again and kissed between her shoulder blades.

"But—but this is for you."

"And I want to take care of you. Any more objections? Should I gag you?"

"Nope. No gagging necessary, thank-you-very-much. I'm shutting up." She turned and buried her face in the pillow, only to throw her head back with a gasp when he used his teeth to graze the spot his lips left.

He feathered touches along the sides of her breasts and rubbed his cheek against the smoothness of her back. He caressed down her ribcage, until his thumbs met at her waist and his fingers were on her hipbones. "Like warm silk, you are. Can't have enough of touching you." He rained open-mouthed kisses first to the back of her neck and then down her spine, sliding his body backward at the same time. He spread her legs with one knee and kept retreating until he was kneeling between her calves. Unable to stop himself, he bit one of her buttocks. "Sorry, love," he told her wriggling form. "Too tasty, for me to resist."

She giggled and swayed from side to side, but he held her down and gave her one playful bite after the other.

"Hey. Stop that."

"Make me."

The easy, playful atmosphere was forgotten when he tried to bite her again, and her movements brought his mouth to her pussy.

*

"I want you." Lexi bucked her hips. She ached for more contact.

He swiped his wicked tongue along her slit. "Not yet, pet. Haven't had my fill of you, have I?"

"But I want my fill of you," she said, before remembering what the night was all about. "Fine. Have it your way. Just wait till you're at my mercy." Ric nibbled on her inner thigh, and a moan slipped past her lips.

She continued to moan and mewl while his lips went lower, until he flicked his tongue over the inside of her ankle. When he moved to the other leg, this time starting from the foot up, she could only gasp. She pushed her body harder into the mattress below her, seeking some friction to release the pressure his ministrations built inside her.

When Ric reached the apex of her thighs again, she sighed with relief, certain he'd do more this time. He'd finally bury himself inside her.

Nope. *Damn him.*

With a light slap on her ass, he crawled over her body again and turned her on her back once more. He grinned. "You didn't think after this long a wait, I'd hump you like a horny teen?"

As a matter of fact, this was exactly what she thought. "No, I just—"

*

He cut her off with his index finger on her lips. "Liar-liar, pants on fire." He winked, but lost his smugness in a groan when Lexi wrapped her lips around his finger and sucked, circling the tip with her tongue. "Tease." He burrowed his face into the crook of her neck, to worry the flesh there with his teeth. Satisfied he'd left a decent enough love-bite, he ran his tongue around one of her breasts and then the other in ever-narrowing circles, until just the nipples remained wanting.

The perky tips strained upward, begging to be suckled. Ric couldn't say no to their pleas. He placed a palm flat on Lexi's belly, to stop her from arching into his touch, and enveloped one peak with his lips, rolling the other between his fingers. He grazed the rosy tip with his teeth, sucked on it until it was impossibly hard, and then blew on it. Goose bumps rose on her skin. Nodding his approval to himself, he licked his way to the other nipple, flicking the deserted one with his thumb.

He loved how she sucked in a breath whenever he did something different, and made a bet with himself to guess how many such little gasps he could get out of her by keeping busy with her breasts.

He licked and nibbled, nuzzled and bit on the fleshy mounds, making her moan louder. He kneaded and rubbed, one moment laving her breasts with barely-there touches, the next squeezing and flattening them, pinching the nipples between two fingers so he could attack them again with his mouth.

Her breath came out in short pants. No other sound escaped the silent O of her lips. Her eyelids were heavy with desire, but her grip on the bed railings was so tight, her knuckles turned white.

And still Ric wanted to draw out her pleasure.

*

Mind and body in a frenzied state of arousal and need, Lexi wanted more. More of his touch. More of his mouth. More of him. She needed to feel him against her core, but he kept his body a couple of agonizing inches above hers. She raised her legs when he bent low, to dip his tongue in her belly button, and pressed the heels of her feet into his ass to push him toward her.

He wouldn't budge.

Instead, he grabbed her ankles, lowered her feet to the mattress, and stood in one liquid, graceful motion. Lexi whimpered as a caress of cool air replaced the warmth of his body on hers. Her next whimper was for the show he put on as he opened his shirt, letting the fabric reveal his naked flesh a bit at a time. He pulled the plush material out of his waistband and undid his cufflinks, then let it float to the floor in that unique way silk has of defying gravity.

296

Lexi was mesmerized by the contrast of black on white, but instead of following the shirt, her gaze was fixed on his carved muscles. He undid his belt, biceps flexing, pecs and abs coiling and stretching. She ached to caress his body. Feel its warmth on her. Suck on the spot beneath his jawline that drove him crazy.

God help her, she wanted to have the length of him impale her, and the bastard knew it. It was evident in the sway of his hips when he freed his cock. He stroked himself a couple of times, leering at her.

He turned his back to the bed, to take off his shoes and socks. Lexi forgot all about her restraints when the perfect curve of his ass stretched the fabric of his pants and then peeked above it, as his trousers slid down. She longed to dig her nails in the taut flesh, while he pumped inside her.

Ric read her mind, or their thoughts coincided. He stalked to the foot of the bed and climbed to her on hands and knees, covering her body with kisses until they lay face to face. His hips cradled between her thighs, he rubbed his length against her wet pussy and coated himself in her juices.

"Please. Please. Please," she chanted every time the blunt head of his cock brushed her clit.

Finally, he wrapped his arms around her, holding her to him. "I love you," he said and pushed inside her in one smooth, long stroke.

Her vision was blurred. Tears threatened to make their appearance again. More than threatened — they rolled down her cheeks. Fully seated inside her, Ric peppered her face with kisses and murmured soothing words. He didn't move, and if he wanted her half as much as she wanted him, staying still took a lot of effort.

"Ric, it's okay," she murmured, voice choked. "Happy tears. Promise."

*

He studied her face. Her beaming smile underlined the truth of her words. He began thrusting slowly, his gaze never leaving hers. Absorbing and memorizing every reaction, and reveling in the slightest catch of her breath. He expected her to close her eyes, throw her head back as she'd done before, in the throes of passion, but her gaze didn't waver. Their lovemaking was everything he hoped for. Everything she denied them both all this time. A merging of not only bodies, but also souls.

It was what he promised — or warned her — it would be. Both of them taking each other. *For good.*

Sensing she was close, Ric redoubled his efforts and raised her legs to his shoulders so he could plunge deeper and harder within her. He changed the angle of his thrusts, barely staving off his own release as he curled an arm around her thigh to massage her throbbing clit.

She thrashed under him, her body clenching, as if to strangle his cock. Yet it wasn't her orgasm that brought him to completion.

Lexi cried out, "I love you," as the burst of her passion engulfed her.

Ric came hard, ravaging her lips while her lax limbs fell to his sides, allowing the length of his body to touch hers. He didn't know if it was his heart, thudding loud enough to consume all other sound, or if it was hers.

298

He didn't care.

She loved him, and at long last admitted it.

They fell asleep, still linked. At some point in the night, Ric got up from the bed and unlocked the handcuffs. He massaged the blood flow back into her wrists, gathered her into his arms, and buried his nose in her golden mane that came loose during their coupling.

"So, this means we're going steady?" she asked sleepily.

He chuckled. "Couldn't pry me off with a crowbar, love."

"And you love me?"

"And I love you."

"Good. Keep it that way" — she dropped her voice to a whisper — "'cause I love you, too."

Next time he awoke, he was chained to the bed, and Lexi grinned down at him. "Told you you'd be at my mercy." She lowered her body, so her hardened nipples dragged down his chest.

He didn't mind being at her mercy one bit.

Although, he might have begged a little in the end.

Epilogue

Lexi checked her watch and tried to hide a grin. Four twenty seven.

Thirty three minutes to go.

For the billionth time, she wondered what Ric's plan for the evening was. If it was too sappy, she'd bolt.

She snorted. Still living in denial. Sappiness was her second nature these days. She cooed and sniffled at romantic comedies and took moonlit strolls on the beach without whining about the cold. And it was Ric's fault she couldn't wipe the smile from her face.

As a matter of fact, the only time she'd been sad since she and Ric became an item was when she tried to find the book again and got an error message for her efforts. She was in the upper floor, but had taken her PC with her to her new position, and didn't think that was why the book disappeared.

She guessed it was because the reason *Exotic Beast* found her in the first place no longer existed. She'd found her soul mate—and yes, she'd made her peace with that frightening fact.

A new email notification blinked on her phone, and she prayed it wasn't some work-related emergency that'd ruin her date. It wasn't. It was a message from her own email address. It had to be spam, but she opened it anyway. Amazingly, it just read, "*Exotic Beast* has been updated."

Lexi didn't think twice before trying the book's web address. All she found was an advertisement for a place she'd never visited.

The ad said a local bar called Willy's Dreams hosted a party tonight. Lexi brushed it off. The name of the bar nagged at a buried memory, but work and anticipation for whatever her boyfriend had in mind drove the thought away.

She chanced a glance at the heap of papers neatly stacked to her left, and sighed. She had to go through it all by Friday, which gave her three days. A smile formed on her lips as she contemplated the long hours she'd spend at the office. She wouldn't start today. There were much better things for her to do with her evening.

She stood and rounded her desk, to bury her nose in the six long-stemmed red roses that stood in a vase on its far corner.

"Did it change?" the man at the desk opposite hers asked, flashing startlingly white teeth.

"Huh?"

"The scent of this magnificent bouquet the stud downstairs not-so-subtly left you this morning—did it change from five minutes ago?"

"Um... no?" She batted her eyelashes innocently.

"Then why not stop sniffing it, and go do what you have to, to be where the card says you need to be, by the time you're supposed to be there?"

"What I have to do... be where..." She went over the impossible phrase he uttered. "You read the card."

"It was looking me straight in the face. And you were late coming in. Besides, that blue-eyed specimen of British superiority said I could read it, if I let you off early. You're done. Go."

"Hey. That's only" — she checked her watch — "twenty minutes early."

"I couldn't give you the day off. Pedelty'd kill me."

"*You're* my boss now, Larry." She closed the distance to his desk, leaned over it, and pulled him up by his fuchsia tie to give him a smacking kiss on the cheek. "The bestest-*est* boss ever."

"Flattery will get you everywhere. Now off you go. And I want details."

"Ladies don't kiss and tell," she said over her shoulder, already on her way out the door.

"Two things wrong with that sentence, my beauty. A) You're not a lady, and B) Nobody said anything about kissing."

"Ah, shut up." She rushed out the door. She had a place to be in a couple of hours, after all.

****

A few months ago, Lexi was stuck in a position she didn't like, unable to do anything about it even though the company was owned by her stepfather. She expected nothing of her life, and not only career-wise. She refused the possibility a thing such as true love existed, let alone would come her way, and now...

Now she was assistant to the head of the Marketing Department in the same company, and about to celebrate her sixth-month anniversary with the man she loved. A

302

man who'd tried hard to get her to denounce her stubbornness and cynicism, and for whom she'd managed to do so.

Her mother and stepdad bounced with joy every time they saw them together, which was why she finally moved her butt and got an apartment of her own. She still dropped in announced, especially if her insecurities resurfaced and she needed her mom to provide a comforting hug or mental slap.

Lexi wasn't bitchy on purpose when he happened to be a few minutes late; she was afraid this'd be the time he didn't show up. She didn't mean to be snarky when he was right about something and she was wrong; she worried he'd realize she wasn't as smart as he thought, not as well educated, or not as witty, and he'd leave her.

She'd spent her entire adult life trying not to be clingy. Not to depend on others for her happiness. Not to need anyone. The first time she let her guard down, she was badly burned. Since then, her gut reaction if she feared things might go wrong was to attack and lay the groundwork so she could leave first.

Ric would have none of that. He reassured her and grounded her once he realized what was wrong, but there was only so much guessing a man could do. Luckily, her mom's wisdom was always on tap, to snap Lexi out of her funk when trivial things triggered her self-doubt.

As months went by and Ric showed no signs of leaving, the insecurities reared their ugly head with decreasing frequency, and things kept getting better between the two.

Things were better all around, actually. At times frighteningly so. Lexi was amazed at how much she meant it when she told Angie or Sarah she was doing great.

The stunt she pulled when she asked Ric out for the first time meant she couldn't keep working for Sales. She knew it, as did Edmund. Fortunately for Lexi, Larry, head of the Marketing department, had been impressed enough with her presentation, to ask Edmund to appoint her as his assistant the moment he found out about the show she put on.

That moment had been before Lexi even left the building that day — news had a way of traveling fast in the company — so Edmund had made up his mind on the matter before leaving for Milan, though he didn't tell her then.

As it turned out, this solution was for the benefit of everyone involved. Lexi had a job she loved, Edmund had saved face and didn't have to fire his stepdaughter, and Larry had an assistant with whom he got to discuss fashion on slow days.

****

Ric paced the small living room of Lexi's apartment, pretending he wasn't looking at his watch every two-point-three seconds. She was late. Not that it mattered. What he planned could wait a few minutes — or half an hour, knowing Lexi — but *he* couldn't. "Kitten, if you're not out here in ten, I'm coming in and dragging you by the hair." It was the fifth time he'd made the same threat.

304

"Just one more minute. *God.* You're the one who left instructions on what I was to wear."

"Left more than instructions," he muttered to himself. "And did I get a bloody *thank you*? Or an, *oh, baby, it's so pretty*? Nah."

"Did you say something?" Her voice sounded much closer than before. He twirled around to see her at the opening of her bedroom door.

A bit too much of her showed. The red dress he'd surprised with for tonight might be a bit too low cut. Not that he pondered the subject long, once she walked out of the room and he saw her perfect legs beneath the hemline.

The dress was also bordering on too short.

"What was that?"

After dating someone for six months, the breathtaking factor is more or less removed from the equation, but Lexi had a way of stealing his breath every single time she smiled like she did now.

"Nothing. So, where are we going? Or are you still not gonna clue me in?" She made a show of approaching him. He said she should dress to kill, with the little present he left her, and she was following them to the letter.

"Not getting a word out of me. You'll have to wait and see." He helped her put on her leather blazer jacket and held out his hand. "Shall we?"

"We shall." She pulled him to her for a kiss that promised all sorts of wickedness for later, and then led him to the door.

Ric trailed behind her, dazed.

****

305

Lexi had hinted at a classy restaurant near Bay Street she wanted to try, and she hoped this was where Ric was taking her. She soon realized they were heading a different way. Her excitement washed away when he parked on a dark street she'd never been on before.

While Ric rounded the car to open her door, she spotted a bar at the far end of the street. The neon sign over its door read Willy's Dreams.

"You know that's hardly romantic, right?" she asked as he helped her out.

Ric looked at her with a mixture of hope and trepidation. As if he felt she was about to ask something more, he slanted his lips over hers and pressed her between his body and the car. The kiss was full of wonder and untold wishes, and Lexi was at a loss for words when he pulled back.

"Trust me?" He linked their fingers together.

"With my life." So very corny, even to her own ears. "Besides, you're not getting any nookie, if this anniversary date isn't all I hope it'll be."

"Minx."

"But you love me."

"I do, God help me."

A god might need to intervene if the date wasn't amazing.

The moment they passed the doorway, Lexi felt a shift in the air. She couldn't put her finger to it, but she felt like she was someplace other than in an ordinary bar. Unexplainable tingles aside, she considered making good on her threat, because the place looked nothing like what she'd expected for the night.

"You go get a table, and I'll fetch something for us to drink. Yeah?" Ric left her with a kiss to the forehead, and Lexi scrunched up her nose. So he really meant for them to celebrate here.

Self-doubt tried to claw its way to the surface, stepping on her insecurities. This could be Ric's way of showing her six months was no big deal. Maybe he'd given her some sign she missed, like Andrew had with his late nights at the office...

Even as she dragged her feet to the first vacant table she found and dropped herself on a chair, she knew she was being silly. He wouldn't take her out for that. Wouldn't make a big deal out of what she'd wear. And the flowers...

She tried to spot Ric and saw him talking to the bartender. She couldn't see the other man's face, but something about him seemed familiar.

And six months totally was a big deal.

Ric threw back his head and laughed, but just as she could almost make out the bartender's features, he moved out of her line of sight.

The place Ric chose still sucked, whatever his reasons.

He turned and winked at her, drinks in hand. The bartender ducked behind the bar, and Lexi forgot about him, her heart melting at the love shining in her boyfriend's eyes as he walked toward her. She was stupid. He loved her.

"I love you," she said the moment he sat next to her.

"*I* love *you*, kitten." He looked somewhere behind her. Why didn't he look at her during such a tender moment?

She followed his gaze, and what she saw surprised her more than the venue he picked for the night.

Her mother stood there, teary eyed. She leaning on Edmund, who had one arm around her waist. Angie grinned behind them, and Sarah stifled a giggle—or a sob—with a hand strategically placed over her mouth.

Lexi turned back to Ric. "What—"

He was no longer in his seat. He knelt on the floor in front of her, holding up the most beautiful square-cut diamond ring she ever laid eyes on.

And she'd laid eyes on it before. She went to the stores with her mom a couple of weeks ago, to look for cufflinks for Edmund. Her mom kept swooning over engagement rings, and Lexi told her the one now in Ric's hand was the one she loved.

That was very sneaky of her mom. *Very* sneaky.

Lexi would have given her a killer look now, if Ric wasn't saying something very important.

"I love you so much, Lexi, that I want the whole world to know. I want you to be mine, and I want to be yours. I want to go to bed"—he caught her mother's gaze—"to *sleep* next to you and wake up with you in the morning."

Oh, God.

"I want to make you breakfast, and—"

Married. He wanted to get married.

"—and to take you places,"

Like for real.

" —and to have brilliant, beautiful, blond kiddies with you."

But Lexi didn't do marriage. She couldn't.

Could she? After how things had gone before?

And kids? Seriously? She, a mom?

"So, Lexi Adams, will you do me the honor of becoming my wife?"

She opened and closed her mouth, gasping for breath like a fish out of water.

"Honey?" Her mom's voice was full of worry.

"Love? Are you all right?"

The place seemed awash with a warm blue light, as Lexi scrambled for the perfect way to reply to his question. She blinked, and the bartender's smiling face came into focus.

Willy. Or was it…?

"Xochipilli. You guessed it. Give the girl a prize. I knew you'd figure it out, if I got you to my bar." The voice she remembered from her dreams filled her head.

"What should I do?" She was shocked by her lack of shock. As if she expected him to be able to talk inside her head. Or maybe she was losing it.

"I already told you, girl. Follow your heart."

Yes. That was the only thing to do.

And her heart was with Ric.

"Lexi?"

She wanted to bang her head on the table repeatedly for having caused the worry she could see in his beautiful blue eyes. She smiled. "I'm fine, and my answer is *yes.*"

"You'll spend the rest of your life with me?"

"Couldn't pry me off with a crowbar, baby."

"The lady does know her romance." Ric couldn't hide his relief even as he mocked her reply.

"Oh, will you shut up and kiss me?"

"So you sure it's a yes? You won't take it back tomorrow?"

"Of course it's a yes. Kiss." She puckered her lips, and he chuckled as he put the ring on her finger.

"Kiss you? In here? That's hardly romantic. Or proper. What with Pedelty and Joy—"

Lexi sank to the floor in front of him and then was all over him, toppling him to the ground, in an effort to capture his lips.

"Screw proper," she said. "We're Xandra and Rex."

Ric glared at her.

"I mean, we're Lexi and Ric." And she proceeded to ravish the mouth of the man soon to be her husband.

The End

Keep up to date with all the latest news and information from Sotia Lazu at http://www.SotiaLazu.com

Acknowledgments

This book is very special to me, beginning to end. The plot bunny was tossed my way by a friend from the United States. She and I toyed around with her idea, and she liked what I came up with, so she let me have it. I can never thank you enough for that, Carrie. I love you.

Two ladies in particular helped me put my thoughts into words. Thank you, Tina and Kristi. I hope a copy of the finished book finds its way to your hands one day and makes you smile.

A few years ago, I posted an earlier version of the story online, in installments. While writing it—*because of writing it*—I met readers from around the world. I got to know them through their comments and my responses, and forged friendships that kept me going through some dark personal times. You're too many for me to list here, but you know who you are, and you better know you rock.

A comment I got surprised me, because it was from a guy, when I thought I only had female readers. I replied, and that was my first communication with the man who is now my husband and the father of my son.

I've worked on *Magic at Work*, one way or another, since 2008. It was one of the first stories I wrote, before I knew anything about writing, and for that, it was extremely time-consuming to shape up. Points of view were all over the place, grammar and syntax only made guest appearances, and I had no clue how to use speech tags properly.

The first time I decided to rework it, a good friend from the other side of the world helped me and offered directions. Thank you, Kysira. You know I love you and wish you lived closer.

Allyson Lindt, Carla Krae, and Sofia Grey—authors I love and admire—helped me spot the characters' weaknesses and make this book all I wanted it to be. More than that, they were there for me whenever I believed both the story and I sucked. Thank you all from the bottom of my heart. I'm in your debt.

Finally, I'd like to thank a mystery lady, to whom I've never actually talked. Sofia asked her to read what I thought of as the final draft. She did and pointed out why it really wasn't. I'm not sure I did your brilliant suggestions justice, but thank you very-very much, Tigerlilyreader. I was too close to the book to see what you spotted.

About the Author

Sotia loves romances with a twist and urban fantasy novels, always with vivid erotic elements. Her favorite characters to write are not conventional hero-material at first glance, and she enjoys making them fight for their happiness.

She shares her life and living quarters with her husband, their son, and two rescue dogs, one of which may be part-pony. Sappy movies make her bawl like a baby, and she wishes she could take in all the stray dogs in the world.

Also, she hates mornings!

www.ingramcontent.com/pod-product-compliance
Lightning Source LLC
Chambersburg PA
CBHW060520180626

46817CB00002B/421